wild love

wild love

LAUREN ACCARDO

JOVE
New York

A JOVE BOOK
Published by Berkley
An imprint of Penguin Random House LLC
penguinrandomhouse.com

ISBN: 9780593200292

First Edition: May 2021

Printed in the United States of America
1 3 5 7 9 10 8 6 4 2

Book design by George Towne

To Josh,
who has never,
ever stopped believing in me

chapter **one**

Biting, icy wind whistled through the open car windows, and Sydney shuddered. It had to be at least twenty degrees colder up in the mountains. She raised the windows and hunched over the steering wheel, her already tense shoulders tightening further, like a jack-in-the-box about to pop.

Hot food. She needed hot food.

What she really needed was a memory eraser. She'd gladly give up any shred of happiness from the last ten years if it meant losing the last twelve hours.

Connor and the blonde. The sting in her mouth as she realized she'd chewed her lip enough to bleed. The deeply creased pitying stare on her mother's face when she'd arrived like a lost puppy at her door.

A shaky exhale breezed past her nostrils. One thing at a time.

She pulled her BMW into the sparsely populated parking lot of Utz's, a shadowy nondescript bar with a flashing **HOT FOOD TO GO** sign in the window.

Her stomach yawning with hunger, she scurried out of the warm car and into the fresh, pine-scented air. She might have fled to Pine Ridge under desperate circumstances, but she breathed its perfumed atmosphere into her lungs like a tourist on vacation.

A bright blue flier caught the wind and stuck against the leg of her yoga pants before she snatched it up. **Bingo Night at Utz's! Door Prizes. Cheap Drinks. All U Can Eat HOT WINGZ.**

"Jesus," she muttered. "Hot *wingz*. As if they spelled it correctly, nobody would show up."

With a grimace, she tucked the flier in a nearby trash can and hugged her cashmere cardigan tighter around her body, aching for any comfort she could find. But nothing could erase the memory of that asshole's stupid face as he grunted and moaned, the random blonde perched atop his hips.

She shook off the highlight reel running in her head.

Hot food. She'd promised her mother hot food for dinner.

A tiny bell rang over the door as she entered Utz's. Two burly men at the bar in front of her turned over their hulking shoulders and, after a cursory glance, resumed watching the football game blaring from the TV set on the wall.

"Howdy," the elderly bartender greeted her. A halo of gray hair framed his head, and a friendly grin pressed into his ruddy moon-shaped face. "What can I do you for?"

"Do you have a food menu? I'm gonna get some things to go."

He slid a paper menu toward her and turned back to the football game.

Sydney scanned the offerings. **Fried clams. Burgers. Fried chicken sandwiches. Nachos. Pizza. French fries.**

Onion rings. She twisted her lips and calculated probable calorie counts. So much fat. So many carbs. Not a green vegetable in sight. Maybe just for today, while the dull ache in her chest thudded in time with *Connor and the blonde*, she'd take a cheat day.

Ha. A cheat day. Her lips curled into a bitter grin.

What would her mother like? It had been years since they'd spent any real time together. Was she a vegetarian now? Nah. Couldn't be. The last time Sydney had ventured up to Pine Ridge they'd eaten out at the "nicest place in town," and Karen had ordered the cheeseburger.

Sydney ordered two chili cheeseburgers, french fries, onion rings, and something called "mixed vegetables," which probably came from a can but might be worth the gamble.

She climbed onto a barstool to wait for her food and glanced around the space.

TV sets played the Giants game, signs advertised fried-food specials, and the heavy scent of stale beer and cleaning fluid hung in the air. On a typical Thursday evening she'd be sipping drinks with Connor at the plush NoMad bar or cooing over art she didn't understand at an opening downtown.

Since she'd been let go from her job at the law firm a year ago, she'd slipped seamlessly into the role of "Connor's girlfriend." Silk blouses appeared in her closet as her *The Future Is Female* T-shirt found its way to the donate pile. She joined a Tuesday morning book club. Instead of watching football at a dark, dingy bar on Sunday afternoons, she brunched with Connor and his finance buddies. She'd needed a break from the stress of work, but as time passed and she handed over control of her days to Connor, she'd lost little bits of herself without even noticing.

As the booming announcer's voice called the football game and pint glasses thudded dully against the worn wooden bar, Sydney rested. Her body settled into the barstool, and for the first time in a long time, the tension in her neck eased a fraction of an inch.

Maybe Connor had done her a favor by cheating on her. In their apartment. On their bed. In their sheets.

Bile rose up in her throat.

Maybe not.

She turned her attention to the TV screen as the bartender returned.

"Get you something while you wait?"

A cold hoppy beer would be heaven, but in addition to the chili cheeseburger? She'd pay for it in the gym next week. The girls in her book club seemed to survive on raw almonds and green juice.

She scanned the taps, just in case, and recognized a familiar brown logo. Raquette River Brewing. A nearby brewery whose beer she never saw in New York City. She grinned.

"She'll have a cosmopolitan." The behemoth to her right giggled, his voice a bad imitation of Minnie Mouse.

The equally large man to his right nudged him with a meaty elbow. "With extra cranberry!"

They erupted in laughter, and Sydney glared.

"How'd you know what's in a cosmopolitan?"

The laughter halted, and they stared at each other and then at her.

"He's the one who knew!" one of them called out, pointing at the other.

"No way, you're the one who said it!"

A deep, throaty chuckle interrupted the buffoons. Past them, half-hidden by the sheer size of his friends, was a third male patron. How had she overlooked him? A patch of dried mud on his left forearm spoke to outdoor work, and a dark, neatly trimmed beard covered half his face but couldn't hide a full, rosy mouth. He took a sip of beer and licked the residual froth from his lips.

"You have something to say, too?" Sydney's voice cracked midsentence.

As he turned his piercing gaze on her, the breath caught in her throat.

Well, hello, Mountain Man.

"I didn't say anything." His voice reverberated like a needle on an old jazz record.

She held his steady stare for one moment longer before he turned back to the TV.

The bartender cleared his throat, breaking the spell and dragging her attention back to him. "Anything for you, miss?"

"Oh . . . Um, yes, please. I'll have the Raquette River IPA."

The bartender pulled the pint, and the second her hands closed around the glass, a deep breath escaped her lips. As the first spicy, bitter mouthful of beer slid down her throat, her shoulders relaxed. Perhaps she had underestimated the healing powers of this sleepy mountain town.

She sipped steadily at the pint as the New York Giants moved the football down the field. On third down, Derek Tahoe let go of a wobbly pass, and a Dallas Cowboys defender snatched the interception.

"Oh, you piece of garbage!" Sydney exclaimed. "Are you freaking kidding me with that ham sandwich?" She tilted the pint glass nearly upside down as the last frothy dregs hit her tongue. Empty already.

"Another?" the bartender asked.

"Sure, why not?"

Her diet was already shot to shit for the day anyway. He placed the beer in front of her, and she took a grateful sip.

The Cowboys couldn't manage a score on the drive, and the Giants got the ball back, making good progress on the possession. Once again, on third down, Derek Tahoe scanned the field like a scared little boy in Pop Warner football camp. The ball skimmed the tips of his fingers, wobbled, and fell into the hands of the exact same Cowboys cornerback.

"Are you kidding me?!" Sydney leaped off her barstool. "You human wasteland! What do we pay you for?"

She expected the entire bar to be just as outraged as she was, but instead, a trio of blank faces stared at her. She slid back onto her barstool and gritted her teeth. "Patriots fans?"

"Who *are* you?" Mountain Man asked.

All at once she missed the anonymity of a big city. "Who are *you*?"

"Sam Kirkland. Is your identity a matter of national security?"

"No." She tugged at her cardigan. "Sydney Walsh."

"Walsh, huh? Karen Walsh's daughter?"

"Yeah. How'd you know that?"

"Everybody knows Karen's got a prissy daughter living in New York City who never comes to visit her," Behemoth #1 said. "And you look just like her."

Okay, so she didn't come up to Pine Ridge every other weekend to visit her mother, but *prissy*? Because she wasn't sporting last season's L.L.Bean and a camo baseball cap?

She licked her lips and straightened her spine. If nothing else, she could defend half his accusation. "My mother and I don't look anything alike."

"Are you kidding?" Behemoth #1 said. "Around the eyes? Plus, you can tell Karen was a dime back in the day."

Sydney blushed and clutched the cold pint glass.

"If that wasn't perfectly clear, Joe just called you a dime," Mountain Man said.

Sydney stared into his eyes again, this time noticing the depths of the deep brown irises. A baseball cap obstructed some of his brow, but his eyes were like almond-shaped searchlights, peeking out from beneath the navy-blue brim.

Okay, so maybe this town had more than spruce-scented air going for it.

The bartender reappeared and placed a paper bag on the counter in front of her. "That's everything," he said. "It'll be thirty-five seventy-four."

She winced as she handed over Connor's credit card. In a few weeks, the monthly payment on her own maxed-out card would be due, and where would she be then? How soon until Connor canceled this card? Maybe her mother could loan her some money. She shuddered.

For the moment, she brushed the thought away. She'd spend a few days hiding out in Pine Ridge and deal with real life later.

"Aw, you're leaving?" Behemoth #1 said.

"Yeah, but gosh, am I heartbroken to miss the rest of the nail-biter."

The Cowboys had scored on the turnover, and the score was a grisly 45 to 3. Despite the joke, the bar drew her in. If she had to choose between pints and football and the quiet awkwardness of her mother's apartment, there was no choice at all. But duty called.

"Have fun, guys."

She climbed into her car and rested the bag of hot, deliciously greasy food on the passenger seat. Before she turned the car on, she checked her phone. Reception was spotty in Pine Ridge, but the bar must've had Wi-Fi because a bevy of messages lit up her phone. With nausea brewing in her gut, she opened the few from Connor.

I haven't been able to move since you left. Please call me. I love you.

Her eyes glazed over as the bright light of her phone screen dimmed and then ceased. Pure inky darkness hugged her from all sides. The blackness covered her like a blanket, and for a moment, she was safe. Untouchable.

With a sharp expletive she tossed her phone into her purse and slid the car key into the ignition. She punched the gear shift into reverse, hit the gas pedal, and didn't get more than three feet before the earsplitting crunch.

chapter **two**

Are you all right?"

Sydney grimaced. Her rear bumper was crushed on the right side, and the taillight dangled from its broken cover like the last shriveled grape on the vine. Meanwhile, Mountain Man's filthy truck didn't have a scratch.

"I'm fine," she said. "Just feeling like an idiot."

Sam adjusted his baseball cap and placed his hands on his hips, staring down at her busted bumper. "You pulled out of there like a bat out of hell. You late for something?"

"No, and I didn't pull out like a bat out of hell. I pulled out like a normal human on her way to where she's going. I just . . . didn't check to make sure no one was coming. And the fact that there are precisely three cars in this parking lot made my lack of caution all the more understandable."

He laughed, stroking his beard with long, powerful fingers. Even in the dim parking-lot light she saw the calluses and scars on his knuckles and palms. Strong hands capable of tightening lug nuts, gripping tow chains, probing the curves of her hips until her legs lifted and opened . . .

She gulped. *Where the hell did that come from?*

"Come on," he said. "I'll give you a ride."

Attractive or not, no way was she getting in a truck with this stranger. Charles Manson was handsome, too. "It's still drivable. Just a busted bumper."

"You don't know that. What if there is damage to the rear tire? Leave it here, and I'll take a look tomorrow morning, when it's light out."

She was no damsel in distress, and she certainly didn't need a white knight to save her. She'd taken care of herself once, before Connor came along. Now she needed to do it again. Starting over, from scratch.

"Okay, first of all, I don't even know you. So there's no way I'm getting in a vehicle with you. Second of all, I'll take the car to a mechanic. You don't have to do anything for me."

He laughed again and groaned, adjusting his cap.

"Jesus, you're a trip. *First of all*, I know your mother. Everyone in this town knows your mother. If you disappeared or ended up dead, Karen Walsh would find out who did it and have their head on a stake in the town square before the sun came up. Personally, I like my head, and I want to hold on to it for a while. Second of all, I'm the mechanic in this town. So like it or not, you're gonna have to let me take a look at your car. Otherwise, you'll be stuck riding Karen's red Schwinn."

Sydney swallowed down the lump in her throat, eyes darting around the dark parking lot. Not a human in sight. Probably no Uber up here. And she couldn't see herself ambling along the two miles of country road to her mother's building with only a dim phone flashlight to guide her.

Sam tucked his arms across his chest and dropped his chin.

"Fine," she grumbled. "Let me get my shit."

After pulling her car back into the parking space and

cutting the engine, she grabbed her rapidly cooling dinner and climbed into the cab of Sam's pickup. The scent of freshly cut pine overwhelmed her, and she knew that authentic spiciness didn't come from an air freshener.

"It smells good in here," she said, almost to herself.

"*That* smells good." He nodded toward the paper sack in her lap as he pulled out of the parking lot. "No offense, but you don't really look like a girl who eats a lot of chili cheeseburgers."

She shifted in her seat and clenched her teeth. "Oh, are we making snap judgments? Because I have a few about you if you're interested."

His perpetually amused stare drifted over to the passenger seat. Her cheeks burned. With one hand draped over the steering wheel and the other casually tugging at his full, rosy lips, she wondered what his story was. *Probably married to a former prom queen with eight babies waiting for him at home.* But his left hand was bare. No ring. No ring tan line. And this definitely wasn't the ideal mode of transportation for someone with babies.

"No, thanks," he said. "I can probably guess."

They sat in tense silence as his pickup deftly maneuvered the curves of the pitch-black road, careening through the tree-lined path to Karen's apartment. Sydney reached for the gold chain at her neck and winced at its absence. Had it really been only twelve hours since she'd caught Connor in their bed with the blonde gyrating around on his lap like a second-rate porno actress? Between the cheating and her mother and the fender bender, she needed a Xanax or a martini or both.

Sam shifted, settling back into the driver's seat in a position he seemed to have perfected. He commanded the vehicle with little effort, his right thigh flexing slightly as they took a tight turn and his foot eased off the gas pedal. The man radiated self-assurance, filled the cab with his presence. She felt every inch of space between them and wondered, despite herself and the tumult of the day, what it would feel like to be closer.

The pickup sped past pine trees and skidded around slippery bends, the headlights turning to strobe lights in front of her eyes. "Shouldn't you be driving slower? Aren't there thousands of deer around here?"

"Are you trying to give me tips on driving in the mountains, city girl?"

"I grew up in the suburbs of Albany, okay?"

"While we're on the subject of avoiding car accidents," he said, "you never even apologized for hitting me."

"Your truck is fine."

His eyes wandered over to her again, and this time they held no warmth. He tugged at his lips and shook his head. The desire to be closer evaporated like rain in the summer heat. From the second they'd first interacted he'd treated her like an outsider and passed judgment. So what if he was cute? She'd been pushed around enough for one day.

They drove the rest of the way in silence, and as he pulled into Karen's parking lot, Sydney softened. She didn't know how long she'd be in Pine Ridge, but it was far too soon to be burning bridges.

Before she could open her mouth, he opened his. "Don't choke on your burger."

Asshole. The apology dissolved on her tongue.

"Don't hit a deer on your drive home." She grabbed her food, climbed out of the truck, and slammed the door behind her.

She twisted the loose doorknob to apartment five to find Karen dozing in her recliner. She looked tiny, nearly swallowed up by the brown leather monstrosity, with her wiry gray hair sticking out in all directions. She jerked awake as Sydney neared, her expressive eyes lighting up at the sight of the paper bag.

"I smell Utz's chili," she said. "Were they busy?"

"No." The remnants of her rough interaction with Sam

still prickled under Sydney's skin. She dug around in the kitchenette for plates and unpacked their dinner. "I accidentally bumped someone in the parking lot. . . ."

"Suds! What happened? Are you okay?"

"I'm fine. I didn't look behind me before I pulled out and hit this guy's pickup truck. His truck is completely fine, and my bumper is crushed. He gave me a ride home."

Sydney pulled the container of french fries out of the paper sack and, with fumbling fingers, dropped them all over the kitchen floor. "Damn it . . . ," she muttered, scooping up dusty fries and tossing them in the trash. Her nerves were shot.

"Who was the guy?" Karen asked.

"His name is Sam."

"Sam Kirkland?" Karen's voice came out in a breathy whisper, as if Sydney had said George Clooney.

"Yeah."

"Oh, Sydney, he is the nicest boy."

"Actually, he was a real asshole." She set the plate in front of her mother and settled into the couch with her own dinner. She dug into the burger with gusto and reveled in the greasy food. It wasn't a Xanax, but it would do.

"You know," Karen said, "Sam is a mechanic. He can probably fix your car for you."

"Yeah, he mentioned that. I was . . . a little rude to him, though. Not sure if he's willing to help me anymore."

"You were rude?" Karen's voice rose an octave. "Why?"

"Because he was rude to *me*! He insulted the way I look, the way I drive. He was a jerk. So I acted accordingly." If it didn't require spilling her guts, Sydney would've reminded her mother that she'd already been knocked down by a man once today. Her behavior was entirely warranted.

Wasn't it?

Karen's eyes glittered, and an all-knowing smile graced her lips. "Hmm."

"What?"

"Nothing. I just . . . Nothing."

Tension built at Sydney's temples, spreading through the mask of her face as she took another bite of the burger. Whatever pie-eyed opinion of the town mechanic Karen had to offer, Sydney didn't want to hear it.

The following morning, just as the sun peeked over the pine trees, Sydney laced up her running sneakers and set out on a run. The only sounds were the slap of her feet on the gravel road and the chorus of shrieking birds, belting their early-morning calls from tree branches overhead.

As she rounded the bend toward town, the quick snap of a sleek brown head caught her attention, and she grinned at a deer just inside the forest. She breathed in the clean, cold, dewy air and tasted the new day on her tongue. Nothing in New York City rivaled this purity.

She unzipped the collar of her fleece jacket as her body warmed. The cool autumn air tickled her damp neck and sent shivers across her skin. Just a couple more miles and she'd reward herself with hot coffee back at her mom's place.

She didn't particularly enjoy running, but when her thoughts knocked around her brain like hummingbirds on steroids, she'd lace up her sneakers and find herself slightly more centered when the effort was behind her.

Being at her mother's apartment would require at least a 5K. While Sydney loved her mother as any dutiful child should, she also pitied her. Karen's small-town dreams seemed just that: small. Sydney had worked day and night as an undergrad in Chicago and then completed law school in New York to secure a six-digit income, while Karen chatted with locals about the weather and peddled spy novels to meandering tourists. Their lives couldn't have been more different.

As Sydney rounded a bend in the road, brick storefronts

appeared and then the familiar red neon sign at Utz's. There, in the parking lot, sat her black BMW. She jogged closer to find a pair of dirt-splotched jeans and work boots sticking out from under the back end of her jacked-up car.

"Hey." She slowed to a halt next to the jeans and boots and pushed the damp strands of hair out of her face as icy breath burned her lungs. When the body rolled out from under the car, that breath threatened to choke her. *Shit, he's good-looking.*

"Hey." As he stood, sharp early-morning light caught the auburn strands in his wild hair, and long lashes framed his bright chocolate eyes, her view unencumbered by yesterday's baseball cap. With a firm brow he crossed his arms and stared down at her bumper.

She cleared her throat. *Focus.* "I figured after the way we left things yesterday, maybe you'd thought twice about helping me."

"I did," he said. "But I also thought maybe the sooner your car was fixed, the sooner you'd head out of town, so I woke up at the break of dawn to get started."

Her eyes narrowed, but he cracked a smile. His whole face brightened.

"Lighten up."

"Well, thank you. In any case." She cleared her throat again and reached for her absent necklace while her heart continued to race.

His gaze lingered a little too long, like instead of a normal human woman she was a giraffe who'd wandered into town.

"It should be okay to drive." He wiped his hands on his already filthy jeans. "I can replace the bulb in the taillight, and other than that, it's mostly cosmetic. It won't be cheap, but you don't need to have it fixed right away. Maybe wait until you get back to the big city and find a dealer to take even more of your money."

Defiance flared in her chest. "I have a friend who has a

hookup." *If I ever get back to New York.* "So, you're right,
I will wait. But I won't pay more."

He raised his eyebrows and shifted, widening his stance.
Even with his feet spread, the man was tall. At least six feet
two. His broad shoulders stretched the soft flannel of his
work shirt, and peeking out from the sleeves were sinewy,
tanned forearms that belonged in Dodge truck commer-
cials. She'd never been attracted to rugged men before, instead going after slick finance guys, but anyone who found
the male species attractive would be hard-pressed not to
drool in Sam Kirkland's presence.

"You always up this early?" he asked.

"Not really." *Not since I used to wake up at four to work
out and be in the office by six.* She forced the twisted expression from her face. This veritable stranger didn't care
about the ups and downs of the last two years of her life.
"I'm sleeping on my mom's pullout couch, and I think
I clocked a solid forty-five minutes last night. It's awful. I
figured once the sun came up, I could take advantage of the
quiet and the scenery. Clear my head a little. It's so gorgeous up here."

"You like the mountains?" He dropped his chin as his
eyebrows shot up in his forehead.

"Sure. Why? Shouldn't I?"

"Aren't you a lawyer by trade, Sydney Walsh?"

Nausea rose up in her throat, and her hands instinctively
crossed over her stomach. *The stifling conference room, the
creased brows of the partners, Mr. Fulton's assistant with
a phone in her hand, asking if she should call 911.* The visions popped in and out of her head like camera flashes.

"No."

"You seem like you love to argue."

She shook out her tingling fingertips and capitalized on
the sudden urge to run. "I'm gonna go. Thank you so much

for taking care of the car. I'll drive it over to wherever your shop is sometime soon for the taillight."

His face twisted in confusion, but she didn't have the time or energy to explain any further. With a quick turn and a soft crunch of dirt, she ran.

chapter **three**

The key slipped easily into the lock. No gate. No security system. No dead bolt. One simple lock opened with one single brass key and Sydney entered the Loving Page. Crime must be nonexistent in Pine Ridge. What did the cops up here do all day?

The modest bookshop specialized in Adirondack-themed novels, nature books, and field guides, along with posters from local artisans, pine-scented candles, and a handful of greeting cards. Infinitesimal motes floated through the stale shop air, and as Sydney ran her finger across a table display of Larry Harding's newest mountain-themed thriller, *Shoot! An Adirondack Whodunnit*, a clump of gray dust clung to her skin.

Simple metal shelves along the walls and heavy oak tables served as spaces to feature the books, but the true beauty of the room wasn't in what Karen had done to it but in what had been infused into the shop at conception.

Whoever had built this space wanted it to be something special. Exposed beams lined the vaulted ceiling, while textured cream-colored walls transformed the room from bookshop to literary haven, reminiscent of an English cottage by the sea. Loamy autumn light filtered in through heavy glass windows, and at the far side of the room, a green velvet tufted window seat all but disappeared beneath piles of old newspaper. Sydney's fingers itched to find the nearest trash can and uncover the jewel underneath all the clutter.

She found a cinnamon-and-cedar-scented oil diffuser under the register and opened it, immediately regretting her offer to open the shop for Karen. The shop needed some serious tender loving care, not to mention a top-to-bottom clean. The warm, spicy aroma subtly radiated from the diffuser and forced an angry yawn from her gut. First things first. Breakfast.

The street was empty, save for a few straggling tourists on the hunt for an early breakfast. The scent of rich roasted coffee delicately layered with sweetness hung heavy in the air, and she crossed the street toward McDonagh's Bakery, silently praying that the heavenly aroma originated there.

She pushed through the front door, sending a tiny bell jingling merrily over her head, and breathed in deep. The air was perfumed with toasted sugar, ripe fruit, and spicy chocolate, along with the familiar roasted coffee lifting each scent to new heights. Each bakery case boasted a new treat: domed muffins speckled with glittering coarse sugar; fry cakes dripping with chocolate icing; Danish featuring a rainbow of sumptuous fillings. Sydney could barely take it all in.

"Morning." A bubbly young woman greeted her. "What can I get for you?"

"Oh, um, coffee, first of all," Sydney said, her eyes glued to the bakery cases. "And then . . . Oh man, I don't know.

Which of these is low-calorie, sugar-free, dairy-free, gluten-free?" She looked up in time to catch the woman's frozen expression. "Joking."

"Oh, good." Her face melted into a grin. She flipped her short blond hair to one side, revealing an impressive row of ear piercings. "I was about to throw a chocolate chip muffin at your head."

"I want to order everything, but in the interest of not dying of diabetic shock . . . A muffin? Blueberry?"

"Great choice. They're some of our best sellers. Although if you want the real McDonagh's experience, have a donut. We're famous for them."

Sydney choked back a snide remark. "Famous" must've meant a write-up in the local *Pine Ridge Gazette*.

"Okay, you twisted my arm. I'll take a donut, too. Whichever flavor is most popular."

The young woman plucked a fat blueberry muffin from the tray beneath the glass counter and slid it into a white paper bag. A dusting of sugar crystals fell onto the counter, and Sydney had to take a step back to keep from licking them up.

"And let's see . . ." The girl's Barbie-blue eyes scanned the row of donuts in the case adjacent to the muffins. "Chocolate frosted. For sure." She set Sydney's bag on the counter and turned to the coffeepot in the back corner of the tiny shop.

"You in town for the weekend?" She filled a tall foam cup with deliciously dark coffee.

"Mm, kind of," Sydney said. *Am I? Is it just the weekend? If not, where the fuck do I go from here?* She took a deep breath and forced confidence into her voice. "I'm Karen Walsh's daughter."

"Of course," the woman said, her eyes lighting with recognition. "I totally see the resemblance now. Sydney, right? Karen showed me a picture once. I'm Jorie McDonagh. My parents own this bakery."

"Jorie, very nice to meet you."

"So, what have you been up to since you got into town?"

"Oh." Sydney pushed away thoughts of Connor. *Trying not to remember the real reason I'm here.* "I only got in yesterday, so not a whole lot. Doesn't seem like there's much to do around here."

Jorie's smile faded, and Sydney immediately regretted her comment.

"Of course," Sydney continued, "like I said, I just got in. So I'm sure I haven't scratched the surface of Pine Ridge just yet."

"Well," Jorie said. "There is one bar that's pretty fun."

"Utz's? I was there last night. It was . . ." *Dead. Deader than dead.* "Quiet."

"No." One side of Jorie's mouth twitched into a smile. "Not Utz's. This place is called Taylor's, and they have music and pool and drink specials. It's nothing as fancy as what I'm sure you're used to in New York, but you might like it."

"Sounds fun," Sydney said. What was fun anymore? All the events Connor paraded her around at in New York were supposed to be fun but eventually turned oppressive. "Fun" seemed a distant concept, only truly achieved by sinking into a hot bath in the peaceful quiet of her apartment. *No, not your apartment anymore. His apartment. Connor's apartment. Connor and the blonde.*

She swallowed.

"If you get bored you could come with me tonight." Jorie's goodwill confused her. Was she simply being kind to a new girl in town? Sydney couldn't remember the last time anyone had been so unabashedly warm to her.

Should she join Jorie at the local bar? She hadn't been the most gracious guest to Sam or her mother, and she feared she'd be even pricklier toward a group of locals. The sting of Connor's betrayal still ran hot over her skin, and at this point, she'd do anything necessary to protect herself from future pain.

"Thanks so much for the invite, but I might stay in with my mom tonight. I feel bad bailing on her when I just got into town."

"Okay, sure." Jorie shrugged and brushed a few crumbs off the counter. "If you change your mind, though, here's my number." She scribbled a phone number on a slip of receipt paper and handed it to Sydney.

"Thanks," Sydney said. With one last shot at kindness, she added, "If my mom falls asleep early or is just generally sick of me, I'll definitely shoot you a text."

Sydney carried her treats and steaming-hot coffee back to the Loving Page and settled in behind the register. The morning passed by slowly, with only a handful of people wandering in and out of the store, and not a single sale to be had. Lunch came and went, and the only action of the day consisted of twenty levels of Candy Crush completion. How could her mother maintain an income on this level of patronage?

As the sun lowered in the sky and dusk settled over downtown, Sydney rang up the single sale of the day. A middle-aged woman and her two children were forced to buy a small glass Christmas ornament that one of the rascals broke as he raced by in a game of tag. Sydney flipped the sign in the window to CLOSED and glanced around the shop. The ten-dollar ornament barely covered the electric bill for the day.

She found the key to the back office and let herself in, sitting down at her mother's cluttered desk in search of receipts or an accounting ledger. The plug for the ancient desktop computer sat exposed on the cracked linoleum floor, coated in a fuzzy layer of dust. Seemed it wasn't her mother's top choice in bookkeeping efforts.

Growing up, Sydney had no idea she and Karen were poor. Karen made every effort to provide at least a handful of gifts at Christmas, the occasional trip to the movies, and three square meals a day. It wasn't until she got to high school that she met kids who'd never even heard of food stamps and had all vacationed in Orlando. Sydney and Karen's vacations consisted of a tent and tins of baked beans over a rickety portable grill.

On Sydney's first day of freshman year, bright with enthusiasm for her new journey into high school, a group of popular girls pointed and laughed at her off-brand backpack. She looked down at her clothes—last year's sneakers, her toes straining at the fabric, and Walmart jeans. Hot tears of shame sprung up in her eyes. Later that day, she found a part-time job to buy herself the things Karen couldn't. From then on, she promised herself she'd never let anyone view her as less than.

Tucked inside the wooden in-box at the corner of Karen's desk was a stack of envelopes tied together with red string. Sydney paused and peered closer. OVERDUE. FINAL NOTICE. ACCOUNT SUSPENDED. Her mouth dried up. She shuffled through the papers, hoping to see recovery efforts, but found none.

Sydney stared at the monstrous pile of bills sitting in front of her, barely able to soak in the magnitude of debt. Karen covered the rent on the store and her apartment, but everything else was paid for in borrowed money. A small-business loan, credit cards upon credit cards upon credit cards, and the cherry on the sundae—a letter from her sister in Tucson asking if Karen would be able to start paying back the thousand dollars she'd lent her last year.

The room spun, and the walls of the tiny office closed in. Sydney pressed her forehead into the palms of her hands. Not only was her mother in jeopardy of losing the store, but she was on the verge of having to file for bankruptcy. Bitter laughter rose up in Sydney's throat, and she stared at the cork ceiling tiles. She'd actually considered asking Karen for money. They were the blind leading the blind.

Sydney abandoned the red Schwinn bike she'd ridden in on this morning and walked the long, winding road back to

Karen's apartment. Twisted, convoluted scenarios clouded her mind. Karen always talked about the store as if it thrived. What would've happened if Sydney had never poked around in her bills? Would Karen have silently slid into bankruptcy and moved to a different town? Shown up in New York to stay on Sydney's couch? Lived on the streets? The air around her was cold, but she couldn't even feel it.

By the time she entered Karen's apartment, hot tears of fury burned her eyes. The initial anger and disbelief she'd felt at the store had built up as she walked and now threatened to spill over.

"Hi, Suds," her mom said brightly, hunched over a cross-word puzzle in her usual spot in the armchair. "How'd it go today?"

Sydney walked purposefully into the living room, trying to tamp down the emotion churning inside her.

"Mom." Her voice trembled. "I was in the office and happened to see the stack of bills sitting there."

She waited for her mother to look up at her in shame, embarrassment, anger, anything. But Karen kept her pencil poised over the notebook, working at her lip as she attempted to figure out a six-letter word for "flower."

"Mm-hmm," she mumbled. " 'Daisy' . . . no . . . 'peony' . . . 'orchid'! 'Orchid.' Duh."

"Mom." The simmering anger in her voice turned to ice.

Karen finally looked up at Sydney through Coke-bottle glasses.

"Do you have any idea how bad this is?"

"Oh, don't be dramatic." Karen tossed a hand at her daughter. "Do you know how far past due you have to go for them to turn off your lights? It was a slow summer, with the rain and all. Kept the tourists away. I'm going to stay open this winter and catch all those ski bunnies who come in January and February. Then I'll be back in the black."

Sydney's lips parted. Could her mother be this thick?

Years ago, Karen herself had told Sydney that most of the shops in Pine Ridge closed after Thanksgiving because the tourist stream all but dried up. If Karen thought the smattering of shoppers drifting through town on their way to the ski mountains was going to save her business, she was daft.

"You borrowed money from Aunt Patty."

Now Karen looked peeved. Finally.

"I saw the letter."

"You know," Karen began, removing her glasses and glaring up at her daughter. "I survived sixty-four years on this planet without your help. I raised a daughter, I put her through college, I opened a business, and I kept myself alive and fed with a roof over my skull for all that time. Can you believe it? I'm glad you're here, but I don't need you poking around in my finances. *Capisce*?"

"How many of those sixty-four years were we on the verge of being homeless?"

Karen sat bolt upright in her chair, a tic in her jaw. Sydney had seen that look before—right after Sydney got caught making out with Jim Palombo in her bedroom, or the time she blew her curfew by four hours.

"We were never close to homeless." It was as close to a growl as Sydney had ever heard from her mother. "I made sure every single day that we had everything we needed."

" 'Needed' is a very loose term."

Color rose in Karen's wrinkled cheeks, and her jaw twitched again. "Did you ever go hungry? Did we ever get evicted? I did for you what I thought was most important. Okay, so you didn't have a cell phone in middle school or a new car on your sixteenth birthday. Who cares? You think that's what's important?"

The shame sliced deeper, a searing pain in places Sydney didn't know she was capable of probing any longer. Old shame. The first shame. She ran her hands over her expertly faded denim, remembering the deal she got. Fifteen percent off. Only three hundred dollars. A steal. A second dip into the savings and they were hers.

"You were never good with money," Sydney said. She gnawed at her lip, sure by now that it was bleeding. The feeble retort landed between them, and Karen's jaw finally relaxed.

"You'd be surprised how good you have to be with money to raise a kid on one income and still have money left over to put into savings. I scraped every extra penny I had together, and when you were finally off living your own life, I did the thing I'd always wanted to do. The bookstore. I made it work, Suds. Me. By myself."

The anger rose into Sydney's throat. All those pennies and what did Karen have to show for it? A dusty shop that pulled in ten dollars a day on the verge of going belly-up.

"You're going to go bankrupt. Not only will you lose the store, you'll have to declare bankruptcy. You can't pay your bills. And one person bought something at the store today. One single person. She spent ten dollars. Do you understand that? What's wrong with you? It's dollars and sense. No room for interpretation."

Karen stared hard at the crossword, her eyebrows meeting in the middle. "Eight letter word for 'dog' . . . 'Mastiff'? 'Bulldog?' No . . ."

"Mom!"

Karen turned her steel-eyed stare on Sydney and in a low hiss said, "I am done talking about this."

The apartment squeezed Sydney from all sides. No way out. No release. Her "bed" was half a foot from where her mother sat, and the only other safe space was the bathroom, where she could only hide out for so long. In a move of desperation, she retrieved Jorie's phone number from the back pocket of her jeans and punched it into her phone.

Hi Jorie, it's Sydney. We met earlier today. I'd actually love to join you and your friends for a drink,

if you're still doing that. Just tell me when and
where :)

Absolutely! Taylor's in town, in about half an hour. I
can swing by and pick you up if you need a ride?

"I'm going out for a drink," Sydney said.
"Good, have a couple. Maybe it'll loosen you up."
Sydney snatched her purse and slammed the door be-
hind her.

chapter **four**

Thwap. The bottle suctioned against Sam's lips as he pulled it away. Taylor's brimmed with bodies. At least three of them he didn't recognize. *Must be a record.*

"Hey, Jerk-land. You in there?" Greg's voice shattered his thoughts.

"Really? Jerk-land? 'Cause if we're going back to high school nicknames, Pit Stain . . ."

"All right," Greg said. He adjusted his baseball cap and ran a hand over his paunch. "No need to go there, thanks. You need another beer?"

"Nah—" Sam had had his one drink for the night, but Matt interrupted.

"Get a bucket." Matt hung a huge, beefy arm over Greg's shoulders. Heaven forbid this crew walked out of a bar without a full table of empties in their wake. "Jorie's coming, too."

The consistent trio of buzzes coming from Sam's pocket forced a wince. He'd given her number its own text alert and ringtone so that he'd know as soon as humanly possible when she was reaching out. He wanted to be prepared before he read whatever she had to say or before he heard her fragile voice over the line.

"Liv?" Matt asked.

Sam bit down on the inside of his lip. Guess he'd have to work on his poker face. He pushed himself out of the booth and navigated the thickening crowd to make his way outside. The cold air stung his eyes as he pressed the phone to his ear.

"Hello?"

"Hi." Silence dragged across the line, his heart beating louder with every passing second.

"What's going on? Everything all right?"

"I'm fine." She cleared her throat. "We're fine."

He squeezed his eyes shut and leaned back onto the facade of the bar. The weathered siding dug through his T-shirt, but the dull pain provided strange relief. *You're here. She's there.*

"So, uh, what do you need, then, Liv?"

"Right to the chase, huh? No pleasantries? No 'How are you? What's new?' You assume I'm calling because I need something, right? I couldn't just call to say hello?"

Hot fury rose to the surface of his skin, forcing his grip on the phone to tighten. Was she serious? He'd put his life on hold for her, and she wanted pleasantries? He forced his voice into something resembling neutral. "Is this Olivia's Land of Make-Believe?"

"I'm trying." Right now, she probably had a strand of bright blond hair tucked into the corner of her mouth. Stressed or drunk or both, she chewed on her hair. She'd done it since they were young. Other kids made fun of her for it, but Sam had always come to her rescue. He was still doing it now.

"I'm sorry," Sam said. "I don't want to fight with you." In the past year, all they'd done was fight.

"I *never* want to fight with you."

A sense of foreboding knocked at the back of his brain, warning him that the sweet timbre in her voice signaled a turn in the discussion. He wasn't in the mood for casual conversation. Especially with her. He had to right the ship.

"How's Jay?"

She breathed out slowly. "Good. Fine. I don't know."

Blood surged to his cheeks once more, as if he had a sunburn from the inside out. "You don't know how your son is doing?"

"No, I mean, I *know*. I just can never really tell how he's doing. He's got his appetite back, so that's good. His grandparents cook the most disgusting food you can ever imagine, but he's packing it in and gaining some weight. The doctor says he's back in a healthy range for kids his age."

"Well, that's a relief."

"Are we really wasting time talking about Jay's eating habits?"

He tucked his arm across his chest and bit down on his lip again. If not for Jay, he'd ignore her calls completely. When he agreed to this ridiculous charade, he'd had only Jay in mind. Okay, maybe he'd also been thinking of the way Liv helped his mother. How lost he would've been navigating the waters of diagnosis and chemo and hospice without Nurse Liv walking him through it all. Maybe he'd thought about what a great friend she used to be and how some people deserved a second chance.

He couldn't go there now. He cleared his throat, forcing his mind back to the task at hand. "Well, what, then? What do you need?"

"I had to pay out of pocket for Jay's doctor's appointment. The insurance company is going to reimburse me eventually, but it was almost two hundred dollars. I had to give them practically every penny I have to my name, and since I haven't been able to take any shifts at the hospital because of the garbage they're putting me through down here, I'm super low on funds. I'll have the money soon, and I can totally pay you back, but right now, I'm just . . ."

"All right." Money. That he could do.

"Thank you." Her voice squeaked. "God, what would I do without you?"

Sam's stomach churned with nerves. Without him? *Lose any chance of having custody of your son.*

Sam breathed in, counted to ten, and breathed out. Icy air on his tongue and teeth, past his throat, into his lungs. *I'm here. She's there.* Olivia made his head swim.

"I'll Venmo you tomorrow," he said.

"Thank you, Sam. Seriously."

Ser-iousssly. Was she drunk? He narrowed his gaze, as if she stood in front of him instead of hundreds of miles away, and zeroed in on her speech patterns. The speech patterns he knew better than anyone's. If she'd been drinking, even a single beer, he'd lose it.

"Is that all?" he asked.

"Well, yeah. I guess so." This time, no slurring. Her words were clipped and clean. The constant analysis sapped at his strength like donating blood. She wasn't drunk. She hadn't been drunk since the day of the DUI. Someday he wouldn't question it.

"I gotta go, Liv."

"Hang on, someone wants to say hello to you."

He dropped his gaze to the snow-covered gravel beneath his boots and released a labored exhale. Liv's ability to rip him out of a carefree evening was unrivaled, even when she wasn't trying.

"Hi, Sam!" Jay's sweet voice sang across the line, and Sam grinned despite himself.

"Hey, bud. How's it going?"

"Good. Just finished dinner."

"Oh yeah? What'd you have?"

"Grandma made meat loaf." Jay lowered his voice and whispered, "It wasn't very good."

"Meat loaf's the worst."

"Yeah, but I told her I liked it anyway. I didn't want to hurt her feelings."

Sam's heart split in two. This kid didn't deserve half the shit that had happened to him in his eight years on the planet.

"Listen, bud, I gotta go. Tell your mom I said bye, okay?"

"Okay." Disappointment creeped into the kid's voice, but Sam couldn't let himself sink into that world. He'd drawn the lines of this situation, and he had to stick to them.

"We'll talk again soon, all right?"

"Okay."

"And hey, I got that picture you drew me. Put it on my fridge."

"You did?" His voice soared.

"Of course I did. But hey, you traced that, right? There's no way you did that on your own."

"I didn't trace it! Sam, I promise, I didn't trace it."

Sam grinned. "You're too good, Jay. Draw me another one?"

"Okay, yeah! I will. I'll do it this weekend and have Mom send it."

"Amazing. I'll talk to you soon, bud."

"Okay." Jay waited a beat and said, "Bye, Sam."

Sam ended the call, slipped his phone into his pocket, and ducked back inside. Matt's and Greg's narrowed eyes trailed him as he crossed the bar and slid into the booth.

"How's Liv doing?" Matt asked.

"Fine." Sam grabbed the bottle of water Matt had gotten him from the bar, already tucking Liv and Jay into the back of his mind. He took a long drink and grimaced at the bucket of Bud Light on the table. "There's so much good beer around here and you guys drink this piss."

"When that good beer costs ten bucks for a bucket, I'll start drinking that," Greg said. He leaned his heft back in the booth, his beady eyes skipping around the room as if all three of them hadn't seen everything there was to see in this town. "Giants are gonna take a beating next weekend. If they knew what was good for 'em, they'd bench Tahoe and start thinking about their prospects for next year."

"Bench Tahoe?" Matt countered. "You're out of your goddamned mind."

"Why not? He's—" Greg dipped his chin, lips parted, as he gaped at the front door to the bar. "Whoa. Who's that with Jorie?"

"Never seen her before." Matt squinted. "Is that Wainman's sister?"

"Fuck no," Greg said. "Wainman's sister isn't half that hot."

While Sam had enough female problems to last a lifetime, he wasn't above admiring a cute girl in a bar. He tossed a glance over his shoulder, careful not to look overly interested, and huffed. Of course. Sydney Walsh.

Among the plaid- and camo-clad crowd, Sydney stuck out like a cardinal in the snow. She wore tight jeans and a silky black blouse, her diamond earrings sparkling in the low bar light. Every male head turned to stare as she passed by, like a perverted parting of the Red Sea.

"It's Karen Walsh's daughter," Sam said.

"Oh-ho-ho," Greg said, laughing. "That explains it. Her hotness comes courtesy of a rich boyfriend and New York City plastic surgeons."

Earlier today, when she approached Sam in the parking lot of Utz's with her hair pulled off her face, dressed simply in yoga pants and a track jacket, he'd been caught off guard by her natural beauty. If anything about her was surgically enhanced, the doctor deserved an award.

"Hi, guys!" Jorie said, grinning at all of them but finding her rightful place snuggled in Matt's lap. "This is Sydney Walsh; she's Karen's daughter. Be nice to her, and don't try to get in her pants, okay?"

Sydney's cheeks were already pink from the cold outside, but as she met Sam's eyes, the blush spread to her neck. He forced his gaze away from the dip in her blouse, but it hung low enough to expose the slightest hint of a black lace bra. He chugged his water. *Football, fishing, Aunt Tracy's hairy chin mole, muddy boots . . . Liv.* Spell: broken.

"How's the car?" Sam asked, careful to keep his voice even and detached.

Sydney raised her chin and pressed her shoulders back. "It's fine. Drivable. Like you said."

A dry cough caught his attention. Jorie now sat bolt upright on Matt's lap. She was on high alert. Her jaw tightened in a stern look of warning he'd grown to fear over the years. "You two know each other?"

"Yeah, Andretti over here hit me with her car last night outside Utz's."

Sydney rolled her eyes. "I barely tapped you."

"You were both at Utz's?" Jorie cut in.

"Jesus," Sam said on a breath. He raised an eyebrow in his own version of a warning glare. Jorie wanted him to be happy, but she also wanted to keep the situation between Liv and him as peaceful as possible. Occasionally it made her seem like a referee in the game of his life.

"I might need your help after all," Sydney said. "I'm thinking of selling the car, so I'll have to get the bumper and taillight fixed before I do."

Sam ran his tongue across his bottom lip. This girl was a mystery. She showed up in Pine Ridge out of the blue, and now she wanted to get rid of her car. Maybe she was running from the law.

"It's yours?" he asked. "Title and registration?"

"Yes, it's mine." Her steely gaze matched her sharp tone. "Who else would it belong to?"

"Table's open!" Greg said, nodding toward the pool table. He shot Sam a *Chill out* look before nudging him out of the booth.

"Oh, great!" Jorie said. "Perfect timing."

Matt rolled his eyes. "Baby. Come on. Let us play a game, and then you can play next round."

"So unfair." Jorie tossed her purse into the booth, grabbed a pool cue, and chalked the end as she stared daggers into her boyfriend. "I'm playing."

"Well, hell, I'm not playing with her," Greg grumbled.

"I'll play with her," Matt said, literally dragging his feet as he joined Jorie at the table. "And, Sydney, you can play on the other team. That way it's fair . . . ish. Sam? You up?"

Sam ran his hands over the legs of his jeans and cracked his neck. As long as he stayed on the opposite side of the table from Sydney, he'd be fine. No smelling her perfume, none of her snarky remarks. He raised his eyebrows in silent agreement before grabbing a pool cue from the rack and chalking the end.

Sydney grabbed her own cue before leaning over the table for a practice shot, her blouse and bra and everything they were meant to contain suddenly on full display.

Shit.

chapter **five**

Sam grabbed a beer from the bucket on the table and handed it to Sydney. "You drinking?"

"Sure." She took the beer and twisted the cap, squeezing her breasts together as she went. Still trembling from the interaction with her mother, she craved control in any form.

Sam stood before her, smoldering intensity burning in his eyes. Maybe a one-night stand would find her less unsteady in the morning.

"I'm actually better when I'm drunk."

He blinked, and as if a veil had lifted, the heat was replaced by a vacant stare. Had she said something insulting? He turned over his shoulder, leaving Sydney confused and alone.

After a few terse words with Jorie, Matt tossed up his hands, stepped backward, and watched with pursed lips as his girlfriend poised to break. When the cue ball barely grazed the ball at the top of the pyramid, Matt grumbled and reracked.

"This game is going to be endless," Sam said under his breath.

"What makes you think I'm terrible, too?" Sydney asked. "Because I'm a woman?"

"*I* never said you were anything. Matt implied you're at Jorie's skill level."

"Hey." She leaned into him. Time to disprove some stereotypes. "Let's put some money on it."

Sam raised one dark eyebrow. "Yeah?"

She shrugged, a grin curling her mouth. "Let's just say, dudes who thought girls can't shoot pool ended up paying most of my college bar tabs."

With a wild gleam in his eyes, Sam turned to his friend and clapped him on the shoulder. "Yo, Matty. Care to up the stakes?"

A slow grin spread across Matt's full-moon face. "You serious?"

"'Course. Fifty bucks?"

"Whoa-ho-ho!" Greg chuckled from the booth. "Who is this guy?"

"Hell yeah, man," Matt said. "Now I'm having fun."

Sam met Sydney's gaze and held it for a moment, raising his eyebrows. They were in this together. A thrill ran through her veins, and she took a long drink of the cheap beer to calm her frayed nerves. It wasn't strong enough.

"Give me one minute, okay?" she said. She moved through the dense crowd, squeezing through the mostly male patrons, and sidled up to the bar. Before she could order a shot of whiskey, Sam was next to her. Was it the mass of bodies that forced him to press himself against her? As his warm, clean scent drifted over her, she didn't care.

"Shot of Jack, please," she said as the bartender approached.

"And gimme a Coke." Sam tossed a twenty-dollar bill on the bar.

"You don't have to pay for me," she said. The soft skin of his forearm brushed against her elbow and caused the lump in her throat to nearly choke her.

"If you're as good as you claim to be, we'll make it all back." He ran his tongue over his full bottom lip, and she leaned in toward him. The pull was magnetic.

"Here you go." The bartender set down the drinks, and they clinked their glasses together before she threw hers back. The whiskey warmed her throat and stung her nostrils.

"All right," she said through a cough. "Now I'm ready."

As she turned away from the bar to head back toward the pool table, his hand rested on her lower back. The touch sent shivers all the way down her legs and into her toes. Had he meant to touch her? Was it an invitation? She needed to feel good tonight. She needed this attractive mountain man to be the one who made her feel it.

Back at the pool table, Matt broke, sending a single striped ball into the corner pocket. After snagging one more stripe, he missed the third shot and Sam stepped up. Sam set his sights on the purple four ball and sunk it with no problem. He missed his next shot, Jorie avoided hitting anything other than the cue ball, and then it was Sydney's turn.

She surveyed the table and avoided the most obvious shot, the orange five ball hovering near the side pocket. Instead, she used her nondominant hand, aimed at an impossible shot, and missed.

"*Dude*." Sam's scolding voice carried across the table.

"What are you gonna do, right?" she said, sending him a wink.

He ran his tongue over his bottom lip again. His lips pulled into a grin, sharing their pool shark secret. The whiskey burned in her belly, begging her to do the stupid thing.

Matt sunk one more ball, Sam did the same, Jorie nicked the felt, and then Sydney was up again. This time there was no easy shot. She found the most logical choice, set up her angle, and sunk the ball without issue. She looked up in time to see Matt's jaw hanging.

"Hey, nice shot!" Jorie said brightly.

"Where's your loyalty?" Matt teased. He reached out to grab her hand and pulled her into his side, tucking a soft kiss in her blond hair. The sweet sentiment burned into Sydney. *Connor and the blonde.* She clenched her teeth.

Sydney set up her next shot and sunk it with ease. In one single turn, she managed to sink all but the eight ball.

"Oh, okay, cool," Matt said, his gaze level. "So you pool-sharked us."

Sydney shrugged, a devilish smile playing on her lips.

"I never pool-sharked anyone," she said. "You just assumed, since I'm a woman, that I'm terrible at pool. It's kinda more on you than me, I'd say." A few other men from the bar had joined Greg in the booth, and they all hooted and hollered like a pack of monkeys.

"Oh man, a feminist," Matt groaned. "Great. How long are you here for again?"

Jorie slapped his arm, and he ran a hand over his face, clearly embarrassed to have been schooled by a girl. But Sydney was flying. She loved revealing her skills to unsuspecting men who thought they knew better.

After Matt's turn, Sam sunk the eight ball without issue, and as soon as the ball plunked into the pocket, Sydney yelped and thrust her arms in the air. Sam's arms wrapped around her waist and lifted her clear off the floor in triumph. The wind escaped her lungs in a single rush as she swallowed down the sensation of his arms pressing against her ribs, his face in her neck, and his belt buckle against her thighs. She wanted to breathe in his scent and wrap her legs around his waist, but she wasn't drunk enough to completely forget where she was just yet.

He set her down, and his eyes sparkled. She could only imagine what he wanted from her. She'd seen that look before. And she was single, after all. Recently single. *Connor and the blonde.* A new, fresh flare of anxiety burned inside her gut.

"Come on." She cleared her throat and forced Connor out of her head. "Drinks are on us. Or should I say, on Matt?" She watched Sam's Adam's apple bob up and down as he studied her face. His hands trailed across her hips and fell at his sides. She could almost taste the tension.

They spent their winnings on a round for the group, and after her third drink, Sydney settled into the booth next to Jorie. For the first time in a long time, she felt perfectly at peace.

Inhibitions lowered, Jorie chattered away about the bakery and her parents and her older sister who lived two towns over, and Sydney simply let the information wash over her. Jorie was sweet and kind, and her friends were easygoing and fun. No one was concerned about the outcome of a high-stakes case or who was vacationing at which island this winter. Being in Pine Ridge felt like taking a break from real life.

"So, what about you?" Jorie asked, draining her beer bottle. "You have a boyfriend?"

"No," Sydney said. "Um . . . no." *Thirty-six hours ago I watched my boyfriend have sex with another woman on our bed. In our sheets. Possibly wearing my earrings.*

"Okay." Jorie narrowed her gaze. "I feel like there's more there than just a no."

Sydney cleared her throat and studied Jorie's pretty, honest face. She barely knew the girl, but she wanted to open her guts and spill them across the table. Instead, she bit the inside of her cheek.

A hiccup escaped Jorie's mouth. "Oh God, hiccups. Matt will never let me live this down. I'm not even drunk."

"Let me get you some water," Sydney offered.

"Oh, no, Matt will get it for me." She waved across the

bar at Matt, whose eyes never truly left her, and he mouthed, *Water?* She grinned and gave him the thumbs-up.

"Damn, you guys are really in sync," Sydney marveled.

"We've been together since we were sixteen. He knows more about me than I do."

"That's a long time," Sydney said.

"Heck yeah, it is. Twelve years. And here I am, still waiting for this jerk to put a ring on it." A hiccup bubbled up, and she rolled her eyes. "So, what about you? Ever been close to marriage?"

"No," she said, her voice barely above a whisper. She reached for the chain again and cursed herself for forgetting it wasn't there.

"Not much for gossip, are you?" Jorie teased.

"It's not that." Sydney laughed.

"Sorry," Jorie said. "I'm prying."

"You're not." She took another swallow of beer and tried to clear her thoughts. "I just found out my boyfriend cheated on me. Has been cheating on me. God, I don't even know the full story."

"Wow." Jorie placed a cool hand on Sydney's arm, her brow tightening. "I'm so sorry."

"That's why I'm here," Sydney said. "We lived together, and I don't have a job at the moment. Not full time, anyway. When I caught him cheating and ran out with my suitcase, I realized I actually had no place else to go. My friend Bee would probably have let me crash for a couple of nights, but honestly, I was embarrassed. I couldn't bring myself to call her and tell her the truth about what happened."

Her eyes flickered over to Jorie, waiting for the judgmental sneer to appear and cast her off as a gold digger. But Jorie's kind eyes remained steady.

"Well, Sydney, I'll tell you what. You're not the first woman in this position. And you won't be the last." She patted Sydney's arm. "But man, what a shit thing to do to someone. You must be mad as hell."

The relief trickled into Sydney's heart, and she cracked a smile. Was it that easy to open up to a girlfriend here in mountain country? Whenever she bemoaned her lack of full-time work to friends in New York, they gave her pitying stares and changed the subject. In their eyes, the woman who depended on a man to take care of her was the ultimate offense to feminism. Even Bee, the one friend she'd held on to since college, had grown tired of her happy hour invites being turned down for fundraising galas and drinks with Connor's frat buddies. But Jorie had compassion.

Matt approached with Jorie's water bottle and handed Sydney another beer.

"You guys trying to get me drunk?" Sydney asked, gratefully accepting the drink. Her conversation with Jorie was as much emotional outpouring as she could handle tonight.

"Nah, yer man over there told me I was being a jerk by assuming you were a shitty pool player just because you're a girl. So I thought I owed you a drink."

Sydney found Sam sitting at the bar. His limber body perched on a stool as Greg talked at him. Sam nodded along, with his arms crossed over his chest, and as he adjusted, the hint of a tattoo peeked out from the sleeve of his royal-blue T-shirt. Sydney's legs turned to jelly.

As the night went on and the alcohol seeped further and further into Sydney's bloodstream, she nearly forgot about the mess of chaos her life had become. She was having fun. She and Jorie grooved along to the nineties' hits blaring from the jukebox, and only when Matt jumped in to steal his girl away did Sydney collapse into a sweaty heap in the booth.

"You're a lot more fun than I thought you'd be," Greg said. He adjusted the belt around his paunchy middle, his gaze roaming across Sydney's chest.

"Thanks?" Her patience for comments about her uppity appearance wore thin. She didn't have a drink of her own, so with her vision swimming, she focused on the closest beer bottle and took a swig.

"Sure, Greg doesn't mind," Sam said. "Have a sip."

A grin tugged at her lips, and she leaned over the table, fully aware that her blouse dipped low. She pressed her breasts together and watched with dark delight as Sam's gaze lighted on her chest. He shifted, his mouth pressed into a firm line, and leaned back in the booth.

"Guess I'll get myself another drink," she said. The alcohol had released the demons inside her, and she swiveled her hips as she passed by Sam. When he joined her at the bar, she knew it had worked.

"How are you not falling over?" he asked.

She motioned to the bartender for another round. He knew her drink order by now. "I have a very high tolerance."

The crowd in the bar had reached capacity, with bodies and voices clamoring for maximum attention. The heat from Sam's chest radiated through the thin silk fabric of her blouse, and she leaned in closer to him.

There was something about this man. The intensity flowed out of him in waves, whether it was directed toward a game of pool or a conversation or a BMW that had plowed into his truck. He was even and steady, and she craved his muscled body on top of her. After witnessing Connor with another woman, she deserved at least that. Something raw, something animalistic. Something mind-numbing.

She pressed her lips together, the recently applied gloss tugging at her skin as she opened her mouth again. Let him imagine what her lips could do.

"How are you getting home?" His scratchy voice lowered a full octave. She felt it in her bones more than she heard it with her ears.

"Jorie, I guess."

He ran a hand over his short beard and glanced back at their table, where Jorie and Matt were now openly making out.

"Matt'll probably take her home. That's how these nights usually end. Drunk Jorie. Matt swoops in and takes care of her."

The words floated through her ears without sticking. The soft, bristly hair above his lip looked softer than most beards she'd come into contact with. How would it feel against her skin?

"Come on," he said. He snatched the full beer bottle from her hand and set it down on the bar.

Yes. This is happening.

She grabbed her coat and purse and followed him out of the bar, her entire body preparing to have his lips on her, his taste in her mouth, his salty skin under her tongue. Her heart pumped blood through her limbs, but mostly it congregated square between her legs.

He moved at a clip, and when they burst outside, the cold air hit her like a brick. Her damp skin, now exposed to the elements, puckered and shivered, and she wrapped her arms around her body. She needed his heat now more than ever.

He slid the key into the passenger-side door, and she sidled up next to him, leaving only a hint of space between their bodies. He looked down at her, his breath coming in steady puffs of visible air between their mouths. His brow furrowed, and his lips remained still and flat, but his eyes blazed.

"So," she said. "Are you gonna kiss me or what?"

He clasped his hands in front of his chest, and finally, it all became clear. His eyes blazed but not with lust.

Disgust. Repulsion. Pity. Oh God, I'm the pathetic drunk slut, and he's sorry for me. The magnitude of it forced her backward.

"Let's go," he said.

He moved around her to the other side of the truck, but

her feet stayed put, refusing her brain's commands. She was rooted in this spot. Even the dusty parking lot seemed to mock her.

The earth tilted, and for the first time that night, the reality of her intoxication level settled in. The trees in front of her swayed no matter how she willed them to stop, and she reached out to clutch the door handle in a feeble attempt at steadying herself. A single honk rang out in the night, and it took her a minute to realize it had come from inside the cab. Sam waved her in.

She fumbled with the door handle and climbed into the passenger seat, sinking down into the cracked leather. Thank God for the darkness that masked her blotchy face. She wanted to apologize or excuse herself. She wanted to tell him that she never knew when or why her rebellious side would emerge, that she'd been to hell and back this week and it had turned her insides to hot lava and her brain to mush. But instead she sat silent. Her tongue felt thick and spongy.

"I should text Jorie," she said. "So she doesn't think I got kidnapped or something."

"I told everybody I was taking you home."

She looked over at him with hazy, swimming eyes. His right hand draped over the steering wheel while his left hand tugged at his lips in the now familiar pose.

They coasted through the deserted downtown and past the broken-down fence that signaled Karen's apartment building was coming up on the right. He pulled into the parking lot and cut the engine. Fifteen minutes ago, Sydney would've taken this as a sign he might kiss her. Now she expected a lecture.

"Well, good night." She held her purse close to her body like a shield. "Thanks for the ride home."

"Hey," he said. The single word hung in the quiet cab and echoed in her brain. "Are you all right?"

"I'm fine. I told you, I have a really high tolerance."

He blinked a few times, tilting his head. "I can see that. I just mean, are you all right? In general? You seem like maybe you have some stuff going on."

As if he'd flipped a switch, her eyes filled with tears. The reaction shocked her.

"I'm fine." She choked down the sob. "Promise. Thank you again for the ride."

By the time she got upstairs, the tears flowed freely. The apartment was dark and quiet, and she collapsed onto the couch, pressing her face into a scratchy knit pillow. She screamed her sobs, releasing all the frustration of the day, of the year, of her life. All the emotion she'd held on to for the past few days came pouring out of her, and eventually, through the mess and chaos, she fell asleep.

chapter six

Sam took the long way home. His truck hugged the curve of the road, and only once did he have to slow for an oncoming deer. The sleek creature floated through his consciousness like distractions during a meditation. This tiny town was sometimes suffocating, but the freedom of driving the endlessly looping mountain roads soothed him when he felt too cooped up. He put down the windows, the cold, pine-scented air swirling around him.

He pulled into the driveway of his modest lakeside cabin, cut the engine, and sat motionless. The second he checked his phone, the peace would shatter. He'd have a good-night text from Jay, and he'd fall asleep plagued with thoughts of the responsibility of a family he'd committed to helping that wasn't really his.

The icy air eventually sneaked beneath the layers of his coat and shirt and forced him out and into the cabin. He flipped the light switch and clicked the dead bolt behind him. Before Olivia and Jay moved in, a baseball bat near the door had been his only security system. He figured the kid deserved better than that.

He pushed the flashing red button on his answering machine, an antiquated measure he had to take because of the nonexistent cell service in the area, and waited for the messages to start playing.

"Hi, Sam, it's Annette Bethel. Could you give me a call back when you get a minute? My car is making that weird clunking sound again, and Joe swears it's my fault, but I just don't know what the heck I'm doing wrong there. . . ."

As Annette droned on about her car, his mind drifted. The clearest image was that of Sydney Walsh's lacy black bra and cleavage, but he shook the thought. Okay, she was hot. So were a lot of women. Her confidence spilled out, daring any man in her atmosphere not to get sucked in by the intoxicating perfume and that one-of-the-guys bravado. Sam wasn't fooled.

". . . the goddamned carburetor is shot. I'll bring her in Monday morning, but gimme a call back if ya can."

He hit the Repeat button. The voice sounded familiar, but he couldn't be sure who had called about the carburetor.

"Hey, Sam, it's Irv. I was driving down to Utica today and I'll be damned if . . ."

Sydney's lacy undergarments demanded his attention again. And those yoga pants from yesterday. How did a woman manage to stay so covered up and, at the same time, ooze so much sex appeal that the memory of a scrap of lace had forced him to miss the same voice mail twice?

He dragged his hands down his face in an attempt at literally scrubbing the idea of her from his head. She knew what she was doing tonight; plus, she'd drank way too much for his comfort. Sydney Walsh shouldn't even be on his radar.

His cell phone buzzed with a text message as it finally connected to the cabin's Wi-Fi. He glanced down at the screen; Liv. Jay's nightly text. He didn't know if the kid actually wanted to say good night or if Liv told him to. A tiny daily thanks for helping them out. He slumped down into a kitchen chair and buried his face in his hands.

Instead of opening the message, he tapped on the one from Jorie.

Breakfast tomorrow. First thing. No exceptions.

He sighed and rested his forehead on the cool wood of the kitchen table he'd built himself. In this tiny town, a man had to keep himself busy with more than one trade. The automotive work occupied his mind and brought in most of his income, but the woodwork kept his creative side busy. And on nights when Olivia used to drink too much, he'd disappear into his shed for a welcome respite.

". . . call back if ya can." Sam hit the Stop button on the answering machine. Whoever had called after Irv would have to wait. He opened the record player lid, flipped the switch, and let the warm sounds of Coltrane's saxophone ease his troubled mind enough to settle into sleep.

debated coming here this morning." Sam leaned over the counter at McDonagh's Bakery the following morning.

Jorie bustled around behind the counter, preparing the day's baked goods and coffee. Since she'd started working there in her early teens, "breakfast" always meant "meet me at the bakery."

"Why?" Jorie called over her shoulder. She slid a chipped mug toward him, and he inhaled the scent of strong coffee.

"Because I didn't know if the same drunk Jorie who texted me would remind sober Jorie to actually be here on time."

Jorie rolled her wide eyes and tossed her hand in the air

as if shooing away a fly. "Shut your face. You know I don't black out. Plus, I wasn't *that* drunk."

"The patrons of Taylor's might beg to differ."

She took a break from prepping the shop to lean against the back counter and cradle a mug of her own. Her gaze lowered, and she tilted her head.

"So, you took Sydney home last night?"

Sam cracked his neck and took a step backward before running a hand over his beard. Why did Jorie always assume the worst of him?

"Took her home, yes. Slept with her? No."

Jorie grimaced. "All right. I get it."

"I don't need the accusations, all right? You weren't in any position to drive her home, and she was hammered, and I thought I'd do the nice thing and get her out of the bar before some degenerate convinced her to let *him* take her home."

Jorie raised her eyebrows before her gaze dropped to her coffee mug. "Okay."

"Seriously, Jorie, I don't need this shit."

"O-*kay*." Jorie held up her free hand, palm out. "I'm sorry. I had to ask."

"Well, I'm sorry you don't trust me." He sipped his coffee and watched her twist the end of her short ponytail between her fingers.

"I trust you." As she continued to fidget, the haze lifted. He knew what was going on.

"Is there any chance this is coming from Liv? Did somebody tell her there's a new girl in town and that she's good-looking and that we were talking last night?"

Jorie bared her teeth and squeezed her eyes shut. "Maybe."

A burble of anger simmered in his gut. What was Jorie thinking? She knew how fragile the situation was, and the last thing any of them needed was to add a layer of drama.

"Can I ask what the hell you were thinking?" he snapped.

"*I* didn't tell her anything." Jorie stood tall. "Honestly, I don't know who it was. Some dope in the bar who always wanted a shot with Liv, maybe? Who knows? She just texted me late last night asking what the deal was. She's just curious. That's all."

"The deal is that I'm being a choirboy over here. Maybe *that* piece of information can find its way back to her."

Jorie lowered her chin and shot him the motherly gaze she'd used on her male friends since high school. "Don't act like this is something that was thrust upon you, Sam."

His stomach caved. She was right. He'd asked for this mess. He owed Liv. A crystal clear image of her appeared in his mind, clad in purple nurse's scrubs with not a hint of hangover on her fresh face. She'd slipped his dying mother a bag of peanut M&M's with a wink and patted her frail, veiny arm.

"No, you're right," he said. "I asked for this shit."

"So maybe until things are squared away with Liv, you steer clear of Sydney."

Something in him flipped, and the simmering anger rose up in his chest. Steer clear of Sydney? He'd help Liv because she'd helped him, because if Jay and Liv had a shot at being a normal family he'd help them get there, but he'd do it in his own way. In a way that didn't feel like shackles.

He set down his mug, pushed back from the counter, and stalked to the door. "I'm an adult. A *single* adult. And I can do whatever the hell I want."

"Of course you can!" Jorie said. "It's just hard for her, you know? She's far away, she feels out of control with the custody battle and Kevin's insane family brainwashing Jay against her. She just wants to know that everything back here is the same."

He turned to face her. "Everything is the same."

"She's trying really hard, Sam." Her face twisted into

the same glare of pity that everyone in this town seemed to don when talking about Liv.

"I know."

"And I know she has a long way to go in getting back into your good graces . . ."

"It's not even about that, Jorie." He hoped the finality in his voice would get her to stop. "I need to do this my way."

"You're right," she said, holding her hand up again. "I only want what's best for both of you. For *all* of you. But based on what she tells me, she's making headway."

Headway. In the cross-country road trip of getting back into his good graces, Liv had driven a thousand miles in the wrong direction and was now hoofing it backward on foot. Whatever story she told Jorie and her other friends, they couldn't know the half of it.

"Listen," Sam said. "This whole situation is hard enough. I'm not a liar, you know that. So, to keep up this charade in front of the people in the town where I live? To pretend that I'm happy that this responsibility rests on my shoulders? It's exhausting. Add to that the stress of knowing people are watching my every move to report back to Liv? It's too much. Especially after the year I've had."

He hated to go there, never wanted anyone to feel sorry for him. But he needed Jorie to know that helping Liv tested every ounce of his self-control. He wanted to help her, but he didn't want to lose himself in the process. If Jorie wasn't on his side, he didn't know if he could keep this up.

"I'm sorry," she said. She scratched at her wrist and fidgeted against the counter. "You're right. And I'm totally on your side. Just remember the year *she's* had, too. Her life hasn't been a picnic, either."

Sam released one final huff and exited the shop. The bell over the door jingled happily as he shoved his way outside into the cold, drizzling rain. He passed his waiting pickup truck, opting instead to walk the half mile to his body shop. The fury coursed through him.

"God damn it," he said, the rain already soaking his baseball cap. "This fucking town."

chapter **seven**

·

The rain came down in sheets, pelting the front window of the store and daring anyone to venture outdoors. While the rain masked the sunlight, it did little to ease Sydney's pounding headache. She took a sip of her scalding instant coffee and clenched her teeth against the heat. This was a hangover beyond remedy.

A few brave tourists wandered the Loving Page's offerings, rain dripping from their jackets and pooling in random spots around the store. Sydney would have to mop it up before someone slipped, broke their neck, and sued Karen for her last remaining pennies.

She popped another extra-strength Tylenol as the front door burst open and Jorie hurried inside.

"This weather!" she said, shaking her umbrella out over the doormat. She ruffled her cloud of blond hair and muttered a few obscenities as she made her way to where Sydney sat hunched at the register.

"Good morning, sunshine." Jorie's singsong tone grated

on Sydney's sensitive nerves. "I'm surprised to see you here this morning."

"It was this or sit through my mother's morning guitar lesson," Sydney said, gritting her teeth. "Why aren't you hungover?"

"I have a cure-all," Jorie said. "When I get home from the bar, I chug two full glasses of water, eat two slices of toast with peanut butter, and take an Advil. Then in the morning, I have a Gatorade. And then I'm right as rain."

"I'll have to write that down."

Jorie pressed a pink-tipped finger into the dimple in her chin and frowned, a crease forming between her eyebrows.

"So," she said. "You went home with Sam? Last night?"

"No! Ugh, God no. He drove me home. That's all." Her voice careened on the edge of desperate, but she didn't care. Let it be known, far and wide, that less than nothing happened with Sam. Otherwise, people would find out she'd shamelessly thrown herself at a man who was trying to save her drunk ass from making a total fool of herself.

"Ah, okay." Jorie's posture visibly softened. "Not that you even care, but Sam kind of has . . . somebody. Not *somebody* like a romantic somebody, but a situation he's responsible for. Does that make sense? I know you just got out of a relationship and all, and I don't even really need to tell you this, but—"

"Jorie," Sydney said, cutting her off. "Seriously, it's fine. Nothing happened with Sam. Last night, he was just being nice and giving me a ride home. Simple as that." *Except that if he'd given me even the tiniest hint of a go-ahead, I'd have done filthy, disgusting things to him.*

The denial seemed to be enough for Jorie, and she grinned before taking a step back from the counter and glancing around the shop. "Oh, you ladies will love that! It's one of my favorites."

The two tourists dropped the book they were perusing back on the shelf, but it seemed Jorie wasn't having any of it. She walked to the bookshelf and retrieved the discarded paperback.

"Seriously. Do you like romance?"

The older of the two women tugged at her curly gray hair and, with wide eyes, nodded.

"Then you'll love this. It's about a woman in the 1920s who takes over an inn from her grandfather and falls in love with the logger who lives down the river. I know, the cover is terrible. But the love story is swoon-worthy."

Jorie left the book in the eager hands of the tourists and returned to where Sydney sat, slack-jawed and grateful.

"Damn," she muttered. "Can I pay you to hang out in here and sell this stuff?"

"Mm, *Hiking the High Peaks*? Sorry. But romance novels? Those are my jam. I've got a bookshelf at home that would blow your mind." Jorie reached into her purse and pulled out a white paper bag, placing it on the counter with a wink.

"What's that?"

"A treat. I suspected you were hungover and thought this might help."

Sydney could see the grease already leaking through the bag. Whatever was inside, she wanted it.

"You are so sweet."

Jorie pursed her lips together and tossed a hand in the air, waving away the notion. "Just being neighborly."

"No," Sydney said. "You've been really, really kind to me. I appreciate it."

"Well, you're welcome. But I think if you stuck around here, you'd find out most people in Pine Ridge are like this. We take care of each other." With a flash of a smile, she zipped up her rain jacket, turned on her heel, and headed back outside.

The tourists added a balsam-scented candle to their haul of four novels from the romance bookshelf, and as Sydney rang up the forty-dollar sale, gratitude washed over her.

The friends in Connor's New York circle were kind, and she'd enjoyed their company during dinners and the occasional weekend in the Hamptons, but their kindness always concealed a deeper selfishness. It seemed that in order to live in New York, a woman had to care about herself first and foremost. Aside from Bee, Sydney didn't have anyone she could truly count on. Jorie's pure heart was a breath of fresh air.

Diet be damned, Sydney hung up the flimsy wooden plank painted with **BE BACK SOON** in the shop window for lunch and hurried over to Utz's, where she knew a hangover-curing chili cheeseburger awaited her.

The bar was surprisingly packed on the rainy Saturday afternoon. The blare of the college football game on TV reminded her that anyone who might've planned a hike or canoe trip today was here instead.

She found an empty stool at the far corner of the bar and waved at the bartender.

"IPA?" he asked.

Even though the thought of alcohol turned her stomach, a swell of warmth filled her chest. He remembered her drink order.

"I'm still a little drunk from last night, so I'm going to say Coca-Cola, please."

Families and groups of beer-swilling men filled the tables around her, shouting at one another about Super Bowl prospects and deer-hunting season. The dull, incessant roar of voices drowned out her own thoughts. She settled comfortably into the noisy din of the lunch crowd, and as the man next to her vacated his spot at the bar, someone else quickly filled it. She inched farther to the right to give her new neighbor some space.

"Don't worry, I'm not gonna kiss you."

The scratchy voice shot her adrenaline into overdrive. Sam sat on the stool next to her, a shit-eating grin spreading over his full lips. If she thought her hangover was beginning to fade, the appearance of Sam Kirkland threw her body for another loop.

"Oh, good. You. And here I thought maybe I wouldn't have to run into you again while I was here." Was the steel in her voice believable enough to gloss over the previous night's mistakes? God, she hoped so.

"I don't get it. You hate me or you want me to kiss you? I can't keep up."

"Shut up," she said, pressing the heels of her hands into her throbbing forehead. "I had too much to drink, and I barely even knew what I was saying. If Greg had offered to drive me home, I'd have thrown myself at him instead."

Sam's tongue traced his bottom lip as his gaze landed on her lips. She prayed he wasn't remembering her adverse reaction to Greg's flirting at the bar. The truth was, she'd asked for that kiss from Sam because she wanted it from him and him alone.

"Poor Greg," Sam said, the TV grabbing his attention. As he turned his face away from her, she saw the remnants of a tiny hole in his earlobe.

"Is your ear pierced?"

"Ah, yeah." His mouth twitched into a half smile as his calloused fingers touched the earlobe. "Child of the nineties. I begged my father, and he said no a hundred times over. I believe the f-word was dropped once or twice. And then I went and did it anyway."

"The f-word? He cursed at you because you wanted to pierce your ear?"

"Not that f-word." He turned toward her again and raised his eyebrows. "Apparently if you're a boy, the second the needle goes through your ear you're immediately attracted to men."

"Wow, your dad sounds"—she swallowed all the nasty names tugging at her tongue—"enlightened."

"I didn't realize the word 'enlightened' also meant 'asshole.'" He rapped his knuckles on the bar in some unknown rhythm and nodded at the bartender for his usual. "You eating? I assume you're not here to drink."

"Yes. I need something greasy, and I need it immediately."

"Make it the large platter of nachos, please, Hank." The bartender nodded and turned away to place their order with the kitchen.

"That was presumptuous," Sydney said. "I kind of wanted that chili cheeseburger again."

"Trust me on this, all right? These nachos will wreck you. In the best way possible."

He unzipped and peeled off his hoodie, and another tattoo peeked out from his gray T-shirt sleeve. This time she was close enough to see black feathers and the edge of a red flower petal wrapping around a delicious bicep. She swallowed down the urge to trace her fingertips over the art.

He caught her staring, and she quickly turned back to the football game. Even without looking, the weight of his eyes settled into her.

"Yes?" she asked.

"I didn't mean to embarrass you." His voice had that crackling jazz-record quality again, nearly lost in the bustling crowd and football noise that swirled around them. But when she met his gaze, the simple sentiment resonated loud and clear.

"I'm not embarrassed." Her voice cracked in the middle of the statement. *Shit.* "I mean, I'm a little embarrassed."

"I'm uh . . ." He ran his teeth over his bottom lip. "I'm not really on the market."

"What are you, cattle?"

A grin spread across his face. "Oh, so she does make jokes."

"I'm not trying to date you. I promise."

"All right," he said. "Friends?"

"You want to be my friend?"

"Should I not want that?"

"I don't know, I guess I just haven't been all that nice to you since I got here. Maybe you're just really, really lonely."

It was her turn to send him a devious smile, and he shook his head. The drinks had clouded her judgment the night before, but in this moment, the electrical current flowed between them without question. He dropped his chin and stared deeply into her eyes.

"Sometimes this town feels like living on a merry-go-round. Every day is the same. The people are the same, the topics of conversation are the same. So while I admit I was busy judging you for your high heels and your BMW, I also thought maybe you'd traveled. Maybe you'd been to an art museum or skimmed a copy of the *New York Times* in the last year. I thought maybe you'd be cool and that we could talk about something other than deer lure and how bad the winter's gonna be this year. Am I wrong?"

It took a second before she realized her fists were clenched. In fact, every muscle in her body was contracted, held, waiting for a release. He'd studied her, thought about her outside the confines of some girl Jorie brought to the bar. With a deep breath, she ordered her body to relax. This still meant nothing. He was off the market. And she was leaving.

Wasn't she?

"You're not wrong," she said. "I travel when I can. And I have a subscription to the *Times*. Although now that I said that, I'm afraid it makes me sound like some annoying princess from New York who orders cosmos at Utz's."

"Maybe you're part cosmo princess, part sailor-mouthed pool shark. You don't have to be one or the other."

Didn't she? With Connor, she'd had to give up so much of the person she'd become to fit into his world. He'd grimaced at her cursing, rolled his eyes at her trashy magazine subscriptions, and had actually thrown away a box of Twinkies she'd purchased on a nostalgic whim. It seemed easier to let the little pieces of herself go to avoid Connor's criticism. But what had she given up in the pursuit of financial stability?

A sweet, spicy scent floated over the heads of the bar patrons and hit Sydney square in the face, yanking her out of her reverie. She breathed in the flavored air. "Wow, something smells incredible."

"When it comes to food, you should never doubt me."

Hank set down a pizza tray covered edge to edge in crispy tortilla chips topped with melted cheese, onions, and pulled pork.

"The house special," Hank said. "The Kirkland."

Sam sat up straight with a puffed-out chest.

"I order this so much they named it after me."

She watched with delight as he lifted a loaded chip to his curved lips, opened his mouth, and inhaled the entire thing.

"Wow," she said. "That was impressive."

"I'm glad you think so," he said around a mouthful of chips and cheese. "I did it to impress you."

They polished off the entire tray of nachos, and after consuming the last crumb of tortilla chip, she leaned back on the barstool and clasped her hands over her distended belly. She couldn't believe she'd helped him eat the whole tray.

"I actually can't remember the last weekend where I ate so much freaking food," she said. "Muffins, donuts, cheeseburgers, nachos. And there's no gym here, so I'll probably have to rely on running outside for exercise, and with the wonky weather up here, it seems like I won't even be able to do much of that. I'll probably die of a heart attack before I leave."

"Well, if you make it until Tuesday, there's an amazing café about thirty miles north of here. They don't have pulled pork nachos, but everything is locally grown, and you can even get a salad if you want."

He had a smudge of barbecue sauce on his cheek. She wanted to lean forward and lick it off. The sudden urge, despite how full and tired she felt, made her laugh.

"What's funny?" His voice bordered on defensive, like a little boy on the playground. "Having another meal together is laughable?"

"No," she said, tamping down the smile. "I'm sorry. I was thinking of something else. I think I'm losing my mind up here."

"It's probably the cell phone detox. Lack of service. Your brain is learning how to think on its own again."

Your brain is learning how to think on its own again. He couldn't know what that meant to her, and she reached for the chain at her neck. She placed her hand in her lap. The necklace was gone. The man who'd given it to her was gone. All she had was herself and her own instincts.

"I should go," she said, easing her body off the barstool. "How much do I owe you for lunch?"

"It's on me." His eyes softened when he looked at her, that lingering gaze that stripped away all pretense and left her exposed.

"No," she choked out. "Please, we should split it."

"Next one's on you, all right?"

She nodded. *Next one.* "All right. Next one's on me."

chapter **eight**

The rain tapered off in the afternoon, but the earlier downpours had sufficiently scared away any and all shoppers from downtown. Sydney tallied up the day's sales, a whopping $109.32, and tidied the store quickly before heading out into the damp evening.

Despite the deep puddles in the road and the veil of dusk, the bike ride home calmed her nerves. She breathed in the cold, clean air and let the lingering rain mist her face as she sailed past pungent pine trees and dodged tree limbs cluttering up the shoulder.

As she rounded the corner into Karen's apartment building's parking lot, a deer darted in front of her path and she nearly tumbled off the bike. She pressed a hand to her racing heart and laughed. Even the traffic in Pine Ridge charmed.

When she entered the apartment, she expected to see her mother sitting in the same armchair working at her crossword puzzle. But the living room was empty. The closed bedroom door made her pause. She couldn't be sleeping. Her mother always slept with the bedroom door open. Karen always said that if someone was going to break in, she wanted to see them coming.

"Mom?" A thud and a rustling came from the bedroom, and then the door burst open. Karen hurried out, tugging a robe closed around her, her face crimson and her eyes wide.

"Suds, what the heck are you doing here so early?"

She opened her mouth to remind her mother it was well past closing time when a figure appeared in the doorway behind Karen. He was nearly as wide as the doorframe and stood only a few inches taller than Karen, his hair pulled back into a long gray ponytail. He wore a convivial smile and a full-length blue nightgown that looked about ready to burst at the seams. Well. This was new.

"Um." Sydney's mouth pulled into a grimace as she blinked rapidly. "Hello."

"Suds." Her mother swayed back and forth as she did whenever she was lying. Typically an open book, Sydney had only seen Karen caught in a lie a handful of times. "This is Yuri. My friend from the liquor store."

"Friend?" Yuri said. He glared at Karen. "I should say I'm more than a friend. In any case, Sydney, it is such a pleasure to finally meet you." He approached Sydney with his arm outstretched and the same wide grin shining at her.

"Nice to meet you," Sydney said, grasping his hand. He closed his other hand around hers and pumped twice. Was it general exhaustion or the utter absurdity of seeing her mother with a man in her bedroom that caused her field of vision to swim and flicker in and out of focus?

"I've heard so much about you," he continued. "Sydney the lawyer this, and Sydney the beauty that. Your mom is your number one fan."

"Oh, Yuri, shut the hell up and go put some pants on." Karen scurried in between them and shoved Yuri toward the bedroom. When she returned, she faced Sydney with puppy-dog eyes and a flat-lipped smile.

"Mom, why didn't you tell me?"

"Because it's nothing," her mother whispered, leaning in so Yuri couldn't hear. "He really is just a friend. I'm too old for boyfriends, Suds. Plus, why mention him to my daughter if it's no big deal? I don't want you getting attached to somebody if he's gonna disappear in a few weeks."

"I'm thirty years old," Sydney said with a laugh. "You don't have to protect me anymore. I just want you to be happy."

Karen's face melted into pure relief. She placed a hand on her daughter's shoulder and squeezed. Hardheaded and stubborn, self-sufficient and independent. In Karen, Sydney saw glimpses of the kind of woman she'd prided herself on being. Before Connor. Before she'd let her thirst for the finer things surpass her desire to live a full and meaningful life.

Yuri, now fully clothed, told Sydney once again how nice it was to meet her and then made his exit. Sydney pretended not to see him kiss Karen's lips as he waddled out the front door.

As Karen scuttled into the kitchen in slippered feet to put on the kettle, a startling sadness settled over Sydney. She was lost, floating in the loamy blue waters between her old life in New York and a future beyond the horizon that she couldn't quite make out yet. At the same time, she was here, in the steady, reassuring presence of her confident mother, with a bird's-eye view of happiness in its simplest form.

An idea formed.

"Suds," Karen said gently, turning away from the stove, her weathered brow pinched in the middle. "What's going on?"

"What if I stayed here for a little longer?" Sydney whispered, tears blurring her vision. "Just until things settle."

"Baby, stay as long as you like." Karen's cool, dry hand grasped Sydney's elbow and squeezed. "Having you tend to the store gives me some time to relax and do a lot of things I haven't had time for since I moved up here. Playing the guitar, hiking, exploring the neighboring towns."

"Will you let me help you?" Sydney asked. "Maybe think up some ideas for drumming up store business?"

Karen's lips pursed, and she retracted her hand. Unless Karen had swapped personalities with June Cleaver since Sydney had seen her last, she knew her mother wouldn't stand for someone coming into her home and telling her how to run her business.

"I don't know," Karen said. "You've probably got a lot of big-city ideas, and those types of things just don't work with small-town people."

"I'll run everything by you. And it won't be anything drastic. A few small changes here and there. I have some ideas, but I don't want to fully explain yet until I flesh them out a bit more. Okay?"

Karen nodded as the teakettle began its low whistle. As she prepared two mugs of cinnamon spice, Sydney wandered into the living room and collapsed onto the scratchy plaid couch.

She'd stay here. In Pine Ridge. Indefinitely. The past ten years of her life, from undergrad through law school and beyond, had been all but erased, as if she'd never accomplished anything at all.

The tears appeared once again.

"Oh, Suds." Karen settled a mug of steaming tea onto the TV tray next to Sydney. "What is it now? You're not a crier. What's got you? That asshole Connor?"

Sydney swallowed, but the chalky feeling in her mouth remained.

"Look at what I did." Her eyes focused on the ratty blue carpet beneath her feet. "I quit my job. I let Connor take care of me. I'm driving the car he gave me the down payment for. I gave a man all the power even though I told myself since I was a kid I would never, ever do that. I'd take care of myself. I'd be my own person. I worked so hard to make sure I could take care of myself, and then in one year I gave it all away. And now I have nothing."

Silence settled over the room, and when Sydney looked up, she found her mother's eyes filled with tears. Karen ran her hand over her face and turned her gaze toward the window, where tree branches swayed lazily in the inky-blue evening.

"Oh, hun." Karen's voice was a whisper, and she turned her head again, this time staring straight into her daughter's face. "Maybe fancy cars and purses seemed like the end goal, but while you worked toward them you gained independence. You figured out how to do it on your own. You've been doing it since you were fifteen freaking years old."

Karen's mouth pressed into a tight line. "Okay, so you got waylaid. Connor didn't define you, he just sidetracked you for a minute. Took you in a direction you weren't meant for. You'll find your place again. It just might look a little different than you expected."

Sydney gnawed at her lip. She knew her mother was right. And she also knew she was a long way from truly believing it herself.

As Sydney crossed the street toward the Loving Page a few days later, she called out to two women lingering near the front door. "Good morning!"

The early-morning sun reflected off the store window, and she shielded her eyes against it. She suddenly remembered the woman with the curly gray hair. It was the same woman from Saturday, the one Jorie had convinced to buy the romance novel.

"Oh, hello!" the woman said. "I've been so enjoying the book your friend recommended that I wanted to pick up a copy for my sister before I leave town. Do you have an-other?"

Sydney slipped the key into the lock on the front door and grinned. "I sure do. Please come in; I'll grab it for you right away."

The two women purchased another copy of the romance novel plus balsam-, cedar-, and pine-scented candles. When Sydney completed the sale and wished them safe travels, they promised they'd stop back in on their next trip. A surge of hope rose up in her chest for the first time all week. And the seedling of an idea she'd had the day before developed a tiny green sprout.

During downtime at the shop, Sydney dragged Karen's ledgers and notebooks to the cash register out front and tried to make sense of all her outstanding payments.

A flare of determination surged inside her chest as she pored over the books. As North Country headed into the cold weather season, the tourists would eventually taper off, but what about the locals? An entire town lived, worked, and thrived in Pine Ridge twelve months a year. There had to be *something* she could do to pull her mother out of debt and make the store grow.

Around noon, just as her stomach began to growl and she swore she could almost smell Utz's chili cheeseburgers, the front door opened. A wave of adrenaline rolled through her, prickling across the skin at her shins and traveling up across her face. Sam.

Did the man have a literal sparkle in his eyes? She blinked away the dream sequence playing in her mind.

"Don't you work?" She immediately regretted her biting tone.

"I work all the time. Sometimes I start at five in the morning and even allow myself an hour off for lunch."

He approached the cash register, and her eyes lingered on the hint of dark brown chest hair peeking out from the

undone buttons of his Henley shirt. He wore a dark green
army jacket, but even layered up for the cold, the suggestion
of what might be hidden underneath made her legs tingle.

"Decadent." Her voice tripped over the word, mimick-
ing something that might come out of a baby goat.

He cracked a smile but didn't call her on it.

"So, what can I do for you?"

"I told you if you were still here Tuesday I had somewhere to take you."

"You did." *He remembered.*

"Can you take a lunch break?"

She checked the clock. She'd been in the shop for only a
few hours and felt guilty closing up again to go out to eat.
He noticed her eyes on the wall clock and shifted, crossing
his arms over his chest. "Or we could go pick it up and
bring it back here."

"Yeah." She blinked, her brow pinching. Such a simple,
accommodating statement that Connor wouldn't have made
in a million years. "That would be perfect, actually."

His gaze lingered on her for a moment, and his tongue
escaped his mouth to trace his lower lip. He'd done it
more than once in her presence. Was he nervous? Excited?
Did he want her naked in his bed?

The air in the shop grew thick with tension, and she
dragged her mind out of the gutter.

They climbed into his pickup truck, and as he pulled
onto the main road, she opened her window wide and let
the cool autumn air blow through her loose hair. The wind
whipped at her face and tugged her hair in every direction.
She imagined herself catching the right gust of wind and
disappearing over the treetops.

After a few minutes she sat back in the passenger seat
and closed her window enough to quiet the roar of air through
the cab.

"My old dog liked to do that," he said.

"I have a lot in common with old dogs."

They shared a smile. Maybe they could finally drop the cutting remarks and settle into a friendship.

He pulled into the parking lot of a squat white house with a sign over the entrance that read **TREE TORN FRESH**. A patio out front offered seating for warmer days, and through the front window shone a row of gleaming silver coffee machines.

"This is cute," she said as they climbed out of the truck.

"It's good, too. I know we came out here to eat something healthy, but their cookies are out of this world." He ran a hand over his stomach. How hard did the man have to work out to maintain flat abs on a steady diet of nachos and cookies?

They stepped inside the bustling café, heavy with the scent of brewing coffee and freshly peeled oranges, and Sydney scanned the wall-mounted menu, deciding almost immediately on a salad with pomegranate and goat cheese. Her broken heart still craved piles of greasy fries and melting cheese, but Sam had brought her all the way here. Ordering a salad was the adult choice.

As she scanned the café and waited for the couple ahead of them to place their order, she felt Sam's eyes. His pointed gaze was on her throat.

"Did you used to wear a necklace or something?" he asked.

Her shoulders tensed up, and her hand fell from where she'd been tracing her neck.

"What? How could you know that?" She sucked her bottom lip into her mouth and bit down hard.

His eyes narrowed, and he pawed at his own throat. "You do that a lot."

"So? It's a nervous habit. Everyone has them."

His chin raised and lowered, but the skepticism on his face remained.

He seemed to be quiet when he wanted to be. He wasn't

the type of person who needed to fill the silence. In this moment, he gave her nothing but his intense stare and a simple shrug.

They ordered lunch, and she paid, refusing to accept the twenty-dollar bill he thrust at her. As the cashier handed back her credit card, Sam took a step closer to Sydney and in one swift move tucked the twenty into the back pocket of her jeans. His thigh pressed against her hip, and his fingers grazed the top of her butt, sending her nerves vibrating through space. Her entire body turned to fluff.

He pulled away, leaving the faint scent of pine and spicy cologne in his wake. His body wasn't next to hers anymore, but his presence remained. In a low, rumbling voice he said, "Don't you dare give that back to me."

With all the muscle control she had left, she pulled the bill from her pocket and, with shaking fingers, tucked it into the tip jar. Every one of his subtle moves worked itself under her skin, creating a pattern like an intricate tattoo. It stung. But she liked it.

When they headed back toward town, the truck ambling over rocky dirt roads, she peeked into the brown paper bag to check their order and noticed two chocolate chip cookies.

"Did you get cookies?" she asked.

His eyes lit up. "Yes. Pull one out now. They're best when they're still warm."

She pulled a wrapped cookie out of the bag, broke it in half, and handed a piece to him. He popped the cookie into his mouth and grinned at her as he chewed.

"Good, huh?"

She laughed.

He had melted chocolate on his lip.

"You're a messy eater."

"I know. Since I was a kid." He lifted a thumb to his lip and wiped at the chocolate smear. "That place is actually open during the winter months, too, in case you need another break from chili cheese."

She sucked in a breath. Would she be here through the winter?

"I'm sorry. I guess I—" He cleared his throat. "Well, you're still here, so I thought maybe it was for a while. But maybe it's not?"

Her heart beat faster, and she dropped her gaze to the mud-crusted mat beneath her sneakers. "I'm not sure yet."

"I didn't mean to pry."

She looked back at him to find he'd settled into his familiar driving position, plucking his bottom lip and staring out over the road. His easy posture, his ability to back off when something clearly bothered her, his intense but caring stare. Something about him made her feel safe.

"No, you don't have to be sorry. I'm in between things right now. In between jobs, in between apartments, in between . . . lives." A bitter laugh escaped her lips. "But while I'm aimlessly floating, I'd like to try to help my mom's store. She's on the verge of bankruptcy, to be perfectly frank."

"Wow, I didn't realize." His voice softened. "This town can be tough."

"But," Sydney weighed her words carefully, "it seems like maybe if people were slowly introduced to something new at the shop, they might embrace it. Sort of a fresh take on a classic. Would you agree?"

He raised a single eyebrow and looked at her. "I feel like you're looking for something specific here."

She filled him in on a rough outline of her plan for the store, careful not to seem overly excited. If this didn't work, her mom would have to close up shop and find a more practical way to pay back her debts. And Sydney would have another failure under her belt, this time taking her mom down with her.

She waited, holding her breath, as he nodded. Finally, he said, "So that means you'll be in town for at least a few more months?"

His deep brown eyes were nearly black, and they squeezed her heart like a vise. What was his deal? Jorie said he had *somebody*, whatever that meant, but he was putting out strangely intense vibes toward her.

Maybe he was a cheater who did unspeakable things behind his girlfriend's back while he thought she was out for the afternoon.

She swallowed down her own heartache and shoved visions of Connor and the blonde out of her brain. Sam didn't seem the smarmy type. He'd driven her home after way too many cocktails and didn't give in to her advances at all.

"If my mom agrees to let me take over her store and put the plan in place, then yes. A few months."

He pressed his lips together and nodded as his penetrating gaze returned to the road ahead. "A bunch of us are going kayaking this weekend. Jorie, Matt, Greg, me. You should come. If you want. Since you'll probably still be in town, I mean."

She licked her lips to keep from grinning, but the way he fidgeted elicited a spark of joy in her chest. The invitation was casual, easy, unassuming, but his twitching hands gave him away.

"That would be nice. Thanks. I'll be here."

"So, why aren't you rushing back to New York? Thought you had a boyfriend or something?"

The tension in the car thickened, and she shifted the paper sack in her lap. Did he care that she had a boyfriend? Was *that* why he wouldn't kiss her at Taylor's?

"No boyfriend." She turned back toward the passenger window and stared out at the green landscape rushing by. Images of Connor popped into her brain, accompanied by memories of candlelit dinners in the West Village and cocktails prepared by mixologists at swanky rooftop bars. Once upon a time she'd felt safe there, accompanied by a man she thought would take care of things, financially and beyond.

What was he doing now? Was he at work? Out with the blonde? Maybe the other woman had already moved into the apartment Sydney had once shared with Connor and put her expensive blouses into dresser drawers and stacked the medicine cabinets with La Mer and Chanel.

Sydney swallowed down the memories, the worries, the conjured images. It was behind her now. It had to be.

"I'm single," she said. "And it's good. It's just me."

chapter **nine**

The autumn sun hung low in the sky as the caravan of kay-aks made its way to the pullout point in front of Sam's cabin. They'd been careening down the Black River for hours, and despite their winter coats, everyone was beginning to complain of frozen hands and faces. Sam didn't mind the cold. He could've stayed out here for days.

They navigated the gently rolling river and made the necessary turns to end up in Fern Lake. Jorie, Matt, Greg, and Sam had taken this trip hundreds of times since they were kids. This time, though, Sam saw it with new eyes as he pointed out old familiar spots to Sydney.

She'd arrived at the drop-in point that morning without makeup or pretense and hadn't complained a bit as she dragged her borrowed, unwieldy kayak into the river. She'd delighted in every hawk Sam pointed to, every jumping fish, every noteworthy bend in the river. And now, as their trip came to an end, she laughed up ahead with Jorie, and he felt lighter than he had in a long time.

Matt was first in line to pull his kayak onto the lake's grassy edge, and despite his large frame, he leaped out of the kayak like a fox before assisting Jorie with hers.

"How do I do this?" Sydney called out, raising her paddle above her head. Her shoulders tensed up, and Sam watched helplessly as she wobbled toward land before teetering back and forth.

"Quit jerking yourself around!" Matt said. He reached for the end of her kayak to pull her in but caught it at the wrong angle. Sydney lifted herself up to hop out but instead launched her body up and, with an animal yelp, crashed into the water.

"Jesus Christ," Sam said, unable to keep the smile from his face. He'd never seen such an uncoordinated dismount. Like a baby deer trying out its spindly legs for the first time.

He paddled quickly toward the bank, leaving Greg to his own devices, and sprung onto the grass before Sydney had even come up for air.

"Holy shit!" she screamed as she finally bobbed up to the surface, her hair plastered to her face and her mouth sucking air like a trout. "Damn it, it's cold!"

The group howled with laughter as Sam got as close to the edge as possible without climbing in after her and reached a hand out to reel her in. Her freezing hand gripped his with surprising force, and he had no trouble yanking her body to solid ground.

She collapsed at his feet, and he knelt down to make sure she was all right.

"Please don't judge me," she said, wiping at her eyes.

"Jesus, don't cry."

She looked up at him suddenly, beads of river water clinging to her spidery eyelashes, and he realized her body trembled with laughter, not sadness. She clutched her stomach, barely able to get the words out. "Cry? God, I'm not that much of a princess."

The guys dragged the kayaks up to the house, and they

all pushed inside, grateful for the warmth of the indoors. "Get me a beer," Greg bellowed. "Man, am I gonna be sore tomorrow."

Each of them peeled off coats and rubbed their hands together, anxious to regain feeling in their extremities.

"Come on," Sam said.

Sydney dripped water from her hair, coat, pants, and shoes into a massive puddle at his front door, looking like a helpless kid drowning in her dad's oversize ski jacket. "I'll get your floor all wet."

"It's just water." He waved her inside, and she followed him through the living room, down a short hallway, and into his bedroom.

After he'd retrieved his smallest pair of sweatpants and a soft, clean white T-shirt, he stood up from the dresser and turned to face her. She was hunched over his nightstand, reading the spines of his books.

"Snooping, huh?"

As she jerked upright, her soaked clothes squished, and with soggy sneakers, she trudged back to the bedroom door. "No. I mean, yes. I just wondered what you were reading."

He realized, suddenly, that they were together in his bedroom.

He hadn't had a woman in this room for years, couldn't summon the energy and balance it took to maintain a relationship plus his place in Liv and Jay's world. No matter how much or how little the woman asked of him, dating just didn't make sense within the walls of this life he'd created for himself. Liv demanded all of him, whether she was drunk or sober, his girlfriend or not.

In the rainstorm that was Olivia, the single moment of sunlight through the clouds was how she had treated his mother. Liv had washed his mother's hair, secured extra blankets, snuck Sam in after visiting hours were over. When her duties as a nurse ended, her loyalties as a friend and former lover kicked in.

He'd never forgotten it, but it couldn't erase the rest of the shitstorm she'd created in his life. He swung back and forth with her. Forgiveness. Blame. Forgiveness. Blame. Love and sex were no longer on the table, though. They'd both agreed to that.

And now, after many solitary nights in this bedroom, Sydney was here. The low lamplight illuminated her high cheekbones and gave her skin an otherworldly glow. Even with wet hair and frumpy clothes, she was striking.

"I'm stuck in a bad mystery rut," he said finally, stringing together a coherent sentence that didn't have to do with love or sex or his past or her beauty. "Don't judge me by what's on that table."

"I get it. That happens to me, too. Suddenly it's been six months and all I've read are Jack Reacher novels. But hey, if you want something new and exciting, why don't you come into the Loving Page? We have a wide array of scintillating titles." She flashed him a cheesy smile and winked.

"Trust me, I've been in the Loving Page. Your mom caters more to the over-sixty amateur-hiking crowd. Who knows, maybe if she had more of those *scintillating titles*, she might sell more books." He tossed the clean clothes on the bed and headed for the door. "Here's some dry stuff. Try to stay out of my underwear drawer, all right?"

Her lips curved into a smile, and a blush creeped down from her cheeks to her neck. Now that he definitely knew she was single, he'd have to be extra careful around her.

After a few minutes, Sydney rejoined the group in the living room. Her arms were crossed tightly over her chest, and she glanced around with wide, uncertain eyes. The sight of her wearing his clothes made his stomach contract.

"Darlin', you look *good*," Greg said. He smacked his lips together as if staring at a plate of ribs, and Sam had half a mind to force Greg outside and shove his ruddy face in the snow for a nice cooldown.

"Oh, shut up, will you?" Jorie said, whacking the back

of Greg's head. "Has she shown any interest in you whatsoever? No. So back off."

Sydney's shoulders shook with laughter as she doubled
over. "Thanks, Jorie."

"What's wrong?" Sam asked.

With hunched shoulders and arms crossed tightly over
her chest, she took her bottom lip into her mouth and
blinked up at him as he approached.

"You don't happen to have a spare bra, do you?" A grin
played on her mouth. "Or, at the very least, a sweatshirt to
put over this semi-sheer shirt?"

Heat rose from his chest into his cheeks. Of course. She
was a woman. And everything she'd been wearing was
soaked. And now, in addition to a bra, she probably wasn't
wearing . . .

"I'm so sorry," he said. "I didn't do that on purpose, I
promise."

"I know," she said. "It's fine."

He hurried back into his bedroom and tore a black
sweatshirt from the dresser. He spun around to return to the
living room but didn't get more than a foot before he stopped
dead in his tracks.

She stood in the doorway with her arms by her sides.
The peaks of her hardened nipples pressed against the
white cotton fabric. This time he couldn't talk himself out
of the movement below his belt.

"Here." He handed over the sweatshirt and prayed she
couldn't see the erection straining against his jeans. "Do
you need anything else? Socks?"

"Socks would be great." She took the sweatshirt and
slipped it over her head as he rummaged through his sock
drawer. *She's not trying to seduce you, you idiot. And now
she probably thinks you're a creep.*

As the socks passed between them, the tips of her fingers grazed his, and his breath caught in his throat. But her
face remained placid as she took the thick wool socks and

slipped her feet into them. Her toenails were painted bright pink.

Abruptly, he took a step backward. *What is wrong with you? It's been that long since a woman has voluntarily touched you that accidentally brushing her fingers gives you a hard-on?*

He licked his lips as she stood upright and grinned at him. When she smiled, her lips pressed together for a moment before pulling back and revealing her beautifully white teeth, as if she was waiting to see if the recipient was worth the effort of a full smile.

Again, he took a step back, and this time he physically shook his head to rid himself of the thoughts of her. "All right, you good?"

With one last flash of teeth, she nodded.

They joined the rest of the group in the living room, and Sydney settled into the corner of the couch, tucking her feet up underneath her and resting her arms on Olivia's pink pillow. *Olivia's pillow.*

He cleared his throat in a conscious effort to avoid thoughts of Liv. She wasn't there physically, and he'd do his damnedest to keep her away emotionally.

Stew simmered on the stovetop, and Sam dished out large bowls to each of his chilled, starving friends. They tucked into the hearty meal, and a silence fell over the group.

"Damn, this is good," Greg quipped, his mouth full of gravy and venison.

"Amazing," Sydney said. "Sam, you made this?"

"Yeah." Gravy dribbled down Sam's chin, but the food tasted too good to stop for grooming.

"Wow, he cooks." She gifted him with the full smile again, and he snorted a laugh.

"It's a three-step recipe, not rocket science."

"Plus," Jorie cut in, "someone in this house has to cook. Otherwise, they'd all starve."

His eyes darted to Sydney. Did she twitch? How much

did she know about him? Simply looking around the house wouldn't alert someone to the presence of a woman or an eight-year-old kid. He didn't want her to know about Olivia and Jay. At least not yet.

"Well, it's really good," Sydney said. Relief seeped under his skin at her change of subject. Maybe she didn't want to know. "Is it beef?"

"Venison," Matt said, filling his bowl up again from the Crock-Pot in the tiny open kitchen.

Sydney swallowed, and her eyes skipped around the group. "V-Venison?"

"Yeah," Sam said. "We hunt for the meat, and then we cook it."

"Oh God." Her lips turned down as she carefully set the bowl on the coffee table in front of her. "You killed this?"

"Yes."

"Oh man." Her face crumpled further into disgust.

"Can I ask where you think your chili cheeseburgers come from?" Sam said.

"That's different." She pulled her hands inside her sweatshirt sleeves and crossed her arms over her stomach. "Those cows are raised to be meat. Deer are these beautiful creatures that live in the forest and don't hurt anybody."

"You are *such* a city girl." Greg rolled his eyes and dragged a wrist across his gravy-covered chin. "Deer are overpopulated in this area. They're getting killed on highways because they don't have anywhere to go. Hunters around here are encouraged to hunt deer."

Her face softened. "Really?"

"We'll take you hunting," Sam said. "I mean, if you want to. Depending on how long you're here, I guess."

"You're so obsessed with how long I'm staying." A smile played on her lips, and she lowered her gaze, sending a flurry of nerves up inside Sam's chest. Every pair of eyes in the room rested on him.

"How's that?" Jorie asked. Sam knew that steely gaze. It

would be the look Jorie gave her future kids to scare them into admitting lies.

"I'm teasing him." The fire in Sydney's stare faded away, and she picked up the bowl of stew once more. "It's looking like I'll be here at least a few more months. I'm making the Loving Page my new project so that my mom doesn't go completely bankrupt."

"Your mom's the best," Matt said. He leaned back into the couch, and the furniture groaned under his weight. "One time during a bad rainstorm my truck got stuck in the mud and freaking Karen Walsh helped me pull it out. What is she, ninety pounds? I was about to call some buddies, and there's Karen, stomping out of her store wearing a rain slicker and work gloves."

"That's her," Sydney said. Affection warmed her face. "She's a pit bull."

"I wish we could help her," Jorie said. "I hate to think what would happen if she had to close the store. I wonder if she'd stick around or leave town?"

"I did have an idea."

All eyes turned to Sydney. She rearranged herself on the couch to sit a little taller and look out over the group. She caught Sam's eye, and he winked at her for encouragement. He loved her idea. It embraced the small-town values but with a fresh coat of paint.

"Tell me if it's crazy. It would definitely require the help of some locals."

"Some locals, at your service," Greg said.

Greg, despite his quips about a rich boyfriend and plastic surgery, had had his eye on Sydney since the first night she'd shown up at Taylor's. In his own buffoonish way, he'd been flirting. The thought of him asking her out turned Sam's stomach to ice.

"Jorie was in the shop a while back, and some tourists were looking at the romance novels," Sydney said. "They bought a couple and showed up a few days later wanting more. So I thought, what if we encouraged that demographic to shop at the store, supplied a bigger selection of romance than you'd find nearly anywhere else, and started a book club that served as a social gathering in the colder months and encouraged people to spend money at the store? Jorie's been lending me some of her romance novels, and I'm hooked. The writing is amazing. I've been fangirling hard on some of these authors. And romance readers seem like the type of people who might champion a small local bookstore."

Sydney's gaze danced around the circle with hope gleaming in her eyes. The steely veneer she'd worn since she'd shown up in Pine Ridge had finally seemed to fade away, and for the first time, Sam saw the determined but vulnerable woman underneath.

"I love it!" Jorie nearly leaped out of the armchair she'd been sitting in. "And the women in this town would love it, too. You're so right, Syd. Romance readers would absolutely rally around a local bookstore specializing in their favorite genre. And my mom is always complaining that the only places to get together around here in the winter are bars. She'll be over the moon. Brilliant idea."

Sydney's face lit up with joy, and something deep within Sam's gut stirred in response.

"And you're gonna do it up big, right?" Sam asked. He wanted her to keep talking, keep explaining her idea. Anything to prolong the optimism beaming from her eyes.

When she'd initially told him about her plan as they drove home from Tree Torn Fresh, he'd relished the idea of her remaining in town for a while. Even if he couldn't deep dive into why he felt the way he did, the fact was that she was a Monet on the wall of this empty room of a town.

Every space brightened in her wake. His life had been nothing but gloom and doom for over a year. Hell, Jay was eight years old, and Liv had been his personal thundercloud since before the kid was born.

"Yes." Sydney's smile grew a little wider. "I'm going to clean up the store, redecorate. We could have events, knitting parties, recipe swaps. And we could do book signings with romance authors. Pine Ridge is only a few hours' drive from New York City, and this is a huge geographic area that I can't imagine many authors bother to come and visit. I could even drive into the city myself and pick them up."

"Syd, I love it," Jorie said. "I think it's fantastic. I will help you in any way that I can. Obviously, consider your snacks totally taken care of. If we held the book-club meetings at night after the bakery closes, you could have our day-olds."

"Let me know if you need books hauled," Matt said, pushing himself to his feet. "This girly conversation is a little much for me. Gents? Care to join me in the smoking lounge?" He pulled a pack of Marlboros from his coat pocket and nodded toward the side porch.

Sydney and Jorie huddled together on the couch, buzzing excitedly, and Sam joined Matt. As the guys stepped out into the chilly evening air, Greg said, "I think it's a great idea, Sydney. Anything you need help with, you just let me know."

The thick navy-blue darkness wrapped around them as the porch door slammed shut behind Greg. Sam looked out over the lake, tinted black in the nighttime with no moon to light it. "Shit, it's dark out here," Matt muttered, the cigarette dangling from his lips. The tiny flame of the lighter illuminated Matt's round white face.

"Kirks?" Greg offered Sam a cigarette, but Sam refused. He only smoked when he really needed it. He didn't want to need it.

"I'm surprised you're out here with us." Matt clapped a hand on Greg's shoulder. "Thought you'd be sittin' at Sydney's feet offering to lick the shop floor clean if she wanted it to really sparkle."

"Shut up." Greg shoved Matt's arm away. He dragged on

his cigarette and leaned against the porch railing. Sam's eyes finally adjusted to the darkness, and he saw Greg's dopey face gazing toward the window where Sydney and Jorie sat.

"Why don't you just ask her out?" Matt said.

Sam coughed as his throat dried up. Maybe he'd need that cigarette after all.

"She's got a boyfriend, right?" Greg asked.

"Nah," Matt said. "I guess that's why she came up here in the first place. Caught her boyfriend cheating on her."

Bright lights flashed in Sam's field of vision, and it took him a second to realize they weren't real. It was anger. Pure, undiluted anger.

"Cheating on her?" Sam's voice came out on a low growl.

"Jorie told me specifics, but I kinda tuned her out," Matt said. "The important part is, she's single. Ask her out, man."

Sam bit down on the inside of his lip and shifted on his feet. He crossed his arms and then uncrossed them. He leaned against the side of the house and stood upright again. Someone cheated on Sydney. Sam had known her for only a week and his knuckles itched to crack the jaw of this phantom boyfriend.

"I dunno," Greg said, glancing through the window again. "She's been single, what, ten minutes? Plus, she's way hotter than me."

Greg's hand trailed over the curve of his belly and tugged on the edge of his T-shirt. Sam had known the guy so long that he'd missed Greg's transformation from good-looking high school kid to paunchy adult. But when Sam envisioned the type of slick, rich guy Sydney had probably dated in New York, he understood Greg's apprehension.

"So what?" Matt stubbed his cigarette butt out on the porch post.

"Dude," Sam scolded. He ran a hand over the ashy spot. No mark.

"Sorry, man." Matt turned back to Greg. "Jorie is *way*

hotter than me. This I know. But I've got two things going for me: one, I'm great in the sack."

Sam shouted a laugh straight out over the lake, and the echo bounced off the water.

"Two," Matt said, giving Sam the stink eye. "I'm freakin' charming, man. Be charming, and Sydney will say yes. She just got cheated on. Now's the perfect time to capitalize on her probable hatred of sleazy, hot, rich guys."

"Or you could just leave her alone," Sam said. "Give her some space. Let her do whatever it is she's trying to do here."

A silence settled over the trio. Why was he acting this way? Sure, Sydney was cute. All right, gorgeous. But he'd been around plenty of good-looking women before, and none of them had caused this protective, animalistic reaction in him. He only knew he didn't want to hear anything more about Greg's plan to woo Sydney.

He released a long, deep breath and headed inside. Just as he did, the phone in the kitchen began to ring.

chapter **ten**

Sam marched into the kitchen and asked "Hello?" before carrying the cordless phone down the hallway, into the bedroom, and closing the door behind him. Sydney tried to ignore his stern demeanor and turned back to Jorie, who still babbled at a mile a minute.

"Have you ever read the Quinn Jones series? *My Betrothed?* It is *epic*. The main character is this badass empress who beds men and then sends them packing, and one day this hot wanderer finds her getting herself off in a field. . . ."

With one ear on Jorie, she desperately tried to hear through the bedroom wall to Sam's low, grumbling conversation. She heard a distinct, *I don't know, Liv,* but everything else was an angry mutter.

"You want another beer?" Jorie asked, carrying their empty venison stew bowls into the kitchen. She returned with two bottles of Stone IPA. "Sorry, we're out of Bud. Sam drinks this stuff that might put hair on your chest. Tastes like black tar to me."

A tiny smile found its way to Sydney's lips. Stone was one of her favorites.

"So, um," Sydney said, careful to choose the proper detached tone for this question. "Does Sam's girlfriend live here? This place kinda looks like a bachelor pad to me, but there's an extra toothbrush in the bathroom, and I can't imagine he's the one buying lavender-scented hand soap."

Jorie slowly swallowed a mouthful of beer, licked her lips, and settled back into the armchair. She scratched her nose with the back of her hand and picked at the beer bottle label before speaking.

"Olivia," Jorie said. "She's not his girlfriend. Anymore."

Just as Jorie opened her mouth to continue, the bedroom door creaked open. She shrugged and nodded toward the approaching footsteps. Sam burst into the living room, his cheeks filled with angry color and his eyes blazing.

"Everything all right?" Jorie asked.

"Fine." He noticed the bottles in their hands, and the storm on his face passed. "Gosh, are we out of piss beer?"

"I don't know how you drink this," Jorie said, her face twisting as if she were drinking straight grain liquor. "I feel like I have to chew it. And it makes me want to smoke. So thanks, Sam."

She rose to her feet and smacked his arm before joining Matt and Greg on the porch. As the door closed behind her, a fuzzy silence filled Sydney's ears. She wanted to know who Olivia was, if she lived in Sam's house, and, most of all, what about this mystery had her so riled up.

Sam ran a hand over his beard and rested his gaze on Sydney. "Need anything?"

"No," she said. She scolded herself for the tiny mouse voice that squeaked out of her mouth. Where was the powerhouse woman who shut him down when he offered her a ride home from Utz's? Who was this insecure person swimming in his clothes and acting like a scared little girl? It was too much like the woman she'd been with Connor.

Somehow, though, this was different. Sam exposed her true self, leaving her open and vulnerable. Connor had made her feel ashamed until she decided to hide, tucking herself away into a shell of what he wanted her to be. With Sam, there was less fear, more exhilaration. Like the biggest roller coaster in the park.

Sam's mouth curved into a half smile. She squeezed her thighs together to quiet the drumbeat pulsing between her legs.

"Music?" he asked.

"I knew this party was missing something."

He headed toward the dining table, where a record player she hadn't noticed before sat on top of a beat-up hutch. In the space where dishes should've been sat rows and rows of records.

"Sorry, I don't have any Rihanna or Drake," he said, kneeling down and flipping through the vinyl.

"Even after all our hangouts, you've still got me pegged as a basic bitch, huh?"

When he stood upright, a soft breeze carrying his pine-and-cinnamon scent wafted up to greet her. His dark eyes glowed in the dim cabin light.

"Nah. You've managed to surprise me once or twice." His voice was gravel under slow-moving tires. It carried through her brain and down into her rib cage, snuggling up there and finding a home next to her lungs. If she didn't move away soon, she'd ask him to kiss her again. And this time, she wasn't drunk.

"Okay, well, whatever you choose is fine." She clutched the beer bottle and went back to the couch, putting a safe distance between them. He stared at her for a moment before turning back to the records and plucking one from the bottom shelf.

As the evening wore on, the tower of empties accumulated in the recycling bin, Matt's and Greg's voices grew hoarse with each chorus of "American Pie," and Sydney settled further into the warm, comfortable space that smelled like Sam.

When Jorie yawned and announced she should get going if she was ever going to get up to open the bakery in the morning, Sydney's belly ached. She missed Sam's place already.

Sam drove them all to the morning's drop-in point so they could reclaim their cars and go on their respective ways. The boys bounced around, freezing in the truck bed, and Sydney sat squished in the passenger seat next to Jorie, wishing she was in the middle instead.

The cluster of cars came into view at the roadside, and Sam pulled over before turning his hazards on. Sydney hopped down to the road, still hesitant to break away from the happy group, and rounded the front end of the truck to grin at Sam and send him a quick wave.

"Thanks for hosting today," she said.

His hand lingered on the steering wheel as he leaned his other elbow on the ledge of the open window, closing the space between the driver's side and where she stood next to the truck. Maybe he didn't want the others to hear him. She reveled in the closeness.

"Anytime you want to go kayaking, let me know. And you don't have to rent one; I've got a couple in my shed."

She grinned. "Why didn't you tell me that for today?"

He shrugged and dragged his hand across his mouth. "I kinda thought you'd bail on today. You don't strike me as the outdoorsy type."

"I'm starting to wonder where you got all these crazy ideas about me." She took a step closer to the driver's side door as if drawn in by magnets. Being close to him was dangerous but exhilarating. "I only eat salads; I don't like the outdoors; I'm inexplicably a fan of Rihanna. I bet you think I only drink coffee from Starbucks."

"Nah, I don't even really think about you all that often." The words didn't match the subtle smirk on his face.

"We both know that's not true." Her voice came out huskier than she'd intended.

Or had it?

"Yo, Sydney!" Greg's voice snapped her concentration, and Sam sat back in his seat, the devilish smile all but erased from his features.

"Yo," Sydney said as Greg joined her next to the truck. The headlights from Matt's pickup illuminated Greg's silhouette as the couple pulled away with a honk.

"So, uh." Greg placed his hands on his hips and shuffled his feet before turning to Sam. "Hey, uh, thanks for today, man. We'll see you later?"

Sam swallowed as his eyebrows lowered and his gaze darted from Greg to Sydney. He was being dismissed. "Yeah, sure thing. See ya."

He put up his window and drove three feet before the truck stopped again. Sydney waited for him to lean out the window again or hop out of the truck, but he simply sat there, the engine idling and the brake lights casting Greg in a shadowy red glow.

"Hey, um," Greg said, dropping his gaze to the dirt road beneath his feet. Sam's truck hadn't moved. "I was wondering if you'd like to get a drink with me. Just the two of us."

"Oh, gosh." Her voice was a whisper.

The wounds from Connor were still so fresh, and the thought of going on a proper date made her queasy. Beyond that, she wasn't attracted to Greg. He was perfectly nice, but his teeth were stained tobacco-yellow, he'd made more than one lecherous comment about her appearance, and when he looked at her, all she felt was uncomfortable.

"I know you just broke up with somebody," he said. He still wouldn't meet her gaze. "And I know you might leave town soon. But I'd love to take you out. Just have some fun."

Sydney took a deep breath. "That's really sweet, Greg, and I'm really flattered. But I just think it's too soon. I'm not ready to date anyone quite yet."

He looked at her finally, his eyebrows two sad quotation marks framing droopy puppy-dog eyes. She almost said yes just to erase that face.

"That's okay," he said. "I understand."

"I do like you, though," she said. "I hope we can still hang out and be friends."

"Of course." He nodded emphatically, leaning his whole torso into it. "Sure thing. Drive safe, all right?"

He scrambled into his black SUV and peeled out into the night. After the dust had settled, Sam's window came down and he poked his head out.

"Did Greg finally make his move?" He raised his eyebrows suggestively.

"Oh, you knew about that?"

"No offense, but Greg hits on anybody with breasts."

Her cheeks grew hot, and she crossed her arms over her chest. Earlier that afternoon, she'd stood in the doorway of his bedroom and the devil on her shoulder had whispered, *Drop your arms.* She knew the T-shirt was see-through. But he'd been stealing glances at her all day long, and the tingly sensation that gripped her heart and stomach when she caught him was addicting. She'd upped the ante. He hadn't seemed to mind.

"There you go, making assumptions about me when you really have no idea."

He shook his head and let out a loud laugh. "Whatever you've got going on, Sydney—Rihanna fan, salad eater, your anatomy—it's fine by me."

He licked his lips, lowered his gaze. It was just the two of them along this deserted road. An isolated bubble where anything was possible. Her legs pulsed with excitement.

Calm down, crazy. This harmless flirting is melting your rational brain.

"Okay, well, anyway," she said, unlocking her car with buzzing fingers. "See ya later."

He waited until she was safely in her car and on the road before he pulled out and drove away.

"Syd, is here good?" Jorie had arranged the featured titles near the register by dominant cover color, and the rainbow of offerings made Sydney's heart swell. The turquoise blue of *His Other Lover* led to the shocking pink of *Roses Are Red*, and tucked in between, the electric yellow of Sydney's new personal favorite, *The Royal Who Saved Me*.

"Perfect," Sydney said. "That royals book is so good."

"Told you!" Jorie chirped, clapping her hands and standing shoulder to shoulder with Sydney. "I mean, he bucks every family tradition and follows the Duke of Harlington to the front lines. A gay World War Two love story. What's more romantic than that?"

It was eight o'clock in the morning and two weeks had passed since Sydney had told her new friends about her idea to save the Loving Page. In those two weeks, she'd revealed the plan to her mother, who'd reluctantly agreed, as long as she didn't have to put up any of her own money. In response, Sydney sold her BMW and vowed to use as much of the resulting cash to turn the shop into romance land. A large chunk of the money had gone to purchasing romance-book stock, which Sydney occasionally borrowed as her romance obsession grew. Something about the promised happily ever after soothed her in a way she hadn't known she needed.

Before she announced the idea of the book club, the shop had to look impeccable. She wanted to get the word of mouth going about the store's new focus before she asked people to commit to a meeting.

In recent days, many an early morning and very late night, Sydney found herself alongside Jorie or Sam or both, mopping the floors, dusting the shelves, and washing the windows. She'd replaced harsh overhead lighting with glowing floor lamps, arranged clusters of spicy cinnamon-scented candles on every available surface, and even added a rack of book-related T-shirts in the far corner. As soon as the shop started making money, the *Real Women Read Romance* shirt was hers.

"This place looks amazing," Jorie said, glancing around the shop. She'd begun referring to it as the Loving Page 2.0: Romance Rebooted. "It has style, but it's not pretentious."

Sydney had condensed all other genres, expanded the romance titles to cover the entire back wall, and transformed the main space into literary heaven with a little red velvet sofa, brass candlesticks, and a vintage Persian rug she'd found on Craigslist. She envisioned the book club crowded around the area, deep in discussion over that month's selection.

The crowning jewel of the space was the wall of bookshelves that Sam built. She'd run into him at Utz's one evening, and after a few drinks she told him her vision for the space, which included an updated version of Karen's collapsing particle-board shelves. Without hesitation, Sam offered to build the shelves. When she asked him how much she owed him, he'd laughed.

"You're a godsend." Sydney wrapped her arm around Jorie's shoulders. "I just really hope this works."

"Let people hear that the store has changed, their interest will be piqued, and then we'll throw out the idea of the book club. Between me at the bakery and my mother and her big mouth at church, you'll have everyone in town clamoring for a space by next weekend."

Sydney tugged her wool cardigan tighter around her. She'd started turning the heat off overnight to save money on the gas bill, but the chill when she walked in every morning gave her second thoughts. It was barely November, and snow already covered the ground.

"I have to run home before we open," Sydney said. "I

forgot my computer, and I have a lot of social media work to do today. Building these handles from the ground up has not been the easiest task."

"Stop by when you get back and I'll have coffee for you. Oh, and don't let me forget to give you that copy of *Under His Watch*. Cannot believe you've never read Miranda Sands!" Jorie shook her head as she slipped into her coat. "It's a crime."

Sydney rode the red Schwinn the short distance to Karen's apartment and hurried inside for warmth. Soon it would be too cold and snowy for the bike, and what then? *One thing at a time.* She forced the thought from her head as she took two stairs at a time and entered the apartment before releasing an animal scream.

"Jesus Christ!" Reclined on the couch were her mother and Yuri, and had it not been for Yuri's generous size, she definitely would have seen more than her memory would ever let her forget. She stumbled back into the hallway, yanking the door shut and racing down the steps.

She huddled against the front of the apartment building, her heart racing and her palms clammy. Within moments, her mother appeared in front of her. Her face was lined with worry.

"Suds!" she yelped, clutching an old flannel robe closed at the neck.

"Mom." Sydney rested her face in her hands. "Oh my God, Mom. I'm so sorry."

"Don't be sorry. You couldn't have known. I thought you were gone for the day."

"I forgot my computer." The words were muffled as she continued to press on her eyes, begging the image of Yuri's pudgy mass out of her mind. "Oh God, that was awful."

"Oh, stop," Karen said. "It's natural. I'm a human being, Suds."

Sydney took a deep breath and looked up. She finally said out loud what she'd been thinking for a while. "Look, if I'm going to be here for at least another few months, maybe I should get my own place. You need your privacy."

"Don't be silly!" Karen's eyes flew open. Her mascara was smudged, and Sydney looked away, desperate not to envision her mother in any additional sexual scenarios. "We'll just come up with a code or something. I'll hang a sock on the door!"

"No," Sydney said, shutting her eyes again. "Trust me, Mom. It's better this way. I'll find a short-term sublet close by, and it'll be better for both of us. Okay?"

"At least let me start paying you for your work at the shop. You can't pay rent with no income."

"You don't have any money to pay me with. And I have that money from selling the car. I'll be fine. I just need to know that you're okay with this. I don't want you to think I'm leaving because I don't like spending time with you."

It wasn't a line. Without noticing, Sydney had begun to enjoy her mother's company. They actually talked a little about the past, and when they did, Karen explained how she'd been a young single mother and had done the best she could. The shame of judging her replaced Sydney's shame of not having had the newest backpack. How had she missed it before?

"Oh, stop," Karen said. "I don't think that at all. Even if you're a few minutes away, it'll be more time than I've spent with you in years. I'm very blessed."

Sydney nodded, unable to find the words to agree with her mother. She felt lucky, too. Lucky that not a single additional day had passed where she'd pushed her relationship with Karen aside.

chapter **eleven**

Sam wiped a greasy hand on the pant leg of his coveralls. The single bulb hanging over his head wasn't the best light to see by, but the throbbing headache that had plagued him since lunch required minimal brightness.

"Hey yo, fuckwad."

Sam looked up from the engine of Freddy O'Connell's Dodge Ram in time to see his brother check out his own reflection in the shop window as he passed. Jared was only twenty-five years old and still had a young man's bravado.

"Nice to see you, too," Sam said, turning back to the truck.

"I'm joking. How can you see in here?"

"I could probably do this blindfolded."

Jared leaned against the driver's side door of the truck but pulled away immediately to examine a smudge on his navy blazer.

"Did Aunt Nancy call you?"

"No, what is it now?" Sam grumbled.

"She wants us to go to her house for Thanksgiving."

"Sweet old Aunt Nancy—always worried about the poor orphaned Kirkland boys." Sam knew it was the first Thanksgiving since his mother passed. He didn't need Aunt Nancy to remind him.

"We should probably go," Jared said. "The thought of her and Uncle Tony eating deli turkey in their kitchen alone is depressing as hell."

"All right, fine." Sam tightened the oil filter and slammed the hood of the truck down. Jared leaped backward to avoid any errant dust or dirt that might further soil his favorite blazer. Always such a pretty boy.

"Is Liv gonna be in town? Maybe she and Jay would want to come? Or will she do Thanksgiving with her family?"

"I don't know what she's doing." The words came out gruffer than he'd planned, but he didn't have the energy to explain himself. He yanked the chain hanging from the single light bulb, bathing the shop in darkness. Two fingers of bourbon and a dark porch called his name.

"Jesus, I'll kill myself in here," Jared said. "Where the hell is the door?"

Sam opened his phone to light the way for his fragile little brother. Even as a kid Jared hated to get dirty and always preferred video games to touch football or fishing in the creek. Now, as a Realtor, he used his slick swagger to convince people to spend way too much money on property, while his wardrobe remained pristine in a clean white office.

After Jared followed him out, Sam clicked the lock on the shop door and headed toward his truck. On any other night he'd have asked Jared back to his house for a drink. Tonight, he just wanted to escape.

"Hey," Jared said. "Hold up."

Sam turned, the lonely moon casting shadows on his brother's familiar face. Jared was a few inches shorter than

Sam, but despite that, the five-year age gap, and Sam's dark beard, the family resemblance was undeniable.

"What's up?" Sam said.

"Are you all right? You seem off lately."

"I'm fine." *Just spending way too much energy convincing myself I didn't make the biggest mistake of my life by offering help to Liv.*

Jared rolled his eyes. "Is it Liv?"

Shit.

"It's not Liv."

"'Cause anybody in their right mind would be stressed by that situation. Her living with you, the kid, the weird custody shit with her ex . . ."

"It's *not* Liv." Let everyone, including his naive brother, think that he could handle a little situation like Liv. After the year he'd had, he could handle anything. Did he *want* to handle Liv? That was a different story.

Jared held his hands up in surrender. "Is it Mom? It's gonna be weird spending Thanksgiving without her."

"Yeah, it is. But I'm working on accepting it. Last year, spending the day with her in hospice wasn't exactly a holiday to remember, either."

Sam feared it was the only version of the holiday he *would* remember. He and Jared had brought the entire meal with them to his mother's room, but the overpowering scent of antiseptic and death in the hospice care center had prevented any of them from eating a single bite.

Jared nodded and ran a hand over his face, trying to hide the tears glistening in his eyes. "That might've been more depressing than not having her around, actually."

"All right, come on." Sam laid a hand on his brother's shoulder and squeezed. "I'll bring some old photo albums to Aunt Nancy's. Remind us of some of our less miserable holidays. Okay?"

Jared cleared his throat and pinched the bridge of his

nose. The grin tugging at his lips reminded Sam of his brother as a kid, always one disappointment away from tears. Their childhood hadn't been perfect, but at least they'd had each other.

The headache pulsed behind Sam's eyes. Maybe he'd skip the bourbon and go straight to bed. He had to be up early to get all the shop work done so that at night, he could stop into the Loving Page after it closed to sand down the busted shelf.

When Sydney called to tell him she'd nicked the shelf with the claw edge of a hammer, she sounded apologetic. As if the shelves were an extension of him. He'd spent a lot of overtime helping her revamp her store. And he didn't regret a single moment of it.

"Where'd your head go, brother?" Jared said, interrupting Sam's thoughts. "I think you actually smiled there for a second."

Sam forced his features into a neutral expression. "Nowhere. I'm gonna go, all right? My head is killing me."

"Yeah, of course. You want to get a beer tomorrow night?"

"Can't."

Jared waited for his brother to elaborate, but the silence stretched on. "You dodging me or something?"

"No," Sam said. "I'm helping Sydney at the shop tomorrow night, and we have to wait until after closing."

A smile spread over Jared's lips. "Who's Sydney?"

"Karen Walsh's daughter."

"Oh, yeah, okay," he said. "Sydney, right. Greg's got a different name for her."

From the frat-boy glint in Jared's eyes, Sam didn't want to hear it. "Greg's an asshole."

"Either way, dude, I hear she's smokin' hot."

Sam clenched his jaw, the headache turning sinister. Jared had ended up in the bed of nearly every single woman in Pine Ridge under the age of fifty at one point or another.

The last thing Sam wanted was his charismatic brother pawing around Sydney.

"Sure, whatever. She's trying to help Karen get the store out of the red, so I'm helping her with some maintenance stuff."

Jared took a step backward and crossed his arms over his chest, the same shit-eating grin pressed into his face. "What are you charging her for all this work?"

"I can't charge her. She's broke."

"Oh, okay, so you're just doing this out of the goodness of your heart?"

Sam took a deep breath, trying to keep his cool. Jared knew him better than anyone. He'd seen him in his darkest moments, held him as he broke down just once over the death of his mother, and lent a supportive ear whenever Sam needed it. Jared knew when he was lying, when he was out of sorts, and when he was attracted to a woman. He also knew all of Sam's buttons and exactly how to push them.

"Anyway," Sam said. "I'll meet you for a beer at six tomorrow night at Utz's. And I'll go to Sydney's afterward."

"Ah, yeah, that makes more sense anyway. You want to be a little loosened up before you make your move on her, right?"

Sam turned on his heel toward the truck door. "Now I'm really going. Good night, dork."

Aside from the occasional thud of a glass on the worn wooden bar or the droning voices of the six o'clock news, Utz's was quiet. This time of year the tourism stream dried up and locals spent the cold, snowy nights avoiding the icy roads. As much as Sam loved his solitude, he knew it was better for his mental state if he got out every once in a while and socialized. A beer with his brother was as good an excuse as any.

"Jäger bombs!" a deep baritone voice boomed from behind him. He didn't need to turn around to know it was Jared. Patty DiOrio sat at the other end of the bar, sipping her White Russian and rolling her eyes at the town's resident goofball.

"Bud Light, please, Hank," Jared said as he slid onto the barstool next to Sam. He shook the big wet snowflakes from his black wool peacoat. "It's winter, dude."

"Nothing gets by you." Sam sipped his oatmeal stout and shifted his weight on the wooden stool. Somehow the drink tasted better when he knew it was his only one of the evening.

"I'm surprised it took so long," Hank said, setting a bottle of Bud Light in front of Jared. "We've been lucky so far."

"I dunno, snow brings the skiers and snowmobilers," Sam said. "It's good for everybody if the town has more people in it."

"Good for your new *girlfriend* and her store," Jared said, nudging Sam's elbow.

Rage bubbled up in Sam's gut, and before he could stop himself, he reached forward and grabbed the front of Jared's crisp white shirt. His brother's eyes grew three sizes as he tried to back up but couldn't because of Sam's death grip.

"Don't," Sam said. His voice hissed. "You know better."

Visions of manic texts from Liv danced in his head. *Is there someone new in your life? If you don't want to help me, then fine, but please don't embarrass me in the process. I can't handle that on top of everything else.*

He relaxed his fingers, but the stiff fabric of Jared's shirt held the wrinkles, a reminder of the warning.

"Relax," Jared said in a whisper. "Holy hell, dude."

"Oh, so this is what you stood me up for?"

Her voice carried across the bar like the melody of a folk song, and the sound lifted Sam's gaze to the door. Sydney brought a wave of cold, fresh air with her as she ruffled her wavy chestnut hair and clinging snowflakes disappeared from the tresses. Despite the quip, she grinned.

"I did not stand you up," Sam said. He tried to force the blood from his cheeks, but his brain wasn't responding. "This is my brother, Jared."

Sydney slid onto the stool next to his brother and tucked her chin, sending Jared a timid smile. "Hi."

"You must be Sydney," Jared said, extending his hand. Sydney shook it once.

Sam kept his radar up for any sparks that might fly between his good-looking but goofy little brother and the woman he'd developed an unhealthy interest in. Sydney appeared nonplussed, but Jared's gaze dove straight into her low-cut T-shirt.

"Ah, yes, I must be." Sydney pursed her lips and raised a single dark eyebrow.

"What does that mean?" Jared asked.

"She's all butt-hurt because she's been here almost a month and nobody's mistaken her for a local yet," Sam said.

"Well, uh, it looks like you have all your teeth, so no, I'd say you're no local."

Jared flashed his signature lopsided grin at Sydney, and once again, Sam waited for the reaction. But she simply looked at Sam and raised the same eyebrow as if to say, *Is he cool?*

"You closed the store early?" Sam asked.

"Yeah," Sydney said, her posture caving. She reached for the IPA that Hank had pulled her, even though she hadn't asked for it. She might never look like a local, but she was well on her way to becoming one. "No sales today. Not a single one. I even turned down the heat around three o'clock and wore my coat in the store in case it saved me a few bucks."

"Wow, that's bleak," Jared said. He drained his beer bottle and motioned to Hank for another.

"A round of shots, please," Sydney said. "Your finest tequila, sir."

"No way, not for me," Sam said. "I'm using a belt sander tonight."

"Forget the shelf," Sydney said through gritted teeth. "Like it's really going to make a difference." Hank set down three shot glasses. Before the liquid had a chance to settle, Sydney grabbed the glass and tossed back the shot.

"Hit me," she said, staring at Hank with cold, even eyes.

Hank glanced at Sam, as if to ask permission.

"He's not my babysitter. I said hit me. Please."

Jared audibly inhaled. Sam could see his brother's appetite whet. Sydney was exactly his type. If only she wasn't Sam's type, too.

Hank poured Sydney and Jared another round of shots and then quickly capped the tequila bottle and reshelved it. Sam knew Hank had seen one too many skinny women vomit in this place to encourage another.

"So what's the plan for the store?" Jared asked.

"Jorie and her mother are spreading the word around town about the redirection," Sydney said, running a hand through her hair. "And then after Thanksgiving we're going to promote the book section and the book club full throttle. I'll have free snacks every day, I'm having fliers printed up, I've got a new giveaway lined up for each day of Thanksgiving weekend, and our first book-club meeting will be December fifteenth. We'll see what happens from there."

"Do you have a plan if this doesn't work?" Jared asked.

Sam punched him in the shoulder.

"Ow, dude. What's your deal?"

"It's okay," Sydney said. She touched the hair at her temple and dragged it through her perfectly manicured fingers. When had he started noticing things like nail polish? "I've definitely thought about it. If it doesn't work, it doesn't work. My goal is to have three meetings between now and January 31. If by the end of January we don't see a serious uptick in sales, my mom will have to close the store."

And you'll go back to New York City. She'd barely scratched the surface of Sam's life and yet envisioning it without her caused a lump in his throat.

"It's tough around here," Jared said, taking a swig of his fresh bottle of beer. "It's weird because Pine Ridge should have an Aspen vibe with all the tourists and the kitschy shops and all that. But for some reason it has the stink of failure."

"It does not," Sam said.

He knew how his brother felt about the town. Jared was simply building a reputation for himself before he jumped ship and headed for Utica or Albany to make some real money. He didn't want him poisoning Sydney's mind on Pine Ridge just yet.

"Most of us around here don't want it to be Aspen," Sam said. "Overrun with tourists most of the year and real estate prices skyrocketing. It's quiet here. That's the best part about it."

"Yeah, well, the quiet is also the reason people like Karen Walsh can't make a go of it," Jared said.

Sydney's lips turned down, and her gaze dropped to the floor. "Hey, Hank. One more, yeah?"

Annoyance roiled in Sam's gut. The fucking booze. "Slow down. So you have a tough road ahead with the store. It's not worth drinking yourself to death over."

"Hey, big brother, if you're gonna be a total buzzkill tonight, can you hit the skids?"

"Yeah, hit the skids," Sydney said. Her face screwed up as she sucked on her slice of lime. "Who says that anyway?"

After her third shot of tequila, her eyelids drooped. She leaned back on the barstool and ran her hand through her hair, surveying the empty bar. Even Patty DiOrio had finished her White Russian and gone home.

"Shouldn't we get to the store soon?" Sam asked, checking his watch. It was still early, but if Sydney had anything more to drink, this night would be worthless. His patience for drunk women was already painfully low.

"Forget. The. Store," Sydney said, punctuating each word with a jab of her finger. "I'm super busy forgetting about the store right now."

"One day without customers and you're drinking your sorrows away? You're pretty easily defeated." As soon as the words left Sam's mouth, he regretted them.

Her bottom lip quivered. If looks could kill, she'd be on trial for murder in the first degree.

"Thanks for the pep talk, *Dad*." Her words melted together as she lifted the pint glass to her lips and took a long drink while maintaining eye contact with him. It was a challenge.

"All right," Sam said, pushing himself off the barstool. "Have a great night, you two." He threw a twenty-dollar bill on the bar, grabbed his coat, and left.

chapter **twelve**

Well, that hit a nerve." Jared's voice swam through the air and hit her brain like a lazy cartoon dart. She turned her drunken gaze on his symmetrical face. Clean-shaven. Is that what Sam looked like under the beard?

"He's a moody prick," Sydney said.

"That's my brother."

"He acts like he knows everything, but he doesn't know *anything*. I literally watched with my own eyes as the man I moved in with and compromised myself for and turned into a freaking Stepford Wife for stuck his penis inside some woman who was *not me*. Literally saw them having sex. When he thought I was out of the apartment for the day. Does Sam know shit about that? No."

The tequila had hit her with the force of a Mack truck, and she heard the words wobble and slur and drop off her tongue like the last fat raindrops in a storm. She licked her lips and tasted salt. *Great. And now I'm crying.*

"You all right?" Jared asked, handing her a napkin. His

face was so perfectly smooth. He was young. But how young? A woman's hand reached out and gently fingered his earlobe before tracing down his jaw and landing at the crisp collar of his shirt.

She gasped. It was her hand. *What the hell are you doing?*

"I'm a mess." She squeezed her eyes shut and leaned over the bar, resting her head in her hands. She immediately sat back upright. She was too drunk for closed eyes and a lowered head.

"You got cheated on, huh?"

"Yeah." She reached for the beer to soothe her cottonmouth. "I thought he was kind. I thought he was some sort of white knight, saving me when I really needed to be saved. But he tricked me. Turns out he was just a really good liar, and I didn't actually know him at all. But he didn't know me, either. He wanted me to be someone else."

Jared nodded, leaning in as she spoke.

"Who could cheat on you?" His voice was barely a whisper. He reached out and tugged at a hair caught in the corner of her mouth. "You're gorgeous."

"You must be blind," she said, her face screwed up in confusion. "I'm half in the bag and crying in an empty bar. I'm wearing my mother's old sneakers, and I haven't washed my hair in two days."

"Well, it's working for you," Jared said with a laugh. "Seriously, Sydney. You're one of the most beautiful women I've ever seen. Anybody who can't see that must be a total idiot."

"Hey-uh." Hank approached, a wet dishrag in his hand and a tight-lipped expression on his face. "She all right?"

"I'm fine. Why shouldn't I be? So I'm a woman. I can hold my liquor, all right?"

Jared ran a hand over his mouth, and when he leaned back on the barstool, a cool calm replaced the wolfish eyes he'd had for her earlier. What once appeared to be desire now came off as concern.

"Let me take you home," he said.

Through bleary eyes, the bar tilted and spun, shifting around Sydney like the walls of a fun house. Her stomach churned, and she choked down what might've been the beginnings of vomit. "I'm not gonna sleep with you."

Jared's eyebrows shot into his forehead. "Yeah, I know. I thought maybe I'd drive you home so you don't pass out on the street somewhere."

Soupy visions of a distraught Karen surfaced in Sydney's mind, and she shook her head, nearly losing her balance and toppling off the stool. Jared snatched at her arms, righting her with a strong grip. He was so much like Sam in so many ways.

"Sometimes I think your brother hates me." Hot tears brimmed her eyes.

"He doesn't hate you," Jared said. "He doesn't hate anybody. Even the people he should."

With some finesse, he helped her to her feet and draped her coat over her shoulders as her eyelids drooped. "Don't take me home."

"Don't take you home?" he asked.

"No." The vomit threatened again, and she coughed, refusing to allow herself that weakness. "My mom. I don't want her to see me like this. She'll never let me hear the end of it. She already thinks I'm a stuck-up bitch. I can't let her think I'm a lush, too."

"All right." Jared's gaze darted around the bar, as if someone else might take her in. But the bar was empty. "Come on. Let's go. We'll figure it out."

The icy wind nipped at her cheeks and chin the moment the bar door opened, but the cold did little to revive her. Jared wrapped one hand around her waist, and the other fumbled with the key fob. Moments later, they cruised through downtown, Sydney's head lolling forward as the alcohol threatened to pull her under.

She blinked, and suddenly Jared was helping her out of the car, guiding her over the slippery front walk of a squat white ranch home with darkened windows.

"I'm not gonna sleep with you." The voice that croaked past her lips sounded like a distant recording. It was someone else from another world.

"Jesus," he said. "What kind of sicko would I have to be to try to have sex with you now, you crazy woman?"

The world brightened and darkened, and then there was a bed and a pillow and darkness reigned.

Sydney forced open her gummy eyelids, and fuzzy shapes came into view. Dark gray light bathed the room in an eerie glow, but even as her vision cleared, the space remained foreign. Generic particle-board desk. Basketball hoop attached to the closed bedroom door. A ripped John Stockton poster next to the single window.

She propped herself up on the squishy old pillow and ran her tongue over her teeth. Her mouth tasted like gym socks. Where the hell was she?

Still wearing her winter coat, she creeped out the bedroom door and down the carpeted hallway toward a light. When she turned a corner, her heart hammering away against her ribs, she saw a man. Jared. Sam's brother. Legs crossed, feet resting on a sagging maroon ottoman, with a paperback open on his lap.

"Hi." As she spoke, he looked up and pressed his lips into a smile.

"Hey there."

Snippets of the evening tumbled into her memory, but the one that stood out was his frowning face as he helped her to his guest bedroom and asked if she needed a water before closing the door behind him.

"I'm so sorry."

He shook his head and shrugged, setting the book down on the floor and rising to meet her. "Don't sweat it. We've all been there."

"Well, I hope to never be there again." She hugged her arms around herself, begging the nausea to subside. A heavy weight pressed on her temples and blurred her vision. "Is it . . . morning?"

"Nah," he said. "It's around eleven. Looks like the water and nap did you good."

A long breath escaped her pursed lips, and tears threatened once more. What danger had she put herself in? How many other men in this town would've been so kind?

"I should go," she said. "I don't want my mom to worry."

"Your mom's the best." A warm, affectionate glow lit his face from within. "Last year I had a pretty bad breakup, and your mom let me stay with her for a few days while my ex cleared her stuff out of here. She made me breakfast every morning."

The bile threatened again, and this time it had nothing to do with alcohol. It seemed the one person in her life who could've grounded her, reminded her that life was more than this season's "it bag" or who was up for what promotion at which firm, was the one person she'd pushed away. Everyone in Pine Ridge seemed to have fond memories of Karen. All Sydney had was regret.

"Would you mind driving me back to my mom's? I'm sorry to have to ask you for another favor, but . . ."

"Of course. I'm happy to."

As Jared's Camry hugged the curves of the mountain roads and sailed through the empty late-night streets of downtown, pressure settled onto Sydney's shoulders, threatening to crush her. She was adrift and struggling against the powerful forces yanking her in all directions. She had no power of her own. No control. It had been so long since she felt in charge of her life. Even the power she felt with

Connor was simply the illusion of control. He'd held all the strings.

They entered an area of strong cell service, and her phone buzzed with a message. She checked the screen and choked. Connor.

I miss you.

"Shit." The curse slipped out of her mouth, and she raised a trembling hand to her lips as if she could shove it back in.

"Everything all right?" Jared asked.

"Fine," Sydney muttered. "Can you actually drop me at my mom's store? I need to get a few things done."

"You sure? This weather is pretty bad. You don't want to get snowed in."

"Yeah, I'll be all right. Worst-case scenario, I sleep in the office."

"Worst-case scenario, call me and I'll drive you home."

Jared pulled up to the curb outside the Loving Page, and with one hand on the door, she turned to him. What was it about this town? No one owed her anything. For all they knew, she was a drifter and would soon be gone. Yet at every turn, a Pine Ridge local stood by to lend her a hand. She didn't know what to do with that kind of generosity.

"Thank you." She blinked back tears. "You've been more than nice to me, and I don't deserve it."

A sarcastic laugh traveled past his lips, and he shook his head before looking at her. "Everyone deserves kindness. And around here, we help each other out. You gotta stop fighting the cheesy-Hallmark-movie town that is Pine Ridge, Syd."

A snort escaped her nose, and she pressed her fingers against her eyes, delighting briefly in the absurdity of the evening. She grabbed her purse from the floor of the car and sent him one last tight-lipped smile.

"Thank you again. I owe you one."

The snow pelted her in the face as she ran toward the front door and let herself in. The shop was chilly but still a welcome respite from the biting temperatures she'd just escaped. She paused a moment, taking in the new decor, the coziness she'd worked hard to infuse into the shop. She begged the universe to make this work.

She shook the snow off her coat and hung it on the hook near the door to the back office. Despite her better financial judgment, she switched on the office space heater and settled into the rickety desk chair, furiously rubbing her hands together for warmth.

The space heater warmed the little office in no time, and its comforting buzz plus the glow from the standing lamp filled the otherwise eerily silent space. Sydney rested her forehead on the cool wood surface of the desk and took a deep breath. Something had to change. If she continued down this path, she'd end up pregnant or with a DUI or worse.

She turned the electric kettle on and filled a foam cup with instant coffee. "Step one," she said. "Get your shit together, you disgusting lush."

Her laptop sat open on the desk where she'd left it earlier, and she ran her finger over the trackpad to bring it back to life. When she was fresh out of law school and just starting out in her first real job, she'd buried herself in work. She was the first one in the office at seven in the morning and the last one to leave at ten at night.

After a couple of years, when most of her friends had given up on inviting her to happy hours and weekends upstate, she realized her obsession with work was an excuse to avoid emotional relationships. Karen Walsh had been shackled by love. Sydney Walsh would never let emotions get in the way of her independence.

Dating Connor was a compromise: a social life without sacrificing her career. She could never have anticipated the panic attack that preceded forfeiting everything she'd worked for. At the time, financial stability seemed to be first priority, and Connor provided that in spades.

But sitting in front of her laptop, the remnants of a terrible night still heavy in her gut, she wondered if what she needed now was work. All-consuming, intensive, fingers-to-the-bone work. Her mother depended on her. And if she could manage to save the store, maybe she could manage to save herself.

She typed furiously, adding every thought coursing through her brain to the document titled the Loving Book Club. Building a website, gaining followers on social media, promotions, giveaways, fliers in local shops, connecting with authors. Any whisper of an idea that entered her brain went into the computer.

As she put the finishing touches on an email to a book publicist in New York, securing the Loving Page's first official author signing for the day after Thanksgiving, a subtle knock broke through her concentration. She sat up in the desk chair, struggling to hear past the low hum of the space heater, and a moment later the knock came again. Louder this time.

The chair creaked as she stood. She peeked her head around the doorframe to see out the shop door, where Sam Kirkland was standing inside a veritable snow globe. She hurried toward the door and flicked the lock to let him inside.

"What are you doing here?" she said as he stamped the snow off his boots.

"Do you have the newest release in the Lusty Lads of London series? I can't sleep until I find out if Gerald's member really *is* as big as all the other girls say."

A grin spread across his face, and her stomach twisted in response. His cheeks were bright red from the bitterly cold wind blowing outside.

"Hmm, Gerald of the Lusty Lads. I think we're fresh out of stock on that one."

"Foiled again." He raised a gloved fist at the sky, and when his gaze returned to her, he ran his tongue over his bottom lip. She wanted to lean in and lick that tongue.

"What are you really doing here?" she asked. The chill in the front of the store creeped past her T-shirt, and she hugged her arms to her chest.

"I had to drive out to Blue Mountain Lake to jump an old lady's Buick, and I was just on my way back home when I saw the light on in here." It still didn't explain why he'd stopped and knocked. But she wasn't sure she cared.

"Jumping an old lady's Buick, huh? Outside of Appalachia, I think you can be arrested for that."

His eyes narrowed behind long, black lashes. Maybe he'd forgiven her for earlier.

"Don't tell anybody, all right? It's a fetish, and I'm getting help for it."

"Admitting you have a problem is the first step." Her teeth chattered, and he frowned at her.

"If I give you five bucks, will you turn the heat up in here? You're no help to anybody if you die of pneumonia before January."

"I was in the office; the space heater's on back there. It's almost hot."

"Well, then, what are we doing standing here?"

He sailed past her on a breeze of cold, pine-scented air, and she followed, eager to be back inside the warm, toasty confines of the office.

When she moved past the doorframe, she found him sitting in her desk chair, staring intently at the computer screen. Only a foot of space sat between the door and the chair, and she hovered there, reticent to stand on the other side of him, where she'd have to be nearly pressed against his arm. But the heater was on the other side, and here, close to the door, she was still all chattering teeth and goose bumps.

"You took my seat," she said. He looked up, the creases of concentration still pressed into his brow.

"I was reading your game plan." He rose, peeled off his coat, and stood in the eight-inch heated space on the other side of the chair. She sat down, her heart pounding, and tried to forget that his belt buckle and all it contained were a mere head turn away.

"It's not really a game plan." She kept her eyes if not her focus on the computer screen. "It's just some stuff I was thinking about."

"Well, I think it sounds great. Especially the part about promoting on local radio. A lot of people around here listen to the radio, so it's a more effective promotional tool than in some other parts of the country."

Slowly, she turned her head and looked up at him. He'd removed his coat but still wore his wool ski cap, and the ends of his thick dark hair curled out around his ears. A single bead of sweat trailed down her lower back. Was it him or the space heater?

"You think?" she choked out. She pushed her chair another inch toward the door, and the frigid shop air nipped at her, bringing a bit of clarity to her otherwise cloudy brain.

"For sure. I know all the guys at North Country Public Radio if you want me to put in some calls for you."

"That would be amazing."

"And I see you've been working on Karen's social media stuff, too," he said. "That's smart. Coming at it from all angles."

Sydney turned back to her computer and clicked on the tab where a Facebook event page mocked her. Why was it so difficult to get someone on the phone at these social media companies? She'd cleaned up the Loving Page's Facebook page, opened a new event, and now the stupid thing wouldn't let her invite people.

"I'm trying. I pulled up this event page today. . . ."

All the air rushed out of her lungs in one gust as he leaned over her shoulder from behind, his mouth mere inches from her ear. He leaned one arm on the desk and the other on the back of her chair, and she froze. His warm breath breezed against her neck, and she clenched every muscle in a feeble attempt at not falling apart.

"Ah, look." He raised a finger to the screen. "You have to create the event first, put in all your info, and then you can invite people."

The words floated around her head, unable to compete for brain space with the close proximity of his warm body. Every inch of her buzzed, like she'd come too close to an electric fence.

"Oh." It was the only word she could muster. He stood up straight, leaving her slightly shook.

"Your Instagram stuff is pretty good, too," he said. "Beefy dudes and dogs? Can't go wrong with that."

"Don't forget beefy dudes *holding* dogs. Those are some of my most popular posts."

For a moment, she forgot they were discussing the store. What had happened in the five hours since she'd seen him? He'd stormed out of the bar, and now he was here, sharing this tiny space with her and praising her ideas.

"I'm sorry I was an asshole earlier," he said.

"Oh." She blinked. Had she said any of that out loud? "I . . ."

"I'm not really known for my optimism, but it pissed me off to see you so down on yourself about this place. Your ideas are really smart, and I think the whole plan could work. You just have to give yourself a shot at it."

Pressure built in her sinuses, and suddenly the tears were there, threatening at the corners of her eyes. Before she could tell him how much that meant to her, how grateful she was to have someone believe in her, he opened his mouth again.

"Plus," he said, "you seem to drink a lot when you're going through something. It's a little scary."

"What do you know?" she snapped. It was one thing to admonish herself over the drinking. It was quite another for this near stranger to scold her. Even if he was terrifyingly close to the truth.

"What do *I* know?" he said, a smile tugging at his lips. "I watched my dad die of liver cancer after trying to drink his own problems away, so I come from a place of experience, all right?"

The air stilled. He was so cavalier, the statement almost flowed right through her without resonating. He ran his hands over his face and leaned back against the wall, waiting for her response.

"I'm so sorry," she said. "How long ago?"

"He died when I was fourteen. But he was a heavy drinker his whole life. *My* whole life. He was a lot older than my mom and never really wanted kids, so when she had me, I guess it was the push he needed to go from casual drunk to full-blown alcoholic.

"He wasn't abusive or anything, which is usually where people's minds go, but when he finally died, we were all a little relieved. My mom basically got to start her life over. He was a real weight on her. Every time he left the house, she'd wait up for him, looking out the window, worried he'd plowed into a tree or something. The night he died, she slept for eighteen hours."

She nodded slowly. He spoke, face neutral, as if discussing a movie he'd just seen. "Well, wow. That's nuts."

He raised his eyebrows and shrugged. "He's not the first unhappy man to drink himself to death, and he won't be the last."

"Is your mom remarried now?"

A dark cloud rolled over his face, and his jaw twitched before he said, "Mom died last year. Last December."

"Damn," she muttered. "I'm so sorry."

"Thanks." He ran his hands over his face again and huffed out a short breath. "Sorry, man, that took a really depressing turn."

"Don't be sorry."

"All that was to say I have experience with people who drink a lot. I can tell you on good authority, it doesn't make anything better. In fact, it makes most things worse."

Of course it did. She knew that. Had she made things worse for him? She swallowed down her own insecurity and forced some reassurance into her voice.

"I know," she said. "I agree. Definitely doesn't make me feel any better, that's for sure. I think I'm gonna take it easy for a while."

She watched for his response. He nodded.

"Good."

The silence creeped around them like bugs, and Sydney chewed on her lip, desperate for something to talk about. But he didn't seem fazed at all. His eyes never left her.

"How's your mom doing? Is she embracing the changes?"

"No," she said. "The difficult part is that I can't tell if she's skeptical about the actual idea or if she just doesn't like her daughter coming in and running the show. She's been in the shop every day since I started the renovations, looking in every corner and examining every new piece. It's exhausting. It's a wonder she has time to engage in other *activities*."

As she remembered Yuri and her mother on the couch, she nearly gagged.

"Activities?" he asked.

"Do you know Yuri? Who owns the liquor shop next door?"

"Yeah. Your mom's boyfriend."

Sydney tilted her head to the side. "You knew that?"

"Yeah," Sam said. "Everybody knows that. I mean, nei-

ther of them has ever admitted it out loud, but this is a small
town. Once they were spotted together at the bowling alley
wearing matching shirts, it was all over."

The bile rose in Sydney's throat. How long would it take
before everyone in town knew Jared had to carry her out of
Utz's? Hank the bartender was the only one who'd seen
them leave together, but surely Jared had neighbors. Maybe
the snow had blocked the view? She could only hope.

"Well, yeah," she said. "So I caught them . . . you
know . . . on the couch."

"Banging?"

"Ugh," she said, covering her mouth with her hands.
"You can joke, but I have the visual. It's burned into my
brain like I stared at the sun."

"That's cruel." He laughed and ran his knuckles over his
bearded jaw. "Yuri's not the most attractive man, but your
mom still looks all right."

"She's my *mother*. It's just not right. I prefer to believe I
was delivered by the stork." His eyes sparkled in the dim
glow of the standing lamp as he watched her with amuse-
ment.

"Your mom knows you sleep there and she still did it on
the couch?" He laughed again. "Damn, Karen Walsh.
Didn't know she had it in her. Kinky."

"I might throw up." Her voice was muffled as it carried
through her fingers. "Anyway, as you can imagine, I'm not
really comfortable staying with her anymore. She should
have her privacy. And I should have my . . . sight."

"Jorie's got that extra room. I'm sure she'd let you crash
with her for a while until you find a more permanent spot.
Plus, she's at Matt's a lot. And since you sold your car, if
you need a ride, I have a junker that's seen better days, but
she'll get you through the snow better than that bike will."

"Sam," she said softly. "Seriously?"

"Yeah, sure. You need a ride, I've got one."

"How much?"

"You'd be doing *me* a favor by taking it. It's occupying valuable real estate in my shop."

She tilted her head. "Stop. Let me give you a couple hundred bucks."

"I can't take your money." His steady gaze dared her to continue.

"Okay. That would be amazing. All of it." She bit down on her lower lip. "Thank you. You're kind of solving all my problems tonight."

He snorted a laugh. "If I can't solve my own, might as well solve somebody else's."

She licked her lips. Maybe now was the moment to ask about Olivia. In her mind, she'd run through all sorts of scenarios. Olivia was terminally ill, but they were still in love and she'd begged Sam to move on with his life. She was Sam's green card wife and was currently overseas figuring out her visa. She was a man transitioning to be a woman and was having treatments in California. Whatever the truth, if Sydney didn't hear it soon, she'd crawl out of her skin.

The shrill ring of the shop phone broke through her thoughts. "That's weird," she said. "Who would call here this late?"

"It's probably a wrong number," he said.

With visions of her mother in some sort of emergency, unable to get through to Sydney's unreliable cell phone, she reached for the receiver hanging on the office wall and said hello.

"Hi." The voice came on a breath. Crank call?

"Hi, who's calling?"

"It's me, Syd." Recognition hit her like a punch to the jaw. Connor.

"Hi." Her eyes flickered over to where Sam was still standing against the wall, his thoughtful gaze trained on her. He didn't move. "What do you want?"

"I just wanted to talk. I can't stop thinking about you, baby. I miss you so much."

Her hands curled into fists. How dare he.

"How did you know I was here?"

"I haven't been able to get through to your cell, so I thought maybe you blocked me. I called your mom's apartment, and she told me it might've been the bad cell service and that I should try you at the store."

"She knew it was you?" She couldn't believe her mother would give her up like that.

"Yeah, I . . ." He cleared his throat. "I think so?" Connor had never sounded so insecure.

She looked back at Sam, who still hadn't moved. While she didn't necessarily want to have a long, drawn-out conversation with Connor, she knew she couldn't say anything definitive with Sam standing two feet away.

"Can you hang on a second?" she asked.

"Sure," Connor said. She placed a hand over the mouthpiece of the phone and turned to Sam.

"This is not going to be a pleasant phone call," she said, tucking her bottom lip between her teeth.

A tendon in Sam's neck flexed, and he cracked his knuckles as if preparing for a fistfight. "He's not here, is he?"

"What? No, he's not here. How did you know who it was?"

He pressed his lips together and shifted on his feet. If Connor was actually here, what would Sam do about it? How much did he know about her relationship? And where did he find out?

"I heard you got cheated on," he said. "Figured from the sound of your voice that it had to be him. Some asshole calling trying to get you back."

A lump formed in her throat. He was jealous. Or angry. Or both. And damned if the idea of that had her wanting to drop the phone, rip his clothes off, and taste every inch of his skin. The heat radiating from him hit her in the chest and ran through her limbs like hot oil.

"I'll leave you alone." He squeezed past the desk chair

and stepped out into the store, holding his coat to his chest, pausing only to confirm. "He's definitely not here, right? I don't have to wait out front for some tiny dick mobile to pull up with your ex inside?"

The combination of his serious face and the ridiculous sentiment forced laughter to bubble up and out of her like a waterfall. She clutched her stomach as peals of laughter carried through the store and echoed off the walls. When she finally came up for air, tears streamed down her cheeks, and Sam grinned.

"Damn," he said. "I was right, huh? Tiny dick?"

"You're awful," she said, wiping at her damp face. "And you're wrong."

"Eh, he's overcompensating for something. He's gotta be."

She let her head fall back, wishing he didn't have to leave. Whenever she was with him, everything felt easy. Even silence was easy.

"Let me know if you can hook anything up with the radio station," she said. "That would be a huge help."

"It's done." Before he turned to walk away, he raised his eyebrows. She wanted more. But she wasn't going to get it tonight.

chapter **thirteen**

Don't be strangers, you hear? Just because your mom isn't around anymore doesn't mean we're not family. We love you boys like our own."

Aunt Nancy kissed Sam's cheek, her sticky red lipstick leaving a gummy mark on his jaw. When she pulled away from Jared, he had one, too. As if the emotional and mental scars she'd left on them wasn't enough, she had to brand them physically.

"Okay, Aunt Nancy," Jared said in a voice reserved for the very young. "Thanks again for dinner."

"Anytime, boys. Anytime." She watched and waved until the brothers were in the cab of Sam's pickup and halfway down the block.

"Ho-lee shit," Jared said once they'd turned the bend. He pinched the bridge of his nose and released an animal yelp. "That was hands down the worst Thanksgiving dinner ever. *Ever.* Worse than the year Cousin Amber showed up with our old gym teacher and told everybody they were banging. Worse than the year Dad accidentally turned the oven off and we didn't have a cooked turkey until midnight."

"I get it," Sam grumbled. The tension headache pressed at his temples. He hoped he had the presence of mind to get them back home in one piece.

"What was that weird orange stuff? I put some on my plate, but there was no way in hell I was eating it. It smelled like fish."

"I don't know, man. I didn't touch it, either. I only ate the rolls because I saw her pull them out of a package."

"When she said she made most of the meal in her microwave, I loaded up on peanuts. I'm fucking starving."

"Me, too. Everything's closed, though."

"I say we crash Jorie's." Jared had a devious glint in his eyes. "You know even if they're done eating, they'll have tons of leftovers, and her crazy-ass family will party until dawn."

"Good point." Sam tried to hide his smile. Sydney and her mom would be there, too. Karen always spent Thanksgiving with the McDonaghs, and he couldn't imagine this would be the year they'd break tradition.

Over the past couple of weeks, Sam had been finding excuses to swing by the Loving Page. He'd have an idea for a promotion, a friend who could help out, or a stain or paint sample for the reading nook. Simply being in the same room as Sydney soothed his soul, and if he could manage to get her laughing to the point of tears, he found he slept better that night.

The brothers pulled up to the McDonaghs' modest ranch home to find the driveway filled to capacity, cars parked in the street, and light pouring from every window. It looked like the fake party scene from *Home Alone*, only this party was very real and very loud.

"I hope Insane Cousin Mary doesn't try to jump me this year," Jared said, climbing out of the truck. "I shouldn't have worn this sweater. I look way too good in this sweater."

"Would you shut up?" Sam slapped the back of his brother's head as they made their way up the icy front walk. Their shoes crunched over rock salt. "If you're really that concerned, let me mess up your hair. That'll definitely turn her off."

He reached for Jared's perfectly combed and gelled hair, but Jared swatted his hand away. "I'll ruin you."

Sam pressed the doorbell, but after an unanswered minute, the brothers let themselves in. Sam couldn't wait any longer to surround himself with the familiar faces of his surrogate family after the stilted, awkward afternoon with his blood relatives.

"Kirklands!" Jorie squealed. She stood on the bottom step of the staircase and raised her arms over her head. Her mouth was rimmed with purple.

"Hey, drunky," Jared said, squeezing her in a hug. "Is that wine, or were you making out with Barney?"

"Oh, *ha-ha*," Jorie said, rolling her eyes. She turned to Sam and hugged him, lingering just a moment too long. It was only seven o'clock, and he could already tell Jorie had mere minutes until she was passed out cold somewhere. He'd learned to accept the rampant drinking in this town, but he'd never be okay with it.

People milled about in each corner of the house, and Sam knew every single face. He made his way past the tiny entryway into the living room and said hello. A cluster of elderly aunts chatted on the couch; babies slobbered over piles of plastic blocks while their young mothers looked on; ruddy-faced men chugged icy beers in the kitchen; and still seated at the dining room table were Mrs. McDonagh, Insane Cousin Mary, Karen Walsh, and Sydney.

"Sammy!" Mrs. McDonagh said, leaping up from the

table. She stood five feet tall but managed to hug Sam around the neck and squeeze him until he choked. "I'm so glad you're here! Have you eaten? We just finished up, but we've all got bets going on what time somebody says they're hungry and we're busy making turkey sandwiches."

"We're here for the grub," Sam said, leaving an arm wrapped tightly around Mrs. McDonagh's shoulders. "And the company, I guess."

He tried to give everyone in the room equal attention, but his gaze returned to Sydney as if his eyes were magnets and she a steel beam. She stood up from the table, carrying handfuls of dirty plates, and gifted him with her signature lip-press-into-smile.

Tonight she wore light-colored jeans that turned her ass into a perfectly rounded heart and a loose, low-cut navy-blue blouse. Gold hoop earrings swung against the curve of her jaw as she moved past the tightly packed chairs into the kitchen.

"You need help?" Sam asked, following her into the kitchen and reaching for the teetering stack of dishes in her left hand.

She shook her head as she set the dishes into the sink without missing a beat. The kitchen only comfortably allowed four bodies at a time, and with Matt and Mr. McDonagh still arguing over the wishbone, Sam was forced to stand mere inches away from Sydney as she rinsed plates.

"You'll be glad to know I'm totally sober," she said.

"It's seven o'clock at the McDonagh family Thanksgiving and you're still standing and you're *sober*? There's no way you survived this thing without some kind of intoxicant. Tell me your secret."

She dried her hands on the dish towel and turned to face him, cocking her head to the side. "Okay, one glass of wine. But I'm nowhere near drunk, and I plan to drive my mother and me both home tonight. That night at Utz's was a wake-up call. I don't want to put myself in a dangerous situation."

He studied her face as something like pain flickered across her features. In an instant, she'd smoothed her brow and forced a tiny smile.

"Dangerous?" he asked.

"I don't mean, like, men-with-knives dangerous." The forced smile grew. "I'm being dramatic. I just don't want to get like that again."

He nodded. Sometimes it proved difficult to keep up conversation when all he could focus on was the soft skin at the curve of her collarbone, her slightly crooked bottom teeth, and the subtle perfume that reminded him of an expensive hotel he'd stayed at once.

"So," she said, picking up the slack for both of them. "Your aunt's was terrible?"

"It was all my fault. I thought they'd be serving *food* on Thanksgiving, not potting soil and fiberglass insulation. Silly me." A melodic laugh escaped her lips and she leaned in, a wave of her scent wafting over him. He breathed her in like the first inhale after a deep-water dive.

"Well, there's enough food here to feed an army," she said. "You want me to make you a plate?"

He blinked. No one had offered to take care of him in a very long time. "What? No, you don't have to do that. I can make my own plate."

"Okay." She leaned in conspiratorially and whispered, "I was going to steer you away from Cousin Mary's weird potato thing. But go ahead. Live dangerously."

As she squeezed between him and the kitchen island, her breasts brushed against his chest, and he swore she looked up at him while she went, her eyes full of innuendo. She still didn't know all the details of his situation with Liv, but maybe the whiff of another woman in his life kept her at arm's length.

There were nights in her store when the sexual tension was so thick, he could barely stand it. Nothing as brazen as the night at Taylor's when she'd boldly asked him to kiss her, but something between them had grown and deepened since then. He almost wished now that he'd thrown caution to the wind that night and kissed her. At least that would've been only about lust.

She walked away, the curve of her ass taunting him as she went. As he filled a plate with turkey, Mrs. McDonagh's famous corn-bread stuffing, cranberry sauce, green beans, and mashed potatoes, he considered, for the millionth time, what his life would be like without Liv.

Beyond asking Sydney out on a proper date, he could take a long trip by himself, stay out late without the fear of someone in town tattling on him, or even sell the house and leave Pine Ridge altogether.

But that was all a fantasyland, as real and accessible as Narnia. He'd made his bed a long time ago, and now he had to lie in it. He envisioned himself breaking their deal and walking away, the chorus of townspeople chanting after him: *After all she's done for you.*

He owed her. The way she'd taken care of his mother, well beyond the scope of her shift as hospice nurse, was invaluable. And how could he turn his back on Jay? If he had any part in that kid growing up without a mother or, worse, a kid who knew his mother had chosen alcohol over him, he'd never forgive himself. He wished he could shake the debt, the guilt, the promises he'd made. His heart wouldn't let him.

Sam took a seat at the dining table next to Karen Walsh and nudged her shoulder as he tucked into the heaping plate before him. He had a special place in his heart for the woman.

The morning after his mother's funeral, he woke to find that Karen Walsh had snuck in during the night to clean his house of old food and weeks of dust. Cinnamon buns and hot coffee waited for him on the kitchen table with a note that read, *Don't forget to feed yourself, Sammy. We love you.*

"I made those beans," she said brightly. "Good, huh?"

"Amazing," he said, his mouth full to bursting with food.

"So you think my daughter's gonna pull off this romance-club shenanigan?" she asked. "Seems a little far-fetched to think we're gonna be millionaires from a Pine Ridge book club."

He chewed thoughtfully as Karen picked at the half-eaten pumpkin pie on her plate. "I think Sydney's really smart, and that it's a good idea. Millionaires, though? No, probably not."

"I don't want her to get her hopes up," Karen said, and it was then that Sam noticed the hint of sadness in her voice. "She's had enough heartache in her life. It would kill me if the shop closed and Syd thought she had anything to do with it. I tried all my life to shield her from my money troubles. Pretty ironic that at this age, she's knee-deep in them."

"Give her some credit," Sam said. "She was raised by a tough-as-nails, balls-out bitch. She comes from good stock."

Karen cackled and clutched Sam's wrist. She nodded, gesturing toward the other end of the room. "Hey, let me ask you somethin'. How old is Jared?"

"Twenty-five." Sam shoveled more beans into his mouth. He had to hand it to Karen. They were the best green beans he'd ever had. "Are these real fried onions on here? Not the ones from the can?"

"Yeah, real onions," she said in a faraway voice. "Say, what do you think about fixing Sydney up with Jared?"

The food turned to dust in his mouth. He glanced up at Karen and then across the room to where Jared stood, stealing casual glances at Sydney as she crouched on the floor, cooing at the babies, completely unaware.

"He's way too young for her," Sam said. He wiped his mouth with a napkin and settled back in his chair. Why was Jared looking at her like that? "Why? She likes him?"

Karen's eyes narrowed, and for a moment, the fear of exposure crept along his skin. Had his voice been too desperate? Too invested? She ran a veiny hand across her chin and studied his face.

"She hasn't said one way or the other," Karen said. "I just thought, he's a nice kid, successful, and I'm startin' to get worried about her. That jerk Connor's been calling her a lot."

"Really?" The seething anger that always accompanied a mention of her ex rose up inside Sam. He and Sydney never spoke about the phone call she received at the shop, but he thought she'd told the guy to fuck off. Maybe he was wrong.

Karen took a gulp of her coffee and shrugged. "I don't know if she'd go back with him. But if she had somebody new to focus on, maybe she'd leave him in the dust, you know?"

Sam took a deep breath. He wanted to shake Sydney. Anyone who treated her like she was disposable deserved a punch in the mouth. He certainly didn't deserve a second shot.

"Yeah, maybe," he said.

Sydney stood and looked up, surprised, as she noticed Jared. Sam watched as he gave her a tight-lipped smile and wrapped his arms around her in an awkward hug. Maybe she was interested in him after all.

Sam ran his hands over his face. If they wanted to date, what could he do? They were consenting adults and he was an off-limits outsider with a complicated woman in his life.

If they did get together, maybe he'd just burn his eyes with bleach so he'd never have to see them holding hands.

"Jared's an idiot, though," Sam said. "He's just a kid. Don't fix her up with a kid."

A curious smile creeped across Karen's face, and she rested her chin in her hand. "Hmm, okay," she said in a sing-song voice. "Any ideas on who I *could* set her up with? Or, in your opinion, is there no one good enough for Sydney?"

"Karen Walsh," he said. "What are you suggesting?"

Karen shrugged, batting her eyelashes like a schoolgirl with a secret. "I don't suggest. I call 'em like I see 'em. And if I didn't admire the hell out of what you're doing for Liv and Jay, I'd tell you to go up to my daughter right now and kiss her like I know you want to."

A red-hot blush filled Sam's cheeks. Thank God the beard hid the worst of it. He'd always worried about how transparent he'd been, lusting over Sydney. Maybe he didn't have to wonder anymore.

"But my gut tells me you're trying to make life less complicated for Liv," Karen said. "I know it's been over between the two of you for a long time, but I can't imagine she'd enjoy knowing you'd fallen for somebody else. Seems like one of those situations that might have her running for the hooch, right?"

"It's not like that with me and Syd," he said. The words didn't sound convincing even to him. Karen was spot-on. Before he'd met Sydney, he couldn't imagine a scenario that pulled his focus and dedication away from Liv and Jay. Now he was a rabbit in a trap, desperate for a way out. "We're just friends. I'm . . . Liv and Jay are my priority."

"Mm-hmm," Karen said, taking another sip of coffee. "I get it. You've made a commitment, and if Liv can be the kind of sober parent to Jay that you think she can be, then you're a hero for helping 'em out, Sam Kirkland. And if staying away from pretty girls helps you do that, then more power to ya. But when Liv does show up again, try not to stare at Syd so much. That dopey look you get on your face when she's in the room is a dead giveaway."

Karen stood up from the table, leaving Sam frozen in his chair.

D oes anybody have any threes?" Jorie's eyes swam around the circle like half-dead tadpoles in a tepid pool.

"Baby, that's not how this works," Matt said, peering over her shoulder at her cards. "And you have *all* the threes."

"No, only four of them!"

"Man, I can't play this game with her anymore." Sam threw his cards in the middle of the dining table and leaned back in his chair. It was close to midnight, and most of the over-fifty crowd had gone to bed. Those remaining were either half in the bag or too annoyed with Jorie to continue the game.

"I'll get her a water," Sydney said, pushing herself up from the table. Sam's brain told him to stay put, but the perfectly rounded shape of her ass told a very different part of him to get up and go into the kitchen.

He grabbed himself a cold beer from the fridge and handed her a bottle of water. When he stood upright and closed the fridge door, she remained next to him with an open palm. "And another beer, please."

"For you?"

"Yes, for me." Her lips curved into a smile.

He knew this dance very well. Flirting. It began with banter, escalated with teasing, and culminated in her touching him in some way that made him hard and in need of an excuse to leave the room. It always happened at the end of the night. And it always left him desperate for more.

"You sure?" he said.

"Yes, I'm sure. It'll be my second drink of the night. I'm being so responsible."

He pursed his lips and took a long, slow drink of his own beer. She shook her head as if she couldn't believe him.

"I dunno," he sang. They matched each other's dopey grins, daring the other to break first. He hadn't acted like a silly teenager in a long time, but she brought it out of him.

"It's almost midnight and we're playing Go Fish. And Jorie just asked for a *fifth* three card. I need it."

"I'm inclined to say no, Syd."

She lowered her chin, deepened her gaze, and took a step toward him. Her breasts pressed against his crossed arms, her thighs brushed his, and he could feel the three buttons on her high-waisted jeans against his hardening cock. All the breath left his lungs.

"That was easy."

She stepped back holding his beer bottle. He hadn't even felt her snatch it. By the time he remembered that he had a brain and engaging said brain was necessary to form sentences, she was back in the dining room while he trailed after her.

"What was easy?"

The voice shattered the moment like a brick through a window. He spun over his shoulder, and standing in the front doorway, bringing with her a wave of icy air, was Liv.

"*What* are you doing here?" he said. Her little pixie face crumpled as if he'd pinched her, and he immediately regretted his tone. She sucked at her cheeks, eyes dancing around the discarded napkins, empty beer bottles, and food-caked plates scattered around the room.

She cleared her throat before she said, "I just got in. Thought it might be nice to spend Thanksgiving at home."

"Livvy!" Jorie bounded into the living room and crushed her friend in a hug. Liv's eyes shut tight as she clutched Jorie's swaying body.

When Jorie finally pulled back, Liv grinned at the slurring, sloppy group that had tumbled into the living room to see what the commotion was. "Guess I missed all the fun, huh?"

"Not *all* the fun," Jorie's brother said, holding up a half-empty bottle of tequila. "We're gonna put Jorie to bed so the rest of us can keep having a good time."

"Yeah, we're gonna play spin the bottle," Jared said. His eyelids were at half-mast.

"Like hell we are," Sydney said.

Sam's blood pressure rose. Jared had been lurking around Sydney all night, and now he sat directly next to her, grinning like a kid with a crush every time she spoke. She didn't appear engaged, but Sam couldn't be sure enough to rest easy. He wanted his brother clear across the room from her.

"Yeah, dude," Matt said. "That'd be weird, since a lot of us are related."

Sydney rolled her eyes. "I'm gonna head out."

Sam's feet were planted in place, unable to move toward Liv or away from where he stood rooted to the ground. He watched, helpless in his own skin, as Sydney hugged the group goodbye and asked Matt if he was sure he didn't want her to take Jorie home. Matt assured her Jorie would be better off on the couch in case she puked, and Sydney gathered her coat and purse. She avoided Sam's eyes completely.

"Hi," Liv said, approaching Sydney with an outstretched hand. "I'm Olivia. You must be Karen Walsh's daughter."

"That's right. Sydney."

"So nice to meet you," Liv said. She dropped Sydney's hand and twisted her purse strap between her bony fingers. "I'll have to stop by your mom's store soon. I heard you've been fixing it up."

"I'm trying." The contrast between the two women was

staggering. He'd always considered Liv well dressed, but Sydney's style was effortless and expensive in a way Liv couldn't touch.

"I can't wait to see it." Liv worried the purse strap between her fingers, twisting until he feared she might snap it into two pieces. Uncertainty radiated out of her like a freshman standing in front of the head cheerleader.

"We're having a bunch of fun stuff at the store this weekend. You should come by. Tomorrow, actually, Dusty Rose Publishing is sending an author to do a signing, and we're doing a huge giveaway with some books and swag that a publicist sent me."

"Sounds fantastic," Liv said. "I love romance novels, so I'll definitely have to swing by."

Sydney's lips pressed into a smile, but this time, no teeth. "You definitely should."

She sent a cursory smile to Sam, waved vaguely at the group, and left.

She took the warmth from the room with her. All at once, Sam needed to get out.

He drove, slowly meandering around the slick mountain roads with Liv following, both of them driving toward the cabin they called home. He had a brief fantasy of sailing over the edge of the cliff and meeting his blissful end in a fiery crash below. But he didn't want to die. He just wanted to be over all the heartache.

As he entered the dark cabin, the medicinal scent of Liv's flowery perfume stung his nostrils and turned his stomach. He flipped on the lamp near the door, and there, sitting neatly against the wall, was her little pink suitcase framed by a pair of pink Converse sneakers and a pink umbrella. On the dining table he found a child's drawing. The surprisingly neat penmanship read, I miss you Sam! Love Jay.

He pinched the bridge of his nose, the tension headache

thrumming against his skull. The kid was so smart, so talented. He deserved more than custody battles and a mother he was only allowed to see in photos. Liv's sobriety record in the last year had been impeccable. She'd attended every AA meeting, showed up for Jay, and put her life in Pine Ridge on hold to make sure her kid had two physically, mentally, and emotionally present parents. For a single sad moment, he imagined his father having someone believe in him the way Sam believed in Liv. Maybe the old man would still be around.

Liv entered the house behind him and quietly slipped off her wet boots. She'd done nothing wrong, and yet he wondered if there was any excuse believable enough to get him back out of the house.

As he watched her strip off her coat, walk into the living room, and curl her feet underneath herself on the couch, waves of nostalgia pulled him back. She was like a diseased limb; he knew he had to have it amputated, but once it was gone, he'd spend the rest of his life with its ghost.

"I didn't know you were coming back tonight," he said.

She twirled a strand of white-blond hair around her finger and peered up at him with big doe eyes.

"I wasn't really welcome at Thanksgiving with Kevin's family." She jutted out her chin. "No matter what I do, they're convinced I'm toxic. I mean, he's my kid. How cruel do you have to be to keep a kid from his mother on Thanksgiving?"

Sam remembered Kevin's parents from their one and only brief meeting last year—conservative Christians who believed in an early bedtime, vegetables at every meal, and Bible study three times a week. They may not have been warm and welcoming to their grandson's recovering alcoholic mother, but from what Sam could tell, they wanted the best for Jay.

"What did they say?" he asked.

"We got into an argument because I borrowed some money from them and haven't paid it back yet. I'm paying through the nose for rent in Akron, plus the car payments, doctor's appointments, and now that psychologist they're making Jay go to. And the lawyer fees and all that. So when Kevin's mom asked me when I could pay them back, I told her I didn't know, and she said maybe it would be best if I didn't come for Thanksgiving."

Sam took a deep breath as her eyes filled with tears. Before his mother passed away, she'd told him, "You can't maintain a relationship on nostalgia alone."

Part of it was nostalgia—this tiny woman swimming in her oversize sweater with the same platinum-blond hair she'd had since high school—but his mother couldn't have known how he was drowning when she died. How his heart stopped every time the phone rang because any day could be *the call*.

And how Liv smoothed over that pain and fear by simply being there. Slipping his mother snacks, washing her hair, sneaking into the room during doctor's visits to translate the complicated medical jargon that made Sam's head spin.

Liv hadn't wanted anything from him then. And now she needed him for everything.

"So anyway," Liv said, dabbing at her eyes with the sleeve of her sweater. "I figured if they didn't want me around, I'd come back here for a while."

Sam ran a hand over his face. He couldn't bring himself to step into the living room. He didn't want to touch her, didn't want to discuss this with her. Part of him hated her. Part of him wanted to help her.

"Jay's not coming back with you?" he asked.

"No," she said, collapsing her shoulders. "It seems like he's happy there, and when I'm around, things just get messy. If I'm making my son's life complicated, then I'll go."

He scraped his fingers over his beard. Anger mixed with

sympathy, creating a toxic cocktail inside his chest. Her poor kid.

"You're still going to meetings, though, right?" he said.

"I hate those meetings." Her eyes were bloodshot and wild. "I go, Sam, but I'm not like those degenerates. All kinds of sad, ugly people complaining about how their wives left them and they had their driver's licenses taken away. I'm young. Lots of young people drink a lot. Look at Jorie's parents' house tonight. Everyone was hammered."

"You're not like everyone else," he said. His vision clouded with rage. The lines were straight out of a scene from his childhood. "Some people can get drunk one night and then they're fine for weeks or months without having a drop. You have two beers and suddenly you're closing down Utz's and I have to drag your drunk ass home so you don't choke on your own vomit and die."

Her bottom lip quivered, and he raked his hands through his hair. This was what she did to him. She pushed him just far enough to say something he regretted, and yet she hadn't done anything particularly evil. His chest heaved. His head throbbed. She was trying. Didn't that count for something?

He knew sober Liv. The Liv who was her patients' favorite nurse, the Liv who received flowers from the families as thanks for everything she did to make their loss less painful. The clear-eyed, grinning Liv who managed to avoid alcohol and stay present.

But that Liv was temporary, only one drink away from torpedoing everything all over again. How could he trust something so delicate?

"I'm sorry." Her eyes filled with tears. "I know I'm letting everyone down. I don't deserve any sympathy from anyone."

The scene was textbook. Defensive, remorseful, a promise to change, rinse, repeat. Her emotions exhausted him, refused to release him from their tangled embrace. The judge said proving Liv had a stable homelife in Pine Ridge would help her case. If he gave up on helping to save Jay's relationship with his mother, he'd never forgive himself. So he stuck it out.

"I'm going to bed," he said. "There's not much in the fridge, but you can eat what's there if you're hungry."

"Thank you," she said, sniffling. She wiped the tears from her dimpled chin. "Seriously, Sam. Everything you've done for us. Everything you've done for me. I know I treated you terribly when we were kids, and I don't deserve any of this. But I truly can't thank you enough."

He bit the inside of his lip, tamping down all the things he wanted to say to her.

As the product of an alcoholic parent, he knew exactly what Jay was up against and would have to fight for the rest of his life. What Sam had never had was someone fighting for his parent's sobriety the way he and Liv fought for hers. If she could hold herself together long enough to create and maintain a stable homelife, maybe Jay would have a fighting chance at normalcy. This version of Liv was weepy and misguided, but at least she was clean.

Please, God, let her stay clean.

Sam walked into his bedroom and closed the door behind him, savoring the inky darkness. Having Liv in the house again set him on edge and tested his nerves. She was a live wire, reminding him that his life was not his own. He'd accepted her as a friend after their messy breakup years ago, but now she occupied a much more tumultuous place in his world.

A year ago, when she got into her car, drunk beyond reason and with her kid in the front seat, he lost faith in her. She'd spent the past twelve months working for her sobriety, reclaiming a solid place in Jay's life, and regaining the trust her friends and family once had in her. She'd gone from a lover to a friend to a burden, and Sam didn't know how to reconcile that type of relationship. All he knew was that he'd agreed to it.

He kicked off his boots, tugged off his clothes, and went to sleep.

chapter **fourteen**

Sydney's mind wandered. Traffic in the store had been steady all weekend, and the book signing on Friday had been a smash. Tourists and locals alike had sought out the Loving Page after reading about the event on fliers scattered around town and posts on social media. They filled the store to capacity and had all but cleaned out the romance section. Most of the avid fans promised to return on December 15 for the first book-club meeting to discuss their first title, *Years Ago.*

Sydney had slid headfirst into the world of romance novels, spurred by Jorie and fueled by the captivating worlds the authors created. *Years Ago* told the story of a career woman who foolishly gave it all up for love, only to find that the man truly worth her time wanted her success as much as she did. Sydney spent the night before Thanksgiving inhaling the novel and weeping through the final pages.

But now the store was quiet, with most of the tourists having finished their shopping earlier in the afternoon.

They were probably out at the bars or having dinner. And Sydney had time to dwell on Olivia.

The reunion she'd witnessed between Liv and Sam had been less than romantic, but she'd barely heard from or seen him all weekend, and the distance left her rattled. All that had changed was Olivia's presence in town. Whatever had pushed Sam away, it had to do with her. Sydney was sure of it.

"Excuse me." A fragile voice interrupted her thoughts. Sydney turned from her spot at the back of the store to face a tiny grinning old woman with a cloud of baby pink hair.

"Hi there," Sydney said brightly. The gorgeous coif begged to be touched. "How can I help you?"

"I heard a rumor you're starting a romance book club," she said. Her eyes twinkled behind massive red glasses. "Is it true?"

"You bet. Are you interested?"

"Very. My name is Edith O'Hare. I've been reading romance for as long as I can remember. But I've never heard of anything like this book club before. What do I need to do to join, sweetheart?"

"All you have to do is read our first title, *Years Ago*, and show up here at six o'clock on December fifteenth." She snagged a paper flier off the bookshelf and passed it to Edith.

Edith's bright pink lips curled into a smile, and she reached a hand out to pat Sydney on the elbow. "Oh dear, I hope I make it till then. At my age, you never know."

Sydney burst out laughing, and Edith sent her a wink. "I'll stay positive," Sydney said. "And if I may say so, your hair is stunning. What a gorgeous color."

"Oh, thank you," she said, a blush creeping into her papery cheeks. "My granddaughter does it for me. My son thinks I'm batty, but you only live once, eh?"

"Are you into makeup, too?"

"Oh, I love makeup," Edith said. She clasped her hands together, revealing electric purple fingernails.

"Then you'll love this."

Next to the cash register sat a row of cheek stains that Sydney had purchased to entice customers to add one more thing before they checked out. She plucked a vibrant shade of fuchsia for her stylish customer, and as she handed it over, Edith's eyes shone like jewels under water.

"Oh darling, this is beautiful," she said. "I'll have it."

"It's on the house."

"Oh, I couldn't!"

"You could," Sydney countered. "Consider it a deposit. You can pay me in the form of book-club attendance. And tell your friends."

Edith's brow pinched as if she was in pain, but before Sydney could ask if she was all right, Edith leaned in and kissed her square on the cheek. "You're an angel."

At seven o'clock, Sydney shuttered the store and drove Sam's junker back to Jorie's house, where she'd been staying for the past few blissful weeks. Jorie spent half her time at Matt's, leaving Sydney plenty of time to herself, and the rest of the time she was a genial roommate who always brought home pastries from work and kept the common spaces tidy.

Sydney pulled up to the dark house and grinned. Nobody home. She could take a long steamy shower without risk of using all the hot water, watch terribly trashy TV and yell at the idiot characters, and eat cheese and crackers for dinner. She'd never actually lived alone, and staying at Jorie's was proving to be close enough.

After her shower, she slipped into clean gray yoga pants and a cutoff T-shirt and flipped the TV to the Bravo network. Two chattering blondes greeted her. "Hello, friends." Once she had her plate of snacks and a steaming cup of tea nestled on the TV tray in her lap, she released a long, deep breath.

Just as she shoved the first cracker heaped with cheddar into her mouth, her phone buzzed with a text. Since the night Connor had texted her, every buzz, beep, and ring on her phone sent her heart into her throat.

She leaned forward to peek at the screen. **Sam**. Her muscles relaxed. It was one of three messages he'd sent her. Apparently, the others had come in while she showered.

I'm coming over, I need to pick up that book I lent you.

You're home, right?

I hope you're not already sleeping? Put your teeth in, Grandma, I'm outside.

Her palms grew slick with sweat, and her heart began to race. The knock on the door sent her leaping off the couch, the crackers scattering across Jorie's carpet. Sam had no consideration for time or space. He was always popping in and showing up unannounced. While she loved seeing him at any time, she also liked to be prepared. Tonight she wished she'd at least bothered with a bra.

She opened the front door a crack, careful to stay behind the icy wind that slipped in. "Come in, come in," she urged. "It's freezing."

Sam hurried inside and closed the door behind him. When he turned toward her, his face was stony. "Did you get my texts?"

"I just saw them," she said, crossing her arms over her chest. "You're so demanding."

He rolled his eyes, kicked off his boots, and moved past her into the living room. "I'm supposed to see the friend who lent me that book tomorrow, and I need it back."

He tossed his coat on the back of a chair, helped himself to a beer from the fridge, and then settled onto the couch.

"Make yourself at home," she said.

He raised a single eyebrow at her. "My dad built this

house and my best friend lives in it, so if we're playing that game, I belong here more than you do."

The words had bite, but his curved lips told a different story. This was how they operated lately. What began as harmless banter turned into flirting, and she usually fell asleep imagining him taking her roughly into those taut, muscular arms and kissing her like no one ever had before.

"Your dad built this house?" She settled next to him on the couch and tucked her legs up, wrapping herself in a throw blanket.

"Yeah. With Jorie's dad and another buddy of theirs from high school." He took a long pull from the bottle, and Sydney watched his tongue catch a rogue drop of beer as it escaped the corner of his mouth.

"Wow, no one ever leaves this town, do they?"

"Not really."

Except for Olivia. She wished she had a bit of liquid courage in her veins to push her past the fear of the big question. No one, not Jorie or her mother or anyone else in town, had been forthcoming with information on Sam and Liv. She knew she had to ask him.

"So," she said, dropping her eyes to a loose thread at the edge of the couch cushion. "I have to ask. What's the deal with Olivia?"

Her eyes flickered over to where he visibly stiffened. Jaw clenched, both hands white-knuckled around the beer bottle. Had she pushed too far? She didn't care. She needed to know.

"What do you mean?" he asked. He crossed one foot over his knee, paused, and replaced it on the floor.

"I mean, everyone in Pine Ridge has mentioned her, but Jorie told me she's not your girlfriend. And your reunion at Thanksgiving was strangely icy, so . . . I'm wondering." She treaded carefully. They'd become fast friends, but this was foreign territory. He didn't ask about Connor, and she didn't ask about Liv.

"It's—" He took a long pull from his beer, and before the bottle left his lips, he lifted it again until the last dregs released with a wet smack. "Very complicated."

Before she could speak again, he stood up and got another. Maybe she *had* pushed too far. She'd never seen him have more than one drink, especially if he was driving.

When he returned to his place on the couch, she feared the conversation was dead in the water. He ran a hand over his face and said, "I don't really like to talk about it."

"I'm sorry," she said. "It's, um . . . It seems to be something that everyone in town knows about but everyone has their own version of the story, and I didn't want to pry but . . ." *But I like you and I need to know what I'm up against.*

His espresso-brown eyes drifted up to the ceiling and he leaned back on the couch, running a hand over his thick, dark hair. He was probably one of those guys who used a shampoo and conditioner in one, but somehow his hair still looked impossibly soft. She was dying to touch it.

"Liv and I dated when we were younger. She cheated on me and got pregnant, and we broke up. She was really young and didn't feel totally ready to be a parent, so she let the kid's father have full custody."

Sam's eyes remained trained on the coffee table as if reading from a teleprompter.

"She'd always loved to drink, but nobody ever thought she was an alcoholic. I mean, you've spent time with the people of this town. Everybody likes to throw 'em back." He licked his lips. "One day, when Jay was about three, Liv decided she wanted to be a part of his life. She spent a year sobering up and proving she could be a reliable parent, and Kevin, Jay's father, let her have some time with him. She stayed clean for a few years. She was doing so well. And then about a year ago, right after Jay's seventh birthday, Pine Ridge cops pulled her over because they saw her car weaving like crazy on Route Nine. She blew a point-twelve on the Breathalyzer, and Jay was in the front seat without a seat belt."

His lips flattened, and his hands tightened into fists.

"Obviously," he continued, "she lost any chance at custody. She's lucky she didn't get sent to jail. But in the past year, she's worked harder than I've ever seen her work trying to get her kid back. Jay's the sweetest little boy you've ever met, and he's stuck in fucking Akron, Ohio, while his shithead parents try to figure out which one of them is less of a shithead enough to raise him. So far, Kevin's winning because he's got his religious parents on his side. But Liv has a fighting chance because she's got me."

Sydney attempted to swallow the lump in her throat. "She's got you?"

"Her lawyer told her it would look a lot better for her if she had a stable home, partner, steady income. I read all the paperwork, I talked to the social worker, went with her to meet the lawyer a couple of times so that I could hear all the information for myself. This is the only way. So she's living with me, and I'm helping her get back on her feet."

He turned to face her, his stare full of fire and fury. She pulled back as if another inch of space would protect her from the heat.

"Oh." It was all she could muster. Every word of the story was a surprise, like accidentally stepping on a bees' nest and being stung over and over again.

"Yeah. Oh."

"So, Jay's not your kid."

"No, he's not my kid."

She ran her hands over the legs of her yoga pants, trying to soak in every detail. Thousands of questions flooded her brain, and she plucked one out to start. "You and Liv are not really together? I mean, you're not together now?"

"Nope."

"But maybe after the dust settles . . ."

"No." He tucked his bottom lip between his teeth and

stared straight ahead of him, clear through the coffee table and to some unknown universe beyond the carpet. "We agreed a long time ago that we weren't meant to be together. I actually think she really loved Kevin, which is why the whole pregnancy thing messed her up so bad. She wasn't ready for a kid, and she wasn't ready to be anybody's partner. She's ready now. At the very least, she's on her way."

"This is an awfully big responsibility for a friend," Sydney said.

"Oh, don't worry." A bitter smile curled onto his lips. "I'm sure a good therapist would have a lot to say about how my drunk dad factors into all of this."

Sydney knew she had to be gentle, but she crept one step further. "Do you trust her?"

With the faraway stare still fixed on his face, he slowly shook his head. "No matter how hard she tries, no matter how long she's been clean, she's always one beer away from ruining me all over again. I've heard the phrase, 'I'm sorry, I was drunk' more times than I care to count. After a while, they're just empty words. Do I trust her? I don't know." He tipped his head back, letting the beer flow into his mouth in a steady stream. "Does Jorie have any whiskey around here?"

"Someone once told me alcohol doesn't solve problems."

He bent over his knees and buried his face in his hands. A hollow laugh escaped the cage he'd built for himself. "I haven't talked about this with anybody but her in so long that I forgot how fucking ridiculous it sounds."

"It doesn't, actually. It sounds noble."

He sat up and faced her again, his face manic and flushed. "It's not noble. It's me pathetically trying to fix some kid's life because nobody could fix mine when I was his age."

A quiet settled over them as he leaned back on the couch again. An owl called out into the dark, and the haunting sound carried over the lake. She knew what it was like to feel out of control, scrambling to hold on to anything resembling stability. She didn't think any less of him for trying to help Liv and her kid.

"Let me ask you this," she said. "What is it doing to you to stay in this situation?"

"Financially, it's no trouble. Emotionally . . . God, listen to me. What a toddler."

"You're doing a really selfless thing," she said. "My advice to you would be to not let yourself get lost in the shuffle."

He downed the last of his second beer, and she snatched the bottle from him.

"Christ, enough, okay? Jorie's guest room is occupied, so there's nowhere for you to drunkenly crash here."

"Well, well, well," he said, leveling his gaze at her. "Hello, Pot. I'm Kettle."

"As you can see," she countered, "I was sitting here alone with tea. No alcohol."

"Yes, I can see your sad little snack." He motioned to the crackers scattered in front of the coffee table and smirked. "Sorry to keep you up, Grandma Sydney. Was it Sleepytime tea? Did I disrupt your bedtime ritual?"

"Shut up," she groaned. "Either I'm a drunken slut or a boring grandma. I can't win with you."

His eyelids grew heavy, and something sparkling passed between them. God, how she wanted him. How easy it would be to traverse the four inches of barren couch between them, crawl onto his lap, and finally experience the solid muscles and soft skin underneath his clothes.

The tension in the room grew to epic heights, and she cleared her throat. Now that she knew the truth about Olivia, she didn't know how to feel about Sam. Technically, he was single. But for the sake of a fragile little boy and his unstable mother, he was the most committed man in the world.

If she and Sam tended this thing between them, would it shatter everything he'd been working toward with Liv?

A buzzing sound broke through her thoughts, and before she could react, he leaned over to look at her phone. "Sorry," he said hurriedly. "I, uh, I didn't mean to look at it. Force of habit."

She reached for her phone. Connor. A tingling sensation traveled up her jaw.

"So, since I spilled my guts to you . . ." Eyebrows arched, his tone questioning, he waited for her response with crossed arms. A smug smile pressed into his face.

"My story is not so noble." She checked the message, despite her better judgment.

Still missing you, Syd. I need you. I'm taking some time off before Christmas. Please tell me I can come up and see you.

She closed out of the messaging app and replaced her phone on the table.

He'd written close to fifteen messages in the past couple of weeks, all variations on the same sentiment. Her brain screamed at her to delete the messages, block his number, and move on. But something else inside her, something deeper and unresolved, wanted to know how far he'd go to get her back. How much she was worth to him. How much she was worth, period.

"I'm still waiting." Sam raised his eyebrows and shoved a cracker with cheese into his mouth. Tiny crumbs clung to his beard.

"You really are a toddler."

She reached forward and combed her fingers through his soft, bristly beard, sending the crumbs tumbling down to his blue plaid shirt. He licked his bottom lip and the same sparkling thing passed between them again. It was so easy to be around him, to touch him, to talk to him. If she wanted to maintain the platonic nature of their friendship, she'd have to at least resist the touching.

"So, go." His voice came out rough and strangled.

"Connor's been reaching out a lot lately," she said. "That's it."

"And you're considering giving him another shot?"

"No," she insisted. She watched her phone in case another message came through. "I don't know if I could ever be with someone who cheated on me. I'd never forget about it, you know? He fucked her in *our* bed. We'd have to move. And burn those sheets."

"Shit," he said, running a hand over his beard. "In your bed. That's bold."

She shrugged. The memory of Connor and the blonde forced a wave of nausea from her gut. "He's bold. In everything he does. He's bold in business, he's bold in his indiscretions, and now he's being bold in trying to contact me again. He doesn't do anything with caution."

"Maybe he'd like to meet Liv."

She cracked a smile. "Seriously, they might be perfect for each other."

Their eyes met, and she pressed her lips together, wondering if he was thinking the same thing. *Maybe we'd be perfect for each other.*

"I think you should tell him you want to meet for coffee to talk about it but then maybe smash his windshield instead."

A snort of laughter escaped her nose, and she covered her face. She'd never considered herself vindictive or petty, but as she packed a bag immediately after catching Connor in the act, an overwhelming urge to break something came over her. She remembered the weight of his Italian leather loafer as she plucked it from his meticulous shoe rack, the easy slide of his top dresser drawer, and the satisfying crunch of each watch face as it smashed beneath the blows. He broke her heart; she broke his shit.

"I'll consider it."

He licked his bottom lip and watched her. The heat from his stare sent shivers up her legs and into her belly. That was it. The look. She'd seen it in the store, at Thanksgiving, and now here. She wondered if he was sexually frustrated on account of Liv. Or maybe they were still sleeping together. Friends did that sometimes, didn't they? The thought made her more anxious than she wanted to admit.

"I'll get you that book," she said, shattering the silence and the moment. She scrambled off the couch and down the hall to the guest room.

A tattered copy of *Into Thin Air* sat under a pile of clean laundry on her bed, and she retrieved it before spinning around and slamming square into Sam's brick wall of a chest.

"Holy hell," she muttered, taking a step back. She raised a hand to her brow, sure she'd have a lump from where his chin collided with her head.

"Sorry, I thought you heard me behind you."

The bedroom was dark save for the green glow of her bedside alarm clock and the pale moonlight floating in through the window. In the shadows, his sharp cheekbones stood out in stark contrast to his soft, dark beard. He stood a mere six inches away, and in the small space, she smelled the clean pine and faint detergent scent on his clothes, like clean sheets on the forest floor.

"Sam." She wasn't sure if she said it in protest or pleading or both at once.

"I'm here to get my book," he whispered back. "That's all I came for."

She took a step closer, daring him to meet her. They'd been here before but under very different circumstances. She was new to town and very drunk and smitten with his rugged good looks and powerful attitude. Now they were friends, closer in ways than she'd been with anyone in her life.

They rocked toward each other until his breath warmed her cheek. His fingers grazed hers, and then he tucked his hand into her smaller one. It was the sweetness that broke her resolve.

He tilted his head and placed his perfectly curved, rosy lips onto hers. She kissed him back, as gently as she knew the moment called for. The sparkling thing they'd been trading all night cascaded from his lips onto hers and straight down into her chest and spine. Everything about being with him was easy. This was no exception. His mouth caressed hers, and his hand lifted to find its rightful place, buried in her dark hair. When she pulled away, his hand remained.

"Damn it." She squeezed her eyes shut. All the reasons they shouldn't be kissing crashed over her at once. "This is dumb. I'm sorry."

"So dumb," he agreed, taking a step back. His hand fell from her hair, and she immediately missed the sensation. His words said *Mistake*, but his face said *Really?*

"This is the tiniest town. You have Liv. It's all . . . This is just not a good idea." Her head was weightless, as if she'd just swallowed mouthfuls of pure oxygen.

"I know," he said, scratching the back of his head. "I'm sorry. I don't even think of you like that."

She stared at him, her eyes finally adjusted to the darkness. What was that supposed to mean? Shame crept up her legs and landed like a brick in her stomach.

"Yeah, me neither," she choked out. But the sparkling thing still hovered between them. His eyelids remained heavy, the connection still alive. She knew they were both lying. Or at least she hoped.

"We're friends." The finality in his voice felt forced.

"Friends." She licked her lips, desperate for the lingering taste of him. She'd never felt so awkward and inexperienced in front of a man. Typically, she'd flaunt her assets, flirt, put on a show she knew would result in a naked finale. In front of Sam, she was a gangly teenager.

"I should go." But he stood rooted in place, massaging his hands together. His eyes dropped, momentarily, to her chest, and she immediately crossed her arms. He raised a single eyebrow.

"All right, well, get out already," she said, lightening her tone. "I've missed the last twenty minutes of *The Real Housewives of* . . . wherever, all because of you."

He swallowed, his Adam's apple appearing and disappearing behind his beard. A smile crept slowly onto his lips. "Heaven forbid."

With one last smoldering stare, he turned over his shoulder and walked out of the bedroom. She followed him to the front of the house, and before he could reach down for his boots, the door swung open.

"Hey," Jorie said. Her eyes were filled with suspicion as they bounced back and forth between Sam and Sydney. "What are you doing here?"

"Had to pick up a book," he said hurriedly. Sydney realized with a growing sense of doom that he wasn't holding the book.

"What book?" Jorie asked. She'd closed the door behind her but stood just inside, unmoving. They'd barely touched, but the memory of that brief brush of the lips burned her gut with guilt.

"Oh, I—" Sam's gaze lifted to Sydney, begging for a save.

"Oh, duh," Sydney said. "Almost forgot to go get it. Sam claims he came here for the book, but I really think he came for free beer." *Keep it simple. Nothing to see here. Just two friends hanging out in the living room, having a beer. Definitely not kissing in the bedroom.*

Sydney retrieved the book from her bedroom, and when she approached them at the front door, Jorie's face creased with stern warning.

"The book!" Sydney said, holding it above her head as if she'd discovered the Dead Sea scrolls.

"Ah, great," Sam said. He took the book from her, snatched his coat from the back of the chair, and snaked around Jorie before opening the front door.

She knew it was dangerous, but Sydney needed him to look at her just once more. One more deep gaze to get her through the night. But he avoided her desperate stare and raised his eyebrows at Jorie.

"See ya." And with that, he slipped out the door and disappeared.

Sydney's heart pounded loudly against her rib cage. Jorie hadn't moved an inch but continued to stand and stare at Sydney, seemingly waiting for something. Sydney didn't know if she had it in her to lie.

"Okay, that was super weird," Jorie said. "What's going on with you two?"

"Nothing."

Jorie crossed her arms over her chest and tilted her head to the side. "Listen. We haven't known each other that long, but I like to think we've gotten pretty close. If there's something to tell, I'd rather just hear it now. I'm not going to judge you, Syd."

Each sentence was like a hammer to her resolve, chipping away one blow at a time. She believed Jorie. But she also knew her place in the town was fragile. The success of the Loving Page depended on the support of the town, and if anyone found out she was worming her way between Liv and Sam, the store would never recover.

"I'm not lying to you," Sydney said, afraid her nose was growing as she spoke. "I will admit I have a crush on him." She could feel the blush creep from her cheeks down her jaw and across her collarbone.

"I figured that much," Jorie said. "He obviously has a crush on you, too."

Sydney's mouth threatened to curve into a smile until she willed it away. She never thought at this age she'd be so thrilled to hear about a crush.

"I think maybe I'm a little bit awkward around him sometimes," Sydney continued. "He came over to get the book, and he had a couple beers and told me the entire Liv story and I just got super awkward. That's all."

Jorie nodded slowly. "All right."

Did Jorie believe her? She couldn't tell.

"I'm sorry. I thought I was keeping my crush in check, but I guess not."

"The two of you . . ." Jorie shook her head. "The thing is, Sam has always been a little different. Everyone thought after high school he'd move away and settle somewhere like New York or Boston or San Francisco. He's supersmart, he loves to travel and debate, and I always felt like this town was way too small for him. So I can see why he might be interested in you."

It was the highest compliment, and it settled over Sydney like a blanket. "Really?"

"Yeah," Jorie said with a shrug. "But the whole Liv thing. With Sam it's not going to be as simple as I like you, you like me, let's get dinner. You know what I mean? He made a promise to her, and she's been working so hard to prove that she's worthy of that promise. To prove that she's worthy of all of it."

"I know."

"I'm not saying the guy has to turn into a monk while he's helping her," Jorie said. "But I know Sam. He gives his whole heart or he doesn't give anything at all."

His whole heart or nothing at all. Sydney's limbs trembled.

Jorie narrowed her eyes and shifted her weight to one hip. "He told you the whole story, huh?"

"Yeah," Sydney said. "His history with Liv, the lawyer's suggestion that a stable homelife would help her case, her drinking struggles."

The suspicion faded from Jorie's eyes. "Right. Well, wow. He must really trust you."

The hope in Sydney's heart climbed one rung higher. He trusted her. "I guess. I mean, I hope."

"Hey," Jorie said. Her gaze softened with kindness. "If you're really into him . . ."

Visions of a sobbing Liv and a devastated faceless little boy played in her mind. No way would she risk ruining a family like that.

"No," Sydney said "Trust me. I didn't come here looking for a guy." Sydney hoped her voice didn't reveal her defeat. Jorie was being kind, but this much she knew: Sam and Liv had a greater goal, and no one was going to come between them. No matter how much she might want to.

chapter **fifteen**

The store looked good. Really good. Sydney had avoided the cliché tinsel and tacky Christmas bulbs, instead opting for an elevated mountaintop Christmas theme, and the results were spectacular.

Her interview at North Country Public Radio had been a great success, but in her excitement, she'd announced a holiday party taking place at the store that coming Friday. She'd had to scramble to deliver said party, and deck the space out for Christmas, while conserving the cozy shop feel for customers. It would be the first big reveal of the Loving Page 2.0, and the pressure was high.

She'd hung twinkling white lights around Sam's custom bookshelves and wrapped the exposed beams with fresh pine boughs, filling every inch of the shop with the clean, invigorating scent of balsam trees. Fluffy buffalo plaid blankets were draped over the couch, and she placed frosty hurricane lamps around the reading nook, with fake flickering votives inside. On the tiny coffee table she'd arranged holiday-themed romance novels, and on the evening of the party, Jorie would complete the scene with a tray of McDonagh's famous homemade sugar cookies.

"I hope people show," Sydney said, gnawing at her lip.

"I hope so, too." Karen's eyes lifted over the rims of her bifocals. No matter how beautiful the store looked, Sydney couldn't get her mother over the hump of cynicism.

"The party is only a small investment," Sydney reminded her. "I only borrowed a little from what I made off selling my car. Most of the money went to buying book stock, actually."

Karen returned her stare to the newspaper. "Just don't get your hopes up, Suds. Asking the people of Pine Ridge, or anywhere else for that matter, to come out on a snowy Friday night is a lot. Even if free booze is on the menu."

Sydney steeled her shoulders and attempted a calming breath. The party was step one. If she could convince her mother that people would come out, she had a shot at convincing her the book-club idea would stick. "I gave you a stack of postcards, right?"

Karen waved the promotional postcards over her head without looking up. "Got 'em. I'll hand them out at my church group Tuesday night, leave some at the community center for the town meeting on Thursday, and Yuri's got a stack at the liquor store."

"And Mrs. McDonagh's got a stack for her Bible study Wednesday night," Sydney said, going over her mental checklist. "Jorie has some at the bakery. Matt promised to drop some along his route through Sherwood."

And Sam doesn't have any because I haven't heard a peep from him since Saturday night. She tamped down the churning anxiety and tried to forget about Sam. He was giving her space. It was logical. But it still hurt.

"You've blanketed all of North Country," her mother said. "Now you just gotta pray."

"Pray" was right. The success of the party, and the ultimate success of the store, relied hugely on the support of the town. She didn't know anyone well enough to know if they'd show up for her and her mother. All she could do was hope.

The week sped by, and Friday evening found Sydney racked with nerves. She tried to tell herself that even if no one else showed, she and Jorie and her mother would have the best party ever. Just the three of them. She'd gone on a long run this morning, despite the whipping wind and snowdrifts, in an attempt at clearing her head. Anxiety still flared.

Sydney closed herself into the tiny office to change her clothes before the doors officially opened. She'd selected a high-necked, romantic red silk blouse with ripped skinny jeans and heels. If she was going to be the brains behind a romance book club, she wanted to look the part.

At six o'clock, half an hour before the party was set to begin, Yuri arrived with cases of wine and beer. He'd sold it to them at cost, but the three times Sydney had attempted to pay him, he'd pushed her off. "I don't want to carry cash on me right now, Syd; just hold on to it." She suspected she'd eventually have to just leave the money in his shop before he'd accept it.

"You want the drinks on the counter, right?" Yuri asked, wheeling over the hand truck. She'd set up a makeshift bar on the counter alongside a few trays of meats, cheeses, olives, and crackers. She hoped the small investment she'd made tonight would result in a few sales and even more word of mouth.

"Yup, on the counter," she said. "And Yuri? You're taking the money tonight. No excuses. You have to stop doing us so many favors."

"If favors keep your mom in business, expect a lot more." He flashed his gap-toothed smile at her, and she softened. He made Karen so happy, and he seemed genuine and pure of heart. Her mother deserved him.

Sydney hurried around the shop, flipping on the sound system to Christmas party songs, adjusting items on shelves for maximum exposure, and lighting scented candles on a high shelf where they were sure to burn without catching on anyone's hair or clothes. The shop was festive and glowing and homey. They were ready.

At 6:31 p.m., Sydney's heart raced and her stomach churned. "This is it," she said with a nervous glance outside at the dark, empty town streets. "No one's coming."

"You gotta relax," Karen said. She handed her daughter a plastic cup filled with red wine. "Here. Drink this, please. You're making me nervous."

Sydney clutched the cup, but she didn't feel like drinking. She'd been drinking less since the disastrous night with Jared, and she wanted to keep the streak alive. She didn't really miss it, and she loved the deeper sleep and clearer skin. It was obviously worth sticking with.

She took a timid sip. Then another. *Okay, maybe one drink would do me good. And just one.*

She checked her makeup in the office mirror, and just as she fluffed her hair, the front door burst open. "Merry Christmas!"

Jorie, Matt, and Mrs. McDonagh all trounced into the shop, stamping the snow off their boots and peeling off their coats. Sydney breathed a sigh of relief. Even if no one else showed, at least the night wasn't a total wash.

"Welcome, welcome!" Karen said, ushering them in. "Please, hang your coats by the door and come in. Syd set up food and drinks, and there's a raffle to win a fifty-dollar gift certificate to Yuri's Liquor."

"Well shit," Matt said, hurrying over to the raffle bowl. "Now I'm glad I came."

Jorie hurried over to Sydney and squeezed her in a hug. "You look beautiful," she said. "And this place looks beautiful. I saw all the photos you've been posting to social media."

"Seems like it might be catching on," Sydney said. "I got follows today from three huge Adirondack accounts, and then one of them reposted the event info. I got a bunch of new followers."

"The hot guys holding puppies is a pretty brilliant marketing strategy. Let me know if you want Matt to pose with my parents' Yorkie." Jorie winked.

A laugh burst out of Sydney's mouth.

"I'll let you know." She exhaled slowly. "I just want this to work so badly."

Jorie laid a hand on Sydney's wrist and smiled. "It's already working. You've managed to rally an entire town behind you. Just have a little faith."

The breath sailed out of Sydney's nostrils on a steady stream, and for the first time all day, the tension in her shoulders eased. Jorie was right. She'd done all she could. Now was the time to have a little bit of faith.

Mrs. McDonagh poured Matt and Jorie drinks, and by the time they'd made a toast to the success of the Loving Page, the front door opened again, and another group of people burst in. This time Sydney didn't recognize any of the faces.

The group was the first of many. By seven thirty, Sydney could barely move through the crowd of people packed into the place, and Karen rang up sales in a steady stream, her stony cynicism momentarily softened by the influx of cash.

Folks had driven in from as far away as Utica, having heard Sydney's radio pitch. They loved romance novels and wanted to see the place for themselves. The party was a great excuse to make the trip.

"Sydney," Jorie cooed, sidling up to her friend at the back of the store. "What did I tell you? Look at this place. Half the people I know and half the people I don't. That's an amazing turnout, if I may say so myself."

Sydney surveyed the crowd. Happy faces grinned at one another, sipped drinks, and screamed with laughter. Some people perused the shelves, and some simply enjoyed the festivities. No matter their reason for showing up, they were here. And if they came tonight, maybe they'd continue to show for a book club.

What about Sam? The fly in the ointment. He hadn't shown. Sydney thought that despite their ill-advised kiss last weekend, he'd be here to support her. She wanted to call him, to make sure he was okay and that he hadn't missed out on tonight due to some terrible accident. But something told her it wasn't that.

As the party reached fever pitch and Sydney had to lean into each person as they chatted with her, the front door opened once more, and an icy wind snaked through the bodies. From her spot near the door, she paused her conversation with someone who'd driven down from Potsdam to greet the new guest. Her gaze lifted, and her lips curved into a smile. And then her breath stopped in her throat. Connor.

"Hi, Syd." Goose bumps rose on her skin, starting at her jaw and working their way down to her toes.

"Hi," she whispered. He clutched a bottle of champagne in his gloved hands and moved slowly toward her, his green eyes bright and hopeful. As he entered her space, the scent of Molton Brown soap wafted over her. Her throat seized up in response. She didn't know if it was nostalgia or longing or hatred, but it stirred her to the core.

"Man, it's so good to see you," he said as quietly as the roar of the room would allow. "I've missed you so much."

Words escaped her. The last time she'd seen him he'd been wrapped up in sheets and another woman's legs. But the anger and shame that had consumed her then was curiously absent now. Connor was everything Pine Ridge wasn't. He was fitted wool coats and designer shampoo and gallery openings with expensive champagne. That world had been a part of her, as much as she'd tried to deny it, and now the physical incarnation of all that glitz and glamour stood in front of her, smiling.

"Did I surprise you?" he asked.

She released a long-held breath. Surprise? Understatement of the century. "Yes. What are you doing here?"

"I needed to see you."

I needed. He'd never cared what she needed. Only what he needed her to be to him.

"I don't want to do this right now," she said. She caught her mother's eyes from across the room. "This is a big night for me, for the store."

"I know. I heard you on the radio."

She narrowed her eyes. "You? You were listening to North Country radio?"

"Well," he said. He dropped his chin, and a lock of dark blond hair fell over his eyes. He offered her a half smile. Those beautiful white teeth he'd paid a fortune for. "A colleague of mine has a house up here, and he said he heard you. I googled it and found out what was going on. That Instagram page has *Sydney Walsh* written all over it."

"Well, then you know this is an important event for us." She straightened her spine, determined to stay strong in front of him. He wasn't allowed to bulldoze this night, to plant the seeds of doubt he was so good at sowing. "I have to get back to the party."

"Sure," he said. "If it's okay with you, I'd like to stay."

She stared at him, lips parted. In all their time as a couple, he never wanted to do anything with her that wasn't already in his best interest. If he wanted to stay at her little holiday party alongside the residents of North Country, he must've been making one hell of an effort.

"Do whatever you want." She turned on her heel and dove back into the sea of bodies. Her head spun, and the collar of her shirt tightened like a noose. She made her way to the office and closed the door, bracing herself against the wall with one trembling arm.

Connor was here. Connor, who had cheated on her, deceived her, pulled a rug out from under her that she didn't even know she'd been standing on. She'd carefully guarded her heart against someone who'd managed to sneak in anyway. And now he was here. Asking for forgiveness. Or at least she figured that was coming next.

A knock on the office door shook her out of her haze, and she opened it just a crack.

"Y'all right?" Jorie asked. "I'm assuming the smoking-hot blond guy with the Veuve Clicquot is Connor?"

Sydney swallowed down the bile in her throat. "That's him."

"Wow," Jorie said. Her jaw tightened. "He's got some balls coming up here tonight."

Sydney gnawed at the inside of her lip. She should agree with Jorie, plot how they were going to get rid of him, and then laugh about it later over a bottle of wine. But the part of her that might someday be strong enough for that was still in training.

"Yeah, I . . . I don't really know what to do."

"You want him out of here? Matt and Greg would be more than happy to toss his ass."

"No," Sydney said. "I mean, just don't do anything. Let him hang out. I don't care."

Jorie's eyes narrowed. "Okay."

"I'll be out in a second." She pushed the door closed again and squeezed her eyes shut, begging the sickening pull of anxiety to subside. *Where is Sam?* Her mind returned to Sam again and again. He brought her strength and peace even if he didn't know it. No one would bolster her resolve in this moment like Sam.

She took one last deep breath and rejoined the party. A

few people had formed a makeshift dance floor near the cash register and twirled each other around to the sounds of Bing Crosby. It should've been the happiest scene. Sydney's insides were torn to shreds.

"You should make a toast!" Yuri said, appearing at her side with a full glass of wine. He handed it to her and motioned to a step stool nearby. The last thing she wanted was every pair of eyes in the place on her. But when Karen also noticed the step stool, she shouted out, "Speech!"

Sydney cleared her throat and grabbed the glass of wine, taking one long, grateful drink. She stepped up onto the stool and looked out over the room. Someone turned down the music, and the crowd fell silent.

She spotted Connor in a small group of burly men, looking like an out-of-place history professor in his slim-cut navy sweater and tailored jeans. His beautiful mouth turned up at the corners, and he winked at her. Her legs turned to jelly.

"I'll make this quick," she said, forcing a smile. "I just want to thank you all so much for coming. I want to thank my mom, Karen Walsh, for begrudgingly agreeing to let me give her shop a face-lift, to Yuri of Yuri's Liquor for the booze." A cheer rose up, and several people patted Yuri on the back.

"I want to thank Jorie and Mrs. McDonagh of McDonagh's Bakery for the incredible treats," she continued. Her eyes scanned the rapt crowd and then she saw it. Outside, stalled at the curb. A pickup truck. With a flash of brake lights, it pulled away. Sam had shown up after all. And left just as quick.

Unreal.

"And, um," she said, suddenly remembering all the eyes on her. She'd deal with her simmering anger later. "Thanks to the town of Pine Ridge. The community here is second to none. I hope that all of you who love romance come back

December fifteenth for the first meeting of our book club, and if you can't make it then, I hope you'll continue to stop by any time you're in the area. Thanks again."

Everyone cheered and raised their glasses, and Connor shouted, "To Sydney!" She tucked her lip between her teeth and stepped down off the stool, afraid if she didn't do it quickly, she'd tumble right off. Her head swam.

Most of the out-of-towners departed a little after eight, and as the crowd dwindled, Karen gleefully began checking receipts.

"We made more in one night than we did in all of October!" she said. "And, Suds, look at your book-club sign-up sheet. You've got thirty names! Maybe we'll get this sorry little shop out of debt after all."

The joy Sydney should've felt flitted around her, just out of reach, as a physical reminder of her painful past lingered near the door. By nine o'clock, it became impossible for Sydney to avoid Connor any longer. Yuri locked the front door, and Mrs. McDonagh, Jorie, and Karen started cleaning up discarded plates, cups, and spent liquor bottles. Connor hovered near the door, running a nervous hand through his meticulously coiffed hair.

"Sweets, why don't you go take care of this?" Karen said. She nodded toward Connor.

"I don't know how," Sydney said, hiding her face. She refused to cry over him anymore.

"It'll come to you," Karen said. "You're a strong girl. Much stronger than when you got here, that's for sure. Just listen to your heart, and it'll tell you what to do. And give him hell."

The warmth from her mother's face filled her up, and she carried that strength with her to the front of the shop. Connor stood a little taller as she approached.

"Do you have to stay and clean up?" he asked. "I was hoping we could go somewhere and talk."

She nodded. "Let's talk."

They grabbed their coats and headed outside, neither of them saying a word as they made their way through downtown. She wanted to stand up to him and let him know how much he'd hurt her. She also didn't want him to see her weakness. *Let him think I don't care one way or the other who he's with or what he's done to me.*

She led them to the Butler House, a bar located in an old hotel on the edge of downtown that played no music whatsoever and featured an ancient list of wines that appealed to the over-eighty crowd. They wouldn't run into anyone she knew here.

They settled into a table in the far corner of the spacious, musty bar, and Sydney immediately busied herself with the menu. More than the alcohol, she needed a glass to occupy her trembling hands.

"We're closing up soon," the waitress said. Her jowls hung low, her posture stooped, and she looked to be as old as the faded carpet under her orthopedic shoes.

"The sign says open until eleven," Connor said. He had so much to learn about this place.

"The sign *should* say open until whenever I feel like it. And I feel like nine thirty. Satisfied?"

"I'm leaving you a terrible Yelp review," he said, furrowing his brow.

"Would you shut up?" Sydney said. She looked back at the waitress. "Can we just have two glasses of red? Pinot noir or whatever you have back there that's already open? We won't be long. And I've got cash."

The waitress turned with a grunt and left them alone.

"Jesus," Connor said, his upper lip curled in a sneer. "You come here a lot?"

"Why do you always have to be such a jerk to waiters?"

Dining out with Connor was always a tense experience. He expected the best, and when he didn't get it, God help the person on the other end of his wrath.

"I'm not." He spoke slowly through gritted teeth. "It's a

customer-based business. If the customer is unhappy, why shouldn't the establishment go a little bit further to fix it?"

She shook her head and stared down at the weathered, dark wooden table. Someone had carved their initials into it: GHN. She didn't miss his condescension. Left to his own devices, Connor wouldn't give a second look to a place like this, let alone step inside and order a drink.

"What are you doing here?" she asked. She looked up as the tightened edges of his face softened.

"I came to see you." His voice was laced with sweetness, and he reached across the table to take her hands in his. Like slipping her hands into old gloves. "I miss you, Sydney. And I'm so, so sorry for what I did. It's inexcusable."

What I did. Would he say the words? Would he admit it? Or would he cop only to what she'd seen and try to explain it away? "Why don't you try?"

He blinked at her as if caught off guard. "What?"

"Try an excuse. Any excuse. Beyond the bullshit one you gave me when I caught you."

"I'm an asshole?"

"Yes, Connor. This we know."

His grip on her hands tightened. "Honestly, Syd, I don't have an excuse. I was bored, I was horny, she threw herself at me, and I let myself go ahead with it. It was the dumbest thing I've ever done."

She. Just the mention of the blonde woman with the perfect ass forced the acid up into Sydney's throat. Her well-meant red blouse and makeup felt suddenly foolish and gaudy. She could play the part of wealthy finance wife, but the tag of her off-brand backpack would always be visible. "You were bored with me?"

"No," he said, leaning in toward her. The waitress appeared and set down their wine, along with a check.

"No hurry," she said, the sarcasm dripping from her words.

Connor glared at her. The second she was gone, he turned back to Sydney.

"I wasn't bored with you," he said. "I don't know. I don't know what else to tell you. It was lust, pure and simple."

If he'd been satisfied with her, he'd never have strayed. But what was the problem? Was it her hair? Her weight? Her topics of conversation? She combed her memory for instances when he'd seemed tired of her. She came up empty.

"But," she said, her voice tiny and meek, "you said things between us were shit. That I'd changed."

He pressed his lips together before pulling his hands back and crossing them over his chest. "Do you deny those things are true?"

There it was. The shame. It poured over her like hot syrup, coating her skin and dragging her down. Sure, she'd changed. Didn't people change? She'd worked most of her adult life at being a lawyer and then found out she couldn't take the pressure and needed to find a career she could handle and enjoy. But feeling adrift didn't change her heart, her core, or her values. It had simply muted them for a while.

Or had she let herself be muted by *him*?

"I thought it was a phase," she said. "My career trajectory had completely changed. I'd gone to law school, worked endless hours at the firm, and lost tons of friends for nothing. Everything I'd done to achieve that goal was for naught. It was a huge thing to go through. If I wasn't myself, that was why."

He shrugged. "I don't want to rehash old issues. I wanted to come here and apologize and see if maybe we can move forward. I couldn't live with myself, thinking you'd disappeared to this shithole because of me."

The faces of all the Pine Ridge residents who had welcomed her and taken care of her, prioritized her needs before their own, surfaced in her mind. How dare he insult these kind people and their town?

Before she could rattle off stories of Edith O'Hare and Hank and Mrs. McDonagh, the front door to the bar opened and Sam walked in. She blinked. She barely believed the figure before her until he sat down on a barstool, leaned over the counter, and grinned at the waitress as she cooed, "Sammy!"

"Oh sure, she's nice to the locals," Connor said.

"Cindy, my love," Sam said. "You about closing up?"

Cindy placed a cold, uncapped beer in front of Sam and shook her head. "I would be if it wasn't for these hoity-toity out-of-towners."

Sam followed Cindy's thumb until his eyes landed on Sydney and Connor. The cheerful grin melted away, and his face went slack.

Sydney raised a single hand to wave at him, not sure how else to react. He was impossibly handsome. His hair was combed to the side, and his red plaid shirt was unbuttoned just enough that she caught the edge of another tattoo on his chest. Nothing else in the room mattered but him.

He ran a hand over his face and dropped his gaze to the bar top, avoiding her stare altogether. The sadness creeped over her, weighing down every limb.

"Hello?" Connor said, interrupting her thoughts. "Syd?"

"I want to go home," she said on a whisper. She feared if she tried to speak any louder her voice would break and the tears would fall.

"All right," he said. He swallowed the glass of wine in two huge gulps and grimaced. "Wow, that's bad."

She stood up from the table, grabbed her coat, and threw what cash she had down onto the scratched wooden surface. She wanted to run. The twinge in her calves and thighs urged her to take off and never look back. She pushed past Connor, past Sam at the bar, and out into the freezing cold night.

She made it as far as the Loving Page before Connor caught up with her. He grabbed her arm, forcing her to spin around and face him. The tears streamed down her cheeks.

"I'm done fucking around," he said, his breath coming

in rapid-fire clouds. "All I want is you, babe. You're the one I've always wanted, and I don't want to lose you again. You can do whatever you want: work at a bookstore, go back to law, or don't work at all. I don't care. I just want you. I think we should get married."

"What?" The laughter caught her by surprise. It flowed out of her in waves, and after a minute she folded over, clutching her stomach as it threatened to choke her. Married. Even the word sounded hilarious to her now.

"Babe, I know it's crazy," he said. "But I want this. I want you."

Finally, she stood upright, wiping at the tears with the back of her hand. She could see it all so clearly now. Her mother was right. She had finally listened to her heart, and it rejected Connor like a virus.

"No," she said. "*Hell* no. Marry you? Are you insane?"

His face turned dark as he stepped away and crossed his arms over his chest.

"Insane is living in this town trying to scrape together enough money to make a fucking bookstore survive."

She'd been here too many times to react. A reaction was what he craved.

"Insane is marrying someone you don't trust," she said. "And I don't trust you. I don't trust you not to cheat on me, and I don't trust that you believe in me, either. You never have."

"I paid for your entire lifestyle," he snapped, pointing at his own chest with fervor. "I shelled out for any stupid activity you wanted to do. Your hair, your nails, your clothes, your coffee, your lunch dates. All of it. On my dime."

"Yeah, to push me into being the woman you thought you should have on your arm. Not to make me happy."

"Fuck this," he said. "I come all the way here to Shitsville to give you the opportunity to come home, and you spit in my face."

"Oh, was this for me? Showing up on a night that was

super important to me and disrupting everything and shaking my confidence? This apology tour was never about me, Connor. Everything has always been about you. Even when it masquerades as generosity, everything you do is selfish."

He sneered, looking down his nose at her as if she were a stain on his perfectly pressed white shirt. "You're a bitch."

He brushed past her, crossed the street to his car, climbed in, and drove away.

chapter **sixteen**

Sam had planned to get an early start to the day, but Liv's snoring woke him far sooner than he'd hoped. He dressed quickly, grabbed the backpack he'd filled the night before, and tiptoed past her tiny unconscious body sleeping soundly on the couch.

She snored like that when she was drunk, he remembered. But after searching the kitchen, the trash, and her room for empties, he found nothing. The suspicion turned to guilt, and he disappeared before she woke. He didn't have the time or energy to dive into Liv's addictions today.

A short, quiet drive later he arrived at the trailhead. His was the only car in the parking lot. Just as he'd hoped. The weather report was a balmy thirty-four degrees but called for heavy snowfall, and that suited him just fine. The worse the weather, the better. Sunny skies wouldn't fit his mood today.

He pulled his knit hat over his ears, tightened the laces on his hiking boots, and started out onto the snowy trail.

Every few feet he looked up at the flat, motionless gray sky. A vast reminder that the world kept turning. The trees kept growing. Animals lived and died. Spring came and went. Nature was a constant, the ever-changing landscape that continued on, even when his mother did not.

He trudged through the knee-high snow, keeping a steady pace. He had nowhere to be and no designated arrival time, but the energy of the morning and the date on the calendar pushed him forward.

He craved the burning sensation in his legs, the heat radiating from his chest. In a while he'd have to remove his outermost layer, his body temperature climbing to an uncomfortable degree.

Today was about his mom. Exactly a year ago on this day, she'd given in to the cancer and slipped away. With the news of her death came anger. He was angry that she hadn't held on for one more Christmas, angry that none of his other friends had lost parents and now he'd lost both of his. Angry that despite everything she'd done for him, in her moment of need there was nothing he could do for her.

Despite dedicating his morning to trekking out to his mother's favorite spot, he couldn't force thoughts of Sydney from his mind. Forget that his mother would've loved her. What was Sydney doing with that jerk at the bar last night? It had to be Connor. That cocky asshole didn't fit in at the Butler House or in Pine Ridge, and the way he'd held her hands from across the table was too intimate to be someone new.

His rage at seeing them together was dampened only by the disappointment. She was too good for someone who would cheat on her. And she'd looked so beautiful in her red blouse, makeup done for the party. Had she invited Connor to come? Did she want him there?

The thought propelled him forward harder and faster, and he closed in on his destination in record time. The trail led most casual hikers to the edge of a lake, where in warmer months they could spread out a picnic and even take a dip in the water if they were brave enough.

Sam had a different destination in mind. Fifteen feet away from the water's edge, down a rocky ravine and half-covered by a tangle of tree roots and mountains of powdery snow, was a lean-to.

His father had built the rickety structure for his mother despite the land being state property. It could've been torn down at any time. His mother always said the fact that it still stood after all this time was a testament to their love. It might've always been fraught with tension, but it lived on. He couldn't imagine a more perfect spot to pay tribute to his mother on this day.

As he approached the lake and made his way down the slippery embankment that gave way to the lean-to below, he paused. Until now, the air held a sharp stillness, only occasionally interrupted by a bird rustling in the bushes. Now he heard shifting and breathing. A person.

"Hello?" His voice echoed over the frozen lake.

"Hello?" a female voice called back. He stood rooted in place, just outside the lean-to, until Sydney Walsh's head popped out.

"What are you doing here?" The statement was sharper than he meant, but his surprise was palpable.

"What are you doing here?" she said. "I was promised this would be an empty spot where I could be alone."

"Who told you that?"

"My mom. She said it's popular in the summer but once it snows, nobody comes down here."

Sam took a deep breath, the air crystallizing in front of his face. Her cheeks were blotchy and red from the cold, her eyes glassy. He wondered how long she'd been here. His anger toward her still smoldered.

"The middle of the wilderness, and I still can't find a spot to be completely by myself," he said.

"Just forget it," she said, climbing to her feet and brushing the snow from her gloves. "I'll go. I'm getting cold anyway."

"Stop," he said. He forced a gentleness into his voice that he didn't quite believe he pulled off. "Sit down. I was gonna make a fire."

The lines around her eyes softened, and she stared back at him. Only a few square inches of her face showed, most of it obstructed by a scarf and hat. What he could see reminded him of their kiss.

"If you want to be alone, that's fine," she said. "Seriously, I don't mind. I wanted to be alone myself."

"Let's be alone together," he said.

She pressed her lips together and studied him again.

"I have food," he said. "Does that change your mind?"

"Do you have any water? I'm kind of thirsty."

"You didn't bring any water on a hike?" He leaned forward as he spit out the words.

"I figured it's winter and I wouldn't need it," she said, crossing her arms over her chest. She wore an oddly small pale pink puffer coat, the sleeves a few inches too short and the buttons straining at her chest. It had to be Karen's.

"You know, that's one of those things that'll tip people off to you not being from Pine Ridge."

She cocked one eyebrow and pursed her lips. "Live and learn."

He pulled off his backpack and unhooked the small pack of firewood he'd brought with him. After stomping out a flat area just outside the roof of the lean-to, he pulled over the large flat rock just inside the structure and built a small teepee of sticks. He tucked a fire starter inside the teepee and lit a match.

"Is this something else I should know in order to be treated like a local?" she asked.

"This is something I was born knowing."

"When I envision you as a baby, I see you with a beard

wearing a tiny red plaid flannel. Now I can add 'making campfires' to that visual."

Annoyance churned inside him. How dare she continue flirting with him when she was spending time with her ex. He couldn't ask to be the only man in her life, but he thought she'd at least have some respect for his feelings.

When he didn't respond, she cleared her throat. "Do you want this to be a no-talking hang? Because I can shut up."

"Can you?" The retort snapped out like a rubber band, and she recoiled.

"Seriously, what is your problem?" Her jaw tensed, and her chocolate-brown eyes flared dangerously. "If anyone should be mad at anyone here, it's me at you. You didn't even bother to show up to the party last night. Thanks for that."

The fire crackled to life beside him as he turned slowly, his lips parted and his eyes wide. The moment the party was announced he knew he couldn't show up. He'd envisioned himself standing awkwardly in the corner, trying not to stare longingly at Sydney while the entire town saw right through him.

"Really? I was supposed to show up to that party?"

"Yes!" Her eyes flew open as her hands raised toward the sky. "I thought we were friends. All my other friends were there."

"Yeah, I know. I saw you and your *friend* at the Butler House."

He turned back to the fire, squeezing his eyes shut in admonishment. *What the fuck are you doing? Turning into a jealous teenager? She's your friend. You have zero claim.*

"I'm sorry." His voice was nearly lost on a breeze.

"That's where all the animosity is coming from? Connor?"

He poked at the fire and tried to come up with a response. Of course it was Connor. It was Connor, it was Liv, it was this town. It was anything standing in the way of him kissing her and touching her and feeling his skin on her skin. The attraction was all-consuming, and every road-block now felt like pure, concentrated torture.

Sam crawled backward into the lean-to and settled down in the dirt next to her. He kept his eyes trained on the fire as the flames licked and danced in their bed, reaching toward the sky.

"My mom died a year ago today."

He didn't mean to derail their conversation about Connor and the party, but he didn't know how to continue talking to her unless she knew the full extent of his torment.

He remembered every hour of that day. How he'd woken up thinking it was surprisingly warm for December and that maybe he'd see if Jorie and Matt wanted to meet him for lunch. He changed Patty DiOrio's flat tire, he stained a coffee table he'd made for a doctor's office in Indian Lake, and he'd even taken a nap. It had been a nice day.

And then at four o'clock on the dot, like you see in movies, his home phone rang. Liv had made the call. She said his mother had "passed on." His mind still cloudy from the nap, he thought she'd been talking about his mother's bowel movements, which he knew far too much about at that point. He'd actually asked, "Passed on what?"

In the months and days leading up to the anniversary, an internal countdown clock ticked away. The closer the date got, the more severe his headaches. As much as he didn't want to admit it, spending time with Sydney was the only thing that gave him any relief.

"I'm so sorry," she said. Her gloved hand found his, and she held it tightly. The tears sprang up in his eyes, and he ran his free hand over them, wiping away any evidence.

"It's why I wanted to be alone today. It's why I'm acting like a total fucking nutjob."

"Dude," she said, her voice full of warmth. "Why didn't you say something? You're allowed to act however you want to act today. You could've brought Celine Dion CDs and cried for hours to 'All by Myself,' and I would've understood."

He lifted his eyes to meet hers, and a smile played on her lips.

"Maybe I'll save that one for later."

"Do you want to talk about it?" she asked.

Her hand remained hooked on his. He didn't dare move. "Not really."

She looked back toward the fire, the reflection of the flames flickering in her eyes. "Well, I'm sorry I commandeered your spot."

"It's ironic, actually." He couldn't tear his eyes away from her face. "My dad built this lean-to for my mom. In much happier days, obviously. But she liked to come here when it was warm out. I figured it would be a good spot for the day, and then I show up and you're here."

"Where's the irony? Her name was Sydney?"

"No," he said, laughing. *She would've loved you. And you're the only person who's made me feel okay since she died.* "Never mind. I'm gonna sound creepy."

She pulled her hand away slowly and stared at him with wide, fearful eyes. "Oh God, what is it? I look like her and you want to peel my face off and turn it into a mask and then wear my skin like a coat?"

"Are you kidding? You are way too small to make a good skin coat."

She gave him her signature lip-press-into-smile and leaned back against the wall of the lean-to. "So what? Go ahead. Be creepy."

He shook his head and trained his eyes on the dirt underneath his outstretched legs. He barely felt the cold. "I don't know how to put this really but . . . I have friends. Good friends. And I'm really grateful for them, but I haven't met anybody in a long time who, um . . ."

He took a deep breath and forced himself to look at her.

A rogue strand of hair had broken loose from her gray knit hat and drifted lazily around her sharp cheekbones. She made him feel things. Things that scared him.

"I haven't met anybody in a really long time," he repeated, summoning all his courage, "who's made me feel the way you make me feel."

The bemused smile faded from her lips. "What does that mean?"

"I don't know," he said, looking back at the fire.

"No, come on. You started this."

Come on, man, say it. You already kissed her. She won't be surprised. "I feel okay when I'm with you. Better. This sounds crazy."

"Stop telling me what I should think sounds creepy or crazy. So far I'm still sitting here."

He yanked off his gloves and ran his bare hands over his face, still refusing to look at her. "I get these tension headaches. Ever since Mom died. I went to the doctor once, and he said it's just stress. That's the only cause. Stress. And when I'm with you, they go away."

He stared at the fire until ten, and then fifteen seconds passed in silence. Finally, he let his eyes drift across the dirt and up to her face. The smile was back.

In a tiny voice she said, "I didn't know that."

He ran a hand underneath his hat and over his hair. Pouring his heart out left him feeling like he had bugs crawling all over his skin. "Well, now you do."

"Did my mom know your mom?" she asked.

His brow narrowed in confusion. "Yeah. Everybody knows everybody in this town."

"Were they friends?"

"My mom was kind of a loner," he said. "She didn't have a ton of friends. But she and your mom were friendly. They said hi in the grocery store. That type of thing."

Her face twisted in thought, and she nodded slowly.

"What?" he asked.

"I don't know. I was thinking it would've been weird and nice if I'd chosen this spot at random. The same spot you were headed for on the anniversary of your mom's passing. But my mom told me to come here today. I wondered if maybe she knew about the anniversary and had a trick up her sleeve."

He thought back to Thanksgiving, when Karen had warned him to start keeping his cool around her daughter if he wanted to keep the peace with Liv.

"I don't think so," he said. He picked up a twig and traced lines in the dirt. "Your mom knows about Liv."

The mood shifted as if he'd thrown a bucket of cold water on their simmering tension. She pulled away and faced out toward the front of the lean-to.

"So how long do you have to remain in your weird forced celibacy?" she said, her voice icy.

"It's not forced celibacy." His heart thudded.

The celibate aspect of his arrangement with Liv was self-imposed. He wasn't in love with Liv anymore, that much he knew. But he couldn't sleep around, much less date, while simultaneously pouring all his mental energy into helping her put her life back together. He also hadn't met anybody worth compromising their agreement for.

Until now.

"Accidental celibacy?" she said. Her face softened. "Or are you guys still sleeping together?"

Talking about sex with Sydney in any capacity made his dick stir. He couldn't help it. After they'd kissed, his imagination had run wild. Now that he knew what her lips and tongue tasted like, he'd spent many solitary hours envisioning what the rest of her would taste like.

"Can I propose something?" he said.

She squinted. "What?"

"I'm tired of tiptoeing around this shit. There are things

I want to know about you. And there are obviously things you want to know about me. Can we just cut the bullshit and be real with each other?"

Her face was still and blank as she nodded.

"No holds barred, all right?" he asked.

She nodded again and shifted once more so that she was facing him.

"You cold?"

"No, I'm fine."

He needed a second to clear his head. The questions he wanted to know, needed to know, rattled around inside his brain like change in a tin can. But the one that he kept coming back to was, *Do you want me?*

He pulled a water bottle from his backpack, took a long swig, and then handed it to her. While she drank, her raspberry red lips sucking at the mouth of the bottle in ways he couldn't begin to let himself linger on, he found granola bars in the front pocket of his pack and tore one open.

"Want one?" he asked as she handed back the water bottle.

"We need sustenance for this conversation?"

"Yeah."

She grinned and accepted the snack. "You first."

"Did you invite Connor to the party last night?" Better to start small.

"No," she said emphatically, her eyes growing wide with the word. "I definitely did not."

His heart rate slowed just a bit. "Okay. Now you."

She bit her lip before asking, "When is the last time you and Liv slept together?"

"Right for the jugular," he said under his breath. "Not since I found out she cheated on me. So, eight years ago. I let her and Jay move into my spare bedrooms about a year ago, after her DUI."

She nodded and toyed with the granola bar wrapper. "Have you slept with anyone since she moved in with you?"

"Hey, I thought we were alternating?" He wasn't sure why it mattered, but this one he didn't want to answer. If he admitted to sleeping with someone else while he was committed to helping Liv, then what was stopping him and Sydney now? If his mind went there, he'd never get it back.

"Okay, fine," she said. "You go."

"Is anything going on with you and Connor?"

"He proposed."

Sam dropped the last half of his granola bar in the dirt. The air halted inside the lean-to, and all sounds were dampened. He immediately looked to her ring finger but couldn't see it because of the gloves.

"What?" It was the only word he could muster.

"And then he called me a bitch when I said no."

Sam's head spun, his vision curled in at the edges like pages of an old book. "Can you fill in the blanks here?"

"He surprised me at the party last night, and I agreed we could talk afterward, which is when you saw us at the Butler House. He tried to apologize for cheating on me, and for some ridiculous reason, I listened. But then you walked in, and I realized I was being a total idiot. After we left, we were standing outside and he said, 'We should get married.' And I laughed. It was so bizarre to me that after all the shit he'd put me through, he'd think that I'd want to marry him. So I said no, that I didn't trust him and probably never would, and I called him selfish, and then he called me a bitch. And then I went back to Jorie's, and I ate all of the day-old muffins she brought home from the bakery."

Red-hot rage boiled up inside Sam. It flowed through his veins and threatened to bubble up and over and force him to do something terrible. If Connor had been in front of him now, he wasn't sure what he would do.

"Wow," he said, running a hand over his head and letting his hat fall onto the ground. "That guy deserves to have something really terrible happen to him."

"He'll get his. Someday." She swallowed, nibbled her

lip, and grinned, the smile stopping short of her eyes. "Connor was the boyfriend that fit my life in New York. The longer I'm here, the more I realize that person wasn't really me. So, while it hurt to be cheated on, and losing everything I'd known in New York was hard, that was a life I was never meant to live. It's for the best."

Despite his anger, he gazed at her in adoration. She hadn't given Connor another shot. She had barely even entertained it. And here she was, the day after, trying to make Sam feel better. His heart swelled.

"My turn," she said. She popped the last bite of granola bar into her mouth.

"Ah, man, you ate the whole thing? I dropped mine."

"Whose fault is that?"

"Yours!" he said, sitting straight up. "You tell me Connor proposed when I'm sitting here telling you I . . ." *Have feelings for you.*

"You still haven't told me shit." She tilted her head to the side and challenged him with her eyes. "My turn."

Despite the cold outside, the fire roared and filled the lean-to with heat. He unzipped the top of his coat and sighed against the relief of cold air on his throat. He was scared of her question. He was scared of his answer.

"Go ahead," he said.

"How long has it been since you had sex?"

He dragged his hand across his face and watched as she licked her lips. It took him a second to count the months. *November, October, September, August.* It was a hot drunk night at an old college buddy's bonfire near Utica. A woman he'd never met came on strong, and he gave in. They were far from home, and he never even got her name. In fact, he'd barely thought about it since.

"Four months."

"Four months?" she said, dropping her chin. "I'm sorry, but the Liv stuff . . ."

"Yes, everything was just like it is now. It was one dumb

night, and it was just sex. I am a human, after all. I have needs. I never told Liv. I figured it would just complicate things. You're the only person I've ever told."

"I'm so confused," she said, yanking off her scarf and unzipping her own coat. Sam was slightly disappointed to see she wore a turtleneck underneath.

"What's confusing?"

"You're so protective over Liv. You're doing all of this to help her, to help Jay. You act like even the hint of something romantic between us would tank Liv's chance at custody. But then you sleep with some stranger? Why doesn't that threaten anything?"

His first instinct was to defend himself and then stick up for Liv. Sydney had no idea the battle Liv fought daily, the tidal wave of addiction crashing against her as she struggled to remain upright. She didn't know how Liv had been there for him when he needed her most and the bottomless debt he owed her because of it, or how Liv's lapse in sobriety came immediately after his mother died and the crushing guilt he felt every moment of every day thinking maybe he had something to do with it.

But as he watched Sydney's impassioned face, her cheeks blushing and her hands waving around in front of her, he suspected something deeper was to blame for the anger.

"My turn," he said.

"Can we stop with the game? I'm trying to talk to you here."

"No, you asked a question, you got your answer. Now it's my turn."

She huffed and slumped back against the lean-to wall like a spoiled toddler. "Go."

He lowered his eyebrows and breathed deeply before lowering the boom. "Why do you care so much?"

chapter **seventeen**

The air rushed out of her lungs. He'd beaten her to the ultimate question. She ran through all the possible answers in her mind. *I don't care. It's not fair to Liv. It's hypocritical.* But ultimately, she knew what she had to say. He'd shown her the break in the dam. Now all she had to do was take one fatal crack at it.

The heat from the roaring fire had her sweating on one side and freezing on the other. "I care because . . ." She licked her lips and swallowed the last of her fears. "I like you."

He dropped his chin. "And?"

"Nope, you got your question. I answered. My turn."

He ignored her protest. He leaned forward, creeping closer to her, and kept his eyes focused square on her mouth. "Do you also care because you're wondering if I'm letting myself sleep with somebody, why can't it be you?"

All feeling flowed out of her limbs in one mass exodus, leaving her body a numb lump of flesh. His mouth had

formed each perfect word as she looked on, hoping he'd get
to what they'd been dancing around for months. Now that
he'd said it, she didn't know what to do.

"Yes." The word was a whisper, a single exhale of breath.
"I care because I am incredibly, stupidly, all-consumingly
attracted to you, and yes, if you're going to sleep with
somebody, why can't it be me?"

A breath escaped his lips, and she felt the puff of air on
her mouth. Before either of them could say another word,
he leaned the last few inches toward her and kissed her lips.
The tip of his nose was ice-cold but the rest of him was
warm, and the heat began to quell the insatiable hunger
raging inside her.

He kissed her greedily, holding her face while his tongue
caressed hers. She tasted chocolate on his mouth, and she
breathed in like it was the last time she might be able to.

They both rose to their knees, and she unzipped his coat
all the way, desperate to feel the tight body beneath his
clothes. She wrapped her arms around his back and let her
fingers explore every tendon and ropy sinew. As she read
his body like braille, his left hand trailed down the front of
her body while he continued to kiss her, spending extra
time sucking on her lower lip.

She leaned in for more. His short beard scratched her
upper lip, the pain quickly eradicated by the sweetness of
his mouth and the thrumming desire flowing through every
vein. She had wanted him for so long, and now his body
was under her hands, his tongue inside her mouth. She almost couldn't believe it.

"In case you wondered," he said, his breathing heavy, "I
am stupidly, fully, mind-bendingly attracted to you, too.
And I kinda have been since we met."

Her lips parted as her brain floated lazily, trying to recover from the rush of endorphins. "Kinda guessed."

They continued to make out, hands roaming, voices
moaning, but she didn't know if she should escalate. What

she really wanted was to tear his clothes off and take every inch of him into her mouth. But they were outdoors, with the fickle heat from the fire their only source of warmth, and even if he only wanted to kiss, she could be happy with that for now.

Just as she talked herself into being okay with first base, his hand snaked down to unzip her coat the rest of the way, and as he tugged the zipper free at her thighs, his fingers paused to trace slowly along the outer edge of her sex through her jeans.

A strangled moan escaped her mouth, and she pulled away to study his face. His eyelids drooped, and his tongue traced his bottom lip. Now she knew what that gesture meant. It made her crazy with desire.

"What do you want to do?" he asked. His voice rumbled in the cold quiet of the lean-to as he tucked his face into her jaw and placed a series of tiny kisses there.

"I thought I was being so obvious." She reached forward and felt for the outline of his hardened cock. It pressed against the woven fabric of his ski pants, and as her fingers trailed up and over it, the pulse between her legs quickened.

"Tell me," he said.

She lifted her face to his while tracing her fingers over his erection again and again. Before she spoke, she flicked her tongue over his lower lip. "I want you to fuck me."

He released a deep exhale and tightened his grip on her ass. His pelvis pressed up against her and she rolled her hips on him, desperate for as much contact as possible.

"God," he groaned, "I think I could come just like this. You feel unbelievable."

She pressed her mouth against his again, and waves of lust rolled through her. This was more than physical desire. This was a deep connection being dug even further. He belonged to her, and as their bodies formed one entity, she gave in completely.

"I have a condom," he choked out. "Just a second." He

frantically grabbed at his backpack and dumped out the entire contents before retrieving an ancient condom from the depths of the pack.

"How old is that?" she asked.

"Not too old to work." He pulled his coat off his arms and laid it on the dirt before leaning back. The outline of his length strained against the ski pants, and her breath caught in her throat. The man certainly had a lot to offer.

She tugged off her own coat and savored the campfire heat. In this moment, she barely felt the chill. She kneeled between his knees and then leaned over him, sliding her hands up his impossibly chiseled abs and firm pecs. He licked his lower lip again, and she craned her neck to kiss it.

He reached under her layers of shirts, sliding his hand up until his fingertips brushed the under curve of her breast. She inhaled sharply, every nerve in her body in overdrive. She ground against him, sure if she didn't, she'd implode, while his thumb rolled over the tightened peak of her nipple. He moved over to the other side, all the while holding her gaze.

"I can't wait anymore," she said, her voice barely above a whisper. "I've already waited so long."

He kissed her gently before removing his hand and reaching for the condom. While he unzipped his pants, she stood up to remove hers altogether. She watched with rapt attention as he pulled out his incredible cock.

"Jesus Christ," she said. "Wait. Just one second."

With one hand clutching the condom, he watched as she knelt down again. This time she lingered at his hips and slipped his head past her lips, across her tongue, and down as far as her throat would allow. He tasted like a dream.

She slid the length of him in and out of her mouth, gripping the base with one hand, and moaning as she went. The sensation of him rolling against her tongue pushed her closer and closer to the edge. Finally, she looked up at him, his face creased in disbelief.

"Jesus, you're unreal," he said.

She buried her face in his stomach, chest, and throat as she made her way up toward his mouth. They kissed again, and now she was desperate for him.

He tore open the condom and rolled it from the tip to the shaft, pausing momentarily to stroke himself. She could barely stand to wait another second.

"You sure you're ready?" he asked, tracing his rough, calloused thumb across her lower lip.

"I am so ready."

With his eyes boring holes into hers, he traced his fingers across her slick seam. He dipped a single finger inside her and she shuddered, tightening around him.

"Don't tease me," she said, on the verge of begging.

"I wouldn't do that."

This time he dragged the tip of his cock along her folds before slowly pressing it into her. She squeezed her eyes closed, savoring each blissful inch as he entered her, filling her up with so much pressure she was afraid to move.

"Look at me," he said.

When she finally opened her eyes, she met his gaze dead-on. His cheeks flushed, and his breath came in ragged gasps. Each exhale hit her nose and mouth, and she breathed in his expelled air as if it could bring them that much closer.

They moved together like ocean waves on a quiet surf, their bodies rocking back and forth, in sync. Both of his hands slid across the soft flesh at her hips, resting finally where he had the best grip. Her thighs tightened around his waist, drawing him even farther inside her and quickening the pace. She wanted it to last, but a deep, clawing desire begged her to speed up.

"Oh God," she said, feeling the climax mounting. She teetered on the edge, begging her body not to give in yet. But the sensation of his cock sliding in and out of her, pressing against her clit and dragging her toward the ultimate release, was too much. She couldn't fight it anymore.

"You close?" he said, dragging his soft lips across hers. Every minute of being with him was intimacy in its purest form.

"Yes," she whispered. He tucked one hand behind her neck and buried it in her hair, the other hand clutching her waist. She'd never felt so connected to someone, so alive and present. It was the highest high.

"Fuck." His face pinched, and the rhythm of his hips rolling into hers increased, but his eyes never left her.

Suddenly, it was on her. The wave had built to epic proportions and now it crested before crashing down over her and carrying her away. "I'm coming," she squeaked as her body shivered in his arms.

"Oh God." He seized up underneath her, and as his hips pulsed and his arms tightened around her, he pressed a kiss against her mouth.

The trembling, pulsating waves finally died down, and she lifted her head from where it had landed on his chest to look at his face. His heavy breathing formed little clouds above him. She felt like she was sinking into a warm mud bath, gravity dragging her further into the sleepy, slippery beyond.

"Holy shit," he said, staring up at the ceiling of the lean-to. He dragged a hand over his face and then raised his head, gazing at her in pure wonderment.

"Yeah. Wow." A tiny tremor flowed from him into her, and she giggled. "Was that an aftershock?"

"Somethin' like that."

He closed the space between them and placed a gentle, purposeful kiss on her mouth. His hand, still buried in her hair, working his fingers through the strands, massaged the back of her neck and kept her close.

"Come on, you must be cold by now," he said. She realized she was naked from the waist down, save for a pair of wool socks, and the heat from the campfire wasn't doing much to warm her up.

She rolled off him, attempting to pull her turtleneck down over her very exposed nether regions. The strangeness of the moment settled over her.

They hadn't stripped each other down or seen each other naked. She still had no idea what the full tattoo was on his chest or if he had any strange birthmarks. The sex was so emotional and yet almost unfinished with all the things they hadn't said or done.

She slipped into her underwear, jeans, and boots while watching him peel off the used condom, tuck it into the empty granola bar wrapper, and slip it into his backpack.

"Saving a memento?" she said.

He zipped up his fly and leaned back on his elbows, one side of his mouth curving into a grin. "Yeah, I have a collection at home. Perfectly preserved used condoms."

"Oh man, you just get weirder and weirder." She tightened the laces on her boots and settled back down into the dirt, on her knees, poised over him and studying his face. He was different to her now. Softer, somehow.

"I was actually going to throw it out when I found a trash can," he said. He tugged at a loose strand of her hair and let his fingers linger at her jawbone.

"Such a responsible outdoorsman."

"What are we doing?" His whisper nearly disappeared on the wind. She didn't want the inevitable conversation to mar this perfect moment. Not now. Couldn't they live inside this warm bubble in the middle of nowhere while nature moved around them but real life did not?

"I don't know," she said.

He sat up and pulled on his coat, inching forward so that she sat between his legs.

"Being reckless?"

"Yeah, that much I already knew." The skin between his eyebrows creased, and she ran her fingers over it before kissing him. Although the physical act was over, the connection forged by sex had not yet broken.

"Was this, um . . ." She swallowed down the awkwardness. What was it about him? With everyone before him, she knew sex was her greatest weapon. Men fell at her feet after she'd had them one time. But with Sam, it was different. She wanted him to want all of her, not just her body. She wanted him to love her.

"Was this what?" he asked.

"Was this a one-time thing?"

He raised a single eyebrow and leaned in closer, resting his hands on the top of her butt. "God, I hope not."

"So then what?"

He breathed deeply, eyes darting around her face. "Liv is still on shaky ground for a while. She has to keep attending meetings, and a social worker can pop up at any time to check out the house, make sure it's fit for Jay to live in, and make sure Liv is still clean. If she can stick with it through all this, she'll probably get shared custody. And then I can back away."

Sydney nodded slowly. "So you're just waiting."

"Yep." He licked his lips and dropped his gaze to her chest. "At least for the next few weeks. And if Liv doesn't get custody, I don't know what happens. If it pans out that way, I'll be worried for her. I'm not sure she can handle it."

The conflict raged in her chest. She admired him for helping a friend, for committing to something so selfless. At the same time, she wanted him to be free of this burden. Free to continue on with his life unfettered.

"Well." She cleared her throat. "I guess that's that."

He snorted a laugh. Perhaps her true emotions were more transparent than she thought. "This is exactly why I didn't want to complicate anything. But I'm not somebody to walk away from my commitments. I said I was going to help Liv get Jay back, and that's what I'm going to do. I can't go back on my word. Not now."

"See," she said, "I told you you're noble. So until the courts make a decision . . ."

A ripple of tension passed between them. This wasn't an affair in any conventional sense, and she tried to tell herself they weren't really hurting anyone. The wrinkles in his brow and at his lips told a different story, and an uneasiness settled into her stomach.

"We'll just go one day at a time," he said. "See how we feel."

She swallowed down the lump that had formed in her throat, but it wouldn't budge. Something between them had shifted, and now, instead of insatiable heat, sadness.

"I should go," she said.

He blinked. "Why?"

"It's cold, I have some errands to run, it's getting late."

His jaw tightened. "Don't run away."

"I'm not running away." Manic laughter belied her words. "I just . . . should go. That's all. Don't read too much into it."

He withdrew his feet and moved backward, farther into the lean-to. She didn't want to push him away or shut him out, but the pinched look on his face told her she'd done something like it.

"Where's your car?" he asked. "Mine was the only one in the lot when I pulled in this morning."

"I parked at the south entrance. It's a shorter hike, and I didn't want to be here that long. Just long enough to, um . . ."

"Make an awkward friendship even more uncomfortable?"

Her heart leaped into her throat as he sent her a strained half smile. "What? No. I was going to say 'lick my wounds after my Connor encounter.' But I guess I, uh, did more than that."

He licked his bottom lip and found his ski cap in the dirt, pulling it over his head. Maybe she didn't know what the lip lick meant after all. Everything she did appeared misguided, and her legs told her to run.

"Okay, well. I'm going to go." She stood up, zipped her

coat, and waited. She thought he'd stand to meet her, hug her, something. But instead he sat in the dirt and traced lines in the dust. "Bye?"

"Bye."

By the time she rounded the curve in the trail toward the parking lot, the uncertainty she'd experienced last night pummeled her once again. This time, for different reasons entirely.

Sleeping with Sam was everything she'd wanted. It was just as easy as every other encounter they'd had, with the added pleasure of all her sexual fantasies of him come to life. He was gentle and kind and careful in a way she'd never experienced before. And the mere thought of his hands gripping her naked hips forced a tremor in her legs.

But the risk was so great. What if Liv found out? What if Sam decided he couldn't be there for Liv and maintain a relationship with Sydney at the same time? What if a little kid lost his mother because of one stupid moment of bliss in a lean-to? And worst of all, what if she lost herself once again to a man, but this time one who had the all-encompassing power to ruin her?

"Suds? Let's call it a night. It's nearly seven anyway. And we've had an okay day."

Sydney and Karen didn't usually close up together, but a large shipment of books had arrived the previous day and Sydney knew the unpacking, shelving, and store closing would go much faster with both of them working.

Their holiday party five days prior had been a smashing success, but the sales tapered off once again the following day and had been puttering along since. This morning, when Sydney checked the mail, two more overdue notices stared her in the face. The fate of the Loving Page would be decided in a matter of weeks.

Sydney had spent hours upon hours hunched over a

computer, researching the effectiveness of Facebook ads,
working Instagram algorithms, and attempting to charm
publishers into donating books and swag for giveaways.
She'd labored over cute book displays, using every shred of
photo skill she possessed to create dynamic content. She
worked every angle, promoting and begging and, occasionally, praying. They were still a cool $9,000 away from be-
ing safely in the black. The number burned in Sydney's
brain as if she'd had it tattooed there.

As Karen flipped the lock on the front door, Sydney
dragged the boxes of books from the office into the reading
nook. As a result of the party, there were now gaping holes
in their book stock. The brief moment of optimism wasn't
enough to pull Sydney out of her malaise.

"Maybe this really won't work," she said. *And what
then?* She'd have to leave Pine Ridge, move back to New
York, get a job as an associate at a law firm, and go from
there. Her throat turned to sandpaper.

"At least you gave it your best shot," Karen said.

Sydney scanned the paperback spines and let her fingers
trail over the smooth edges of Sam's bookshelves. She
missed him. She missed him with every molecule in her
body, from the core of her insides and radiating outward.
He was giving her space again. Whether she wanted it or not.

"Suds." Her mother's quiet voice broke through her
thoughts.

"Mm-hmm?"

Karen approached, placing a cool hand over Sydney's.
"Why don't you call him?"

The panic choked her. "What?"

"Sam. Why don't you call him?"

"What makes you think I haven't? Why would I need
to?" She knew she sounded insane, but her mother was the
best at picking up on unspoken cues. Sydney must have
given herself away.

"I see you checking your phone every fifteen seconds,

and he hasn't been in here in two weeks. I told him to be careful how he acted in front of you, but I didn't think it'd scare him off like this. Did something happen?"

Sydney released a shaky breath and smoothed down her black cashmere sweater. Maybe she should lie. If the words never left her lips, she didn't have to worry about being judged for them. She looked at her mother's wide, honest eyes and knew she couldn't go through with it.

"We slept together."

She expected a gasp, a yelp, a disgusted clucking of the tongue. Instead, Karen laughed. Her eyes crinkled up behind clumpy mascara lashes and she chuckled loudly, sending her high-pitched laugh bouncing off the store walls.

"I'm not kidding," Sydney said.

"I know that." Karen grinned at her daughter. "I'm just happy."

"Mom, how can you be happy about this? I'm the other woman."

"Oh, stop." Karen flattened her lips and tossed a hand in the air. "The other woman. Sam and Liv haven't been romantic in years. Everybody knows that."

"I don't get it." Her voice tightened. "What's his attachment to her?"

Karen shrugged. "First of all, there's the past. She was his first love. And she stepped up when his mom got sick. Liv's had her highs and lows, but she's a terrific nurse, and she went above and beyond to make sure Sam's mom got the best of the best treatment and that Sam had as easy a time as possible with it. You can't put a value on somethin' like that, Suds."

Sydney massaged her forehead and tried to swallow down this new information.

"Liv's DUI came pretty shortly after Sam buried his mom," Karen continued. "And he agreed to help her without a second thought. At that point he'd have done anything for her."

The more Karen talked, the smaller Sydney felt. How could she begrudge him for helping a friend like that in her moment of need?

"The last piece of this puzzle," Karen said, "is Sam's dad. Boy, from what I've heard, he was a drinker. And his mom, God love her, never stood up to him. So maybe our Sammy is trying to help Liv the way he wished somebody would've helped his dad."

Sydney licked her lips. Her mother always saw things so clearly. "I guess it's not as cut-and-dry as I thought."

"Nothing in life ever is, kiddo."

A prickle of guilt danced across her skin as she remembered her quick exit from the lean-to. His hardened face as she turned away from him. *God, what a bitch.*

"He's a good guy," Sydney said.

"One of the best. And anybody with eyes can see you two are hot for each other."

"Oh my God." Sydney collapsed into the little red velvet couch and buried her face in her hands. "Please never ever use that phrase again."

"Well, it's true. I knew if you stayed in town it would happen eventually." Karen settled next to her on the couch and nudged her daughter's shoulder. "So. How was it?"

"Oh my God!" Sydney clutched the ends of her hair. "I might throw up."

"Oh, Suds. You're such a prude."

Sydney shook off the question and leaned back on the couch, massaging her eyes. In the past few years she hadn't kept in close contact with her mother. They exchanged phone calls every now and then, and Karen told her daughter generic stories about the mountains and her shop. Sydney, in exchange, gave her mother platitudes about city life and the ebbs and flows of her relationship with Connor.

They never touched on anything meaningful. Sydney was convinced her mother was content to be a country bumpkin and wouldn't understand her sophisticated metropolitan life. What she'd recently found out, however, was that she'd missed out on years of friendship. Some women would kill to be close to their mothers. Sydney had voluntarily pushed hers away.

"I'm really happy that I've gotten to see your life here," Sydney said.

Her mother's cheeks filled with color as she fidgeted. "You've been here before."

"Yeah, but never like this." She reached across the couch and grabbed her mother's cool, steady hand. Always cool and steady. "I'm sorry it took a cheating boyfriend to get me here."

Karen cracked a smile and kissed Sydney's cheek. "I love ya, Suds. You're my favorite kid."

"Oh, are there others?"

"Nah, just seemed like a nice thing to say."

Sydney matched her mother's grin.

"I know you judged me," Karen said.

Sydney's face fell. "I was a kid. I just didn't understand. All I knew was that I didn't have the things that other people had."

"I hope you're realizing now that things aren't everything. Don't get me wrong, a roof over your head and food in the fridge are important. God knows it'd be nice if we could keep this shop going. But sometimes it's more about *who* you have, not what you have."

Sydney's lip trembled, and she bit down to contain it. *Or who you don't have.*

"Now," Karen said. "What's going on with Sam? You look pretty broken up about something."

Sydney relayed a brief, watered-down version of the weekend's events. She tried to keep her heartache in check, but as her mother's mouth curved further and further into a frown, she knew she'd given herself away.

"Go get him."

Sydney laughed and ran a hand through her hair. "Okay, Mom. Just go?"

"Yes. Just go. I think you're scared shitless about your feelings for him, and you're hurting him in the process. Men aren't all the same, ya know. Sam would never come close to doing to you what Connor did."

"You're right," Sydney said. "I'm scared, but you're right."

"Atta girl." Karen waved her toward the door. "Now get out of here. I'll take care of restocking."

Sydney tucked all her anxieties down deep inside and locked them in a box. If she was going to talk to Sam about what happened, she'd need to be fear-free. Even if she was faking.

chapter **eighteen**

The single bulb over Sam's head flickered.

"Damn it."

He'd have to change it soon, but like a game of chicken, he also wondered how long he could make the sucker last. Tonight the warm, flickering glow kept him company. He needed a friend.

Save for a few snowmobiles Matt had dropped off for routine maintenance, the shop was quiet. Sam was just about to yank the chain on the light bulb when a pair of headlights lit up the space. His junker. A flurry of anger accompanied the tingle below his belt when he spotted Sydney.

After the high of a complete and perfect orgasm had worn off, she'd raced out of the lean-to like a firefighter on a call. Everything about sleeping together was a gamble. Sure, they'd grown close. But she was still Sydney Walsh. She was still a city girl who wore diamonds in her ears and turned down proposals from wealthy stockbrokers.

In addition to the superficial stuff, he'd gotten to know

her. He knew she was scared. Scarred by an absentee father and the fear of being financially dependent on anyone, she was a frightened deer. And women like that could hurt a man just as much as they were scared to be hurt themselves.

"Hi." She crept toward him, barely making a sound on the icy gravel outside his garage. Her face pinched, and she clutched her hands at her throat, tugging at the imaginary necklace.

"Hi," he said. He wiped his grease-smeared hands on a rag at his belt and tried to avoid her laser-beam stare.

"I'm sorry to interrupt you." She stopped a few feet short of where he stood, gnawing at her lip. "I just wanted to come and say I'm sorry."

Now she had his full attention. "Sorry for what?"

"Oh, come on." A bitter laugh escaped her throat. "For running away on Saturday. For acting like nothing happened."

"It's fine." He shrugged. *Fine? It's not fine. Quit letting her get away with everything.*

"Oh, really?" She challenged him instead. "It's fine? You were cool with the way that ended?"

"Well, no." His heart pounded at his ribs as if trying to escape. Was he angry or turned on or both? Damn her. Her full lips glistened in the low shop light as if she'd just applied lip gloss, and the cold air brought out the flush in her cheeks, which reminded him of her face at the exact moment his finger slid inside her for the first time.

"No," she said. It was more of a question than an agreement.

"No, I wasn't cool with it. You're confusing as shit, man."

She stood a little bit taller, but he pressed on.

"I mean, was it not what you'd hoped for? Was it somehow disappointing? Because in my fairly experienced history, if a woman's eyes roll back in her head like that when she comes, it's a good thing."

Her full mouth parted, and the faintest hint of a moan escaped her lips before her hand could fly up to cover it. Something resembling a word came out of her mouth, and he tilted his head, waiting for a real response. She wasn't going to hem and haw and pout her way out of this one.

"It was good." Her voice dropped an octave. "It was better than good."

The stirring inside his jeans forced him to take a step forward and then another. As he inched closer, her breath quickened, the clouds of moisture in front of her mouth coming more frequently.

"Better than good," he said. "So why'd you run away? And don't tell me it was because this is a secret. You knew that before we did it."

"Did it." A smile tugged at the corners of her mouth.

"What are you, fifteen?" Now he was close enough to smell the heady sweetness of her perfume. Like spring plants after the rain. "You knew it was a secret before I had you half-naked next to a campfire, making you moan like a wild animal before you begged me to make you come. Is that better?"

Her eyelids sunk to half-mast, and she released a single, strangled breath that floated across his lips like a ghost. He'd wondered if the sex wasn't good for her, if that was why she'd run. That obviously wasn't the truth.

"I don't know why I did that," she said. He placed a hand on the doorframe to the left of her head and leaned into it, wanting to close the space between them but not entirely confident enough to do so yet.

He'd spent the past four days going over every moment of Saturday morning. The way her hair fell in his face, the way her moans came from deep inside her throat, the way she came hard enough to leave faint bruises on his hips. If she gave him the go-ahead, he'd leap at the chance to have her again. But only on her terms.

"I'm not gonna hurt you," he said.

With this, her eyes closed completely. When they opened again, they searched his face. "Yeah, you say that now. But you might."

"You might hurt me."

As she stood perfectly still, he brushed his lips against hers. She lifted her face to lock in what he'd been unsure about. She covered his mouth with hers and raised her hand to his cheek as she stepped in closer.

He wrapped both arms around her, squeezing her tightly and breathing in every inch of her smell and taste. His tongue worked its way inside her mouth, and she greeted it as eagerly as her hands clutched his waist.

"Come on." He broke away, suddenly aware of how exposed they were in the doorway to his garage, even if the shop was slightly off the beaten path. With clasped hands, they moved inside and toward his office.

"I didn't even know this was here." She followed him from the front office to the back, where he kept a beat-up old sofa, a tiny fridge, and an ancient TV set with an antenna. The guy he'd taken over the garage from liked to spend time away from his wife in there, and Sam didn't have the heart to change it once he became owner.

"I've never really had occasion to use it," Sam said. He closed the door behind her and flipped the switch on a space heater in the corner, praying the rusted old thing still worked. It sprang to life with a groan and quickly filled the dark space with musty warmth.

As he double-checked the lock on the door, she creeped up behind him and slid her hands under his work shirt. She laughed against his back, and he closed his eyes, drinking in the sensation of her delicate body against him.

"Can we take a trip to Bora Bora so that touching each other isn't so much work?" she said.

Her cold fingers slid under his T-shirt, and his stomach contracted in response. His head was a cloudy mess. The smell of her perfume and the sensation of the pads of her

fingers tracing up his sides and across his abs consumed
every inch of his brain space.

He turned in her arms and held her head as he consumed
her mouth, exploring every inch. She was so sensitive, so
reactive, that every time he did something new or touched
her in a different place, a fresh sound emerged and egged
him on. Exploring her was a treasure hunt, each gem better
than the last.

"This time is gonna be different," he said, trailing his
fingers down the sides of her neck. He ran a thumb across
her collarbone and watched as goose bumps appeared in its
wake.

"Different how?" she asked.

She wore a short black puffer coat that hid her body
entirely, and this time around, he wasn't having any of it.
He wanted to see her. All of her. And if they couldn't have
sex in a well-lit bedroom, then he'd have to put in a bit more
work.

"You cold?" he asked.

"No." She kissed him again. Their mouths were like
magnets, always finding each other in the spare moments.
She left a trail of moisture on his lower lip that forced him
to lean down for another kiss.

He unzipped her coat and pushed it off her shoulders,
pausing as it fell to the floor. Tonight, instead of layers of
clothes and a turtleneck, she wore a black sweater with a
deep V-neck that exposed her exquisite neck and the curve
of her breasts.

It was the spot on her body that always turned him into
a puddle, and tonight, he let his hands roam free across it.
She leaned into his touch, and a warm breath escaped her
lips, sending chills across his jaw. He cupped her right
breast and traced his thumb across the edge of her sweater.
The fabric pulled back to reveal the pale pink lace of her
bra, and he hooked his thumb there also, as the dark pink
bud of her nipple came into view.

He placed his mouth over her nipple, sinking into the sound of low moans radiating from her chest. He pulled back in time to see her closed-eyed, open-mouthed face lifted to the ceiling in pure, unabashed pleasure.

"Come here," she said, hooking her hands into his belt and dragging him toward her. Her red-tipped fingers made quick work of the buttons on his shirt and then she tugged at the T-shirt, a pile of discarded clothes growing at their feet.

For a moment, she didn't move. She stared at his naked chest with her fingers poised over his belt and then raised her eyes, a dopey smirk tugging at her lips.

"What are you, chiseled from stone?" she said. She nuzzled into his chest and traced her tongue across the ridge between his pecs, forcing all the blood in his body to one concentrated area. When she arrived at the tattoo over his right pec, she paused again. "Does this mean something?"

He'd gotten the large black-and-white begonias the day after his mother's funeral. She'd always hated his tattoos, but he needed something injected into his skin that would remind him of her. Not to remind him of her face or her kindness or her spirit, but to remind him of what she gave up and that he should never take it for granted.

"Yeah, but I'd rather not talk about my mother again when my chief concern is getting you to come more than once this time."

A strangled animal sound came from her lips, and her hands dropped to his belt, working at the buckle in record time. He took this opportunity to tug at the bottom hem of her sweater and lift it over her head, dropping it into their pile.

Her breasts strained at the edges of her delicate pink bra, and he nipped at the flesh there with gentle bites. His dick was so hard it almost hurt, but more than anything, he wanted her to feel ultimate, otherworldly pleasure. He wanted to pull her toward the edge and hold her as she came again and again in his arms.

As he pulled away, he took her all in. He wasn't afforded this view the first time they had sex, and he wasn't going to ignore it now. Her full breasts gave way to a flat stomach and the rounded curves of her waist. He popped the buttons on her jeans and tugged them down, not content to end the visual tour at the waistband of her pants.

While he was on his knees, working the jeans over her feet, he rested his gaze on her stomach. She had a small brown birthmark to the left of her belly button, and he kissed it gently. Every inch of her was a gift.

"I know," she said suddenly. "I've kind of, um . . . gained some weight since I moved here."

His head snapped up. "Are you joking?"

Her brow furrowed, and she gnawed at her lip as her hands crept across her stomach, blocking his access. "I just mean, I used to work out a lot, and I was super toned and just less doughy."

He stood to meet her, nearly sick to his stomach that she thought of herself that way. "You are perfect. If you apologize to me for the way you look ever again, I will make good on that skin coat thing."

Her lips pressed into a smile, and he snaked his arms around her waist, clutching her body close. She held his neck with both hands and kissed him with more fervor than she'd ever kissed him before. This time was different—in more ways than he'd hoped for.

His right hand moved downward until it cupped her ass, squeezing the smooth flesh and at the same time pressing her hips against his ever-hardening cock. He stepped out of his jeans and carried her toward the couch, setting her down gently and trailing her wavy hair over her shoulder.

"Lie down," he said.

She kissed him again before complying.

He leaned his body against her closed knees until they parted for him. Her eyes shone brightly in the dim light of the back office, and her chest rose and fell with increased exaggeration. If he had to guess, he'd say she was nervous.

"I'm sorry I missed out on this part on Saturday," he said. His calloused fingers traced the edges of her black mesh thong and gently pulled the middle aside so that her soft lips came into view.

"Hey, um," she said in a tiny, timid voice. He dragged his eyes away from her glistening sex and looked up at her. Her face pinched in discomfort. It was not the face of someone experiencing unabashed pleasure.

"What's wrong?" He stood, terrified that he'd hurt her.

"No, no, come back," she said. She reached for his hand and pulled him back to the couch until he sat down next to her. "I don't really like it. Oral sex."

He shrugged. "Okay. That's fine."

She sniffed and centered her gaze on his chest, trailing her fingers through his sparse expanse of chest hair.

A weight settled over him like a wool blanket. She looked so beautiful reclined on the plaid couch. Her hair splayed over the threadbare arm like she was floating through water. But the concern creased into her features alarmed him. He wanted her to feel good. Safe.

"Do you want to stop?" he said.

"No!" she said without missing a beat. "No, I don't want to stop. God, after running away on Saturday and now this, I feel like I'll give you a complex."

"Sydney." Her name fell out of his mouth like a balm meant to soothe. He didn't know how to explain to this woman that she could be whoever she wanted with him and he wasn't going anywhere. He sensed it was something he'd have to show her instead.

"Seriously." The deep wrinkle between her eyebrows never changed. "I want to."

"But you don't have to."

Her hand crept up his chest and landed in the crook of his neck before fingering the curl of hair behind his ear. "I know I don't have to."

"Then let's stop. You're not giving me any sort of complex. The part about Saturday that confused me was when you ran away without explanation and then I didn't hear from you for four days. I thought you regretted it or hated it or that I'd hurt you."

"It was none of that." Her dark brown eyes sparkled with tears, and she continued to touch his hair with gentle fingers.

As much as he wanted her, he also wouldn't mind spending the rest of his life just like this.

"I will never push you to do anything you don't want to do," he said. "Whether that's talking about the ugly stuff in your past or, you know, going down on you."

Her lips curved into a smile. "Is that really messed up? Am I the only woman in the world who doesn't like it?"

"So what if you are? It's not messed up. You like what you like." She looked so fragile in this moment that he wanted to wrap her up in his arms and squeeze the insecurity right out of her. He couldn't envision the man who wouldn't listen to what she wanted and do just that. Or maybe he could.

"Connor was always convinced nobody had ever done it to me the right way," she said, raising a single eyebrow. "He tried and he tried and he tried. I used to fake the orgasm just so he'd stop."

The anger bubbled up inside him again. Connor was the type of guy who ruined good women. The fact that he'd gotten inside Sydney's head made him the worst type of asshole.

"Connor is the fucking worst." He stifled any additional comments. They were still half-naked in the back of his garage office, and everything was a bit too exposed for pure, unadulterated hatred of the ex.

"It matters to me that you don't hate me," she said.

His gaze landed on hers, soaked her all in. She didn't know how impossible that was. "I don't hate you. I couldn't hate you. And if it ever got to that point, trust me, it wouldn't be because you didn't let me go down on you."

She exhaled and slowly nodded, finally seeming to believe him. This was it. The moment had passed. And yet instead of feeling like he'd missed out on something, something else had been gained. She'd laid bare her insecurities to him, and he knew he could handle them. He reached over and grabbed her sweater.

"Come on," he said. "Sit up." She lifted her torso off the couch and raised her arms over her head with a coy smile on her face. He slipped the sweater over her arms and head and tugged the bottom down over her stomach after she'd popped her head through the neck.

"Wow, you dressing me is almost as hot as you undressing me," she said. She leaned into his neck and rested her head there, her warm breath on his collarbone sending electric shocks down his body.

They both finished putting their clothes on, and after he helped her with her coat, she sunk into his arms again. Her face pressed against his chest, and she burrowed in as if sinking into bed for a nap.

"Thank you," she said, her voice muffled by the fabric of his shirt.

"For what?" He held her tightly because he wanted to and also because it seemed to be what she needed. What she was missing. Had anyone ever held her like this? He wanted to believe he was the first.

"For just being kind to me. You are one of the kindest men I've ever met. I don't really know what to do with that sometimes."

He traced his fingers up and down her spine, hoping to infuse some sense of peace and comfort in her. "I care about you. That's what you do when you care about somebody."

She pulled back just enough to look up at him. "Can we spend some time together this week? Maybe just get lunch or something? Everything's been so heavy these past few weeks, and I miss hanging out with you."

"I don't know. Now that I've seen you naked, I'm not really into non-naked hangs. Like, what's the point, right?"

She grinned and gently punched him in the ribs. "Can I retract my previous statement? You're a real asshole."

The following morning, Sam hopped into the cab of his truck with a lightness in his chest he hadn't experienced in a long time. They hadn't slept together, but he had the glow of a man who'd had the best lay of his life.

Instead of getting physically closer, which he was still very much interested in, she'd shown him a side of herself he hadn't known existed. Every preconceived notion he'd had about Karen Walsh's stuck-up daughter dissolved around him. She wasn't arrogant; she had walls built up. She wasn't hedonistic; she was protecting herself with financial stability. And she wasn't a selfish daughter; she was someone who'd had a difficult relationship with her mother growing up and was now working hard to mend it.

He drove through the slushy downtown streets, crisp white snow hugging the roofs and trees lining the road. Winter was a seemingly endless season in Pine Ridge, but at the beginning, the snow was refreshing. Clean.

He parked his truck in front of McDonagh's to grab a coffee before passing by the Loving Page just to check and see if Sydney was inside. The hardware store was his true destination, but he wasn't hurting anybody just passing by.

He tugged on the front door of the bakery, but it didn't budge. The sign in the window told him they were closed.

"Hmm." McDonagh's hadn't been closed on a Thursday morning for as long as he'd been alive. He scanned the street for a telltale reason, but the scene in front of him read as mundane. A few tourists huddled into their coats and scurried between shops and restaurants. Yuri salted his front sidewalk in anticipation of the day's customers. He raised a hand at Sam, and Sam waved back.

"Hey," he said, jogging over to Yuri. "McDonagh's is closed?"

"Just for an hour or so," Yuri said, leaning his heft on the shovel. "The gals are at the Loving Page helping out Sydney with some promotion thing she's running over the weekend."

Sam wondered if Sydney was as starry-eyed as he was this morning. And if she was, how well she was hiding it from Jorie.

"The gals? Jorie and her mom?" he asked.

"Jorie and Liv."

A prickle of fear crept over Sam's flesh as if the grim reaper himself had passed by. "Liv?"

"Mm-hmm." Yuri's mouth set, and he fiddled with the handle of the shovel. Maybe he knew about Sydney. Maybe Syd had told her mother, and Karen had said something to Yuri. Or maybe Sam's poker face was worse than he thought.

"All right, well, uh . . . Guess I'll see ya."

With a deep sense of doom simmering in his gut, Sam crossed the sidewalk to the entrance of the Loving Page. He peered through the big front window to find a scene straight out of a Hallmark movie.

Liv and Jorie strung popcorn on the couch while Sydney stood nearby, sipping from a speckled red mug and laughing at something Liv had said. She leaned against the counter, her bulky gray sweatshirt unable to hide the swell of her perfect breasts. Despite Liv's presence confusing the fantasy, his jeans were suddenly tight.

He adjusted his belt and cleared his throat before entering.

"Welcome to the Loving Page," Jorie chirped. "What's your pleasure? Bosoms, boners, or balsam candles?"

Both Sydney and Liv stared at him, each with a different

hopeful expression on her face. Before he could decide who to speak to first, Sydney turned away to adjust something on the bookshelf.

"Hi," Liv said. She plucked a piece of popcorn from a bowl and pierced it with a needle, working quickly with deft fingers. *Sober.*

"Hi," he said, trying to force the confusion from his voice. "What are you doing here?"

"I was at McDonagh's this morning when Jorie told me she was coming over here to help Syd." *Syd.*

What is going on here? Liv's face shone with hope.

"We're prepping for the weekend event," Jorie said. "Love Letters and Eggnog."

"We're still working on the name," Sydney chimed in. She stood as far away from him as physically possible, but her heavy gaze told him she didn't want to. Her fingers traced the neck of her sweatshirt as the blush in her cheeks deepened.

"It's going to be so cute," Liv said. "Sydney's making eggnog, and Jorie's bringing gingerbread men, and people are supposed to bring their old love letters to read aloud. After the readings, everyone votes on a favorite, and the winner gets a gorgeous Christmas wreath that Karen's going to make, plus two new Christmas-themed romance novels just released. Isn't that such a cute idea?"

"Syd's full of them," Jorie said.

"Why don't you come sit down?" Liv said. "Maybe you can help us think of a better name. You're so good at things like that."

Paralyzed by guilt, Sam choked down saliva. In moments such as these, he conjured up the most painful memories: the glazed indifference in her stare as she confessed she'd slept with someone else; the stench of old booze on her clothes the morning after he'd picked her up from the drunk tank; the innumerable nights she'd passed out cold and he'd lain awake to make sure she didn't aspirate.

Today, with clear eyes and nimble fingers, she proved her sobriety to him once again. He wanted to believe she could do it. She kept showing him and everyone else just how dedicated she was, testifying over and over again that she'd be a great mom to Jay if she could just have the chance. That's what this was all about. But something about Syd and Liv in the same room created a pressure on his chest that he couldn't shake.

"I can't stay," he said, taking a step backward. "But good luck."

He ignored Liv's accusatory stare and Sydney's presence altogether before pushing out the front door into the cold, crisp morning air. The sunshine caused the ice to crackle around him, and he squinted as he crunched across ice-crisped grass. His head felt filled with cement, the tension pressing at his temples with the force of a two-ton truck. He beelined for the hardware store, the space he knew better than his childhood home.

"Hey, Sam," the cashier called out.

"Yo, Earl. What's up."

"Nothing much, my friend." The octogenarian placed a paper cup of coffee on the counter for Sam.

"How did you know?" Sam sipped the hot liquid and breathed a sigh of relief as the warm, familiar taste cascaded across his tongue.

"That tire gauge you were waitin' on came back in stock." Earl thumbed over his shoulder, and Sam nodded a thanks before carrying his coffee back into the shop.

Earl's place was the only destination he ever remembered his dad taking him to when he was a kid, and the smell alone took him back. Everything here had a purpose. Sam ran his hand over the rows of dangling electrical cords the way a woman might touch a row of jeweled necklaces.

His father never had time for ice cream or trips to the water park. But whenever he needed a new garden hose or a replacement part for the toilet, he strapped Sam into the passenger seat of his old Buick and took him along for the errand.

Well beyond the Tootsie Pop that Earl used to hand him when he walked in, Sam loved the order and purpose of the place. The scent of new plastic and sharpened metal, the dust underfoot, the whirring fans overhead. Despite the chaos of his homelife and the anxiety stretched tight between his parents, when he walked into the hardware store with his dad and watched the weathered old man carefully select something he needed to make their lives work, everything made sense.

An ache stretched through his chest. More often than not since his mother had passed away, a sense of loneliness echoed through his bones. It was a loneliness with no origin, aside from the obviousness of absent parents. This town and the familiar faces were his only relief. And now, Sydney.

Because his mom got sick, and then because of his arrangement with Liv, women had taken an official last place on his priority list. He had no desire to attach himself to someone who could ruin his life the way Liv had almost done, and there was no one to meet in this town anyway. Until Sydney.

"Sam?"

He spun around to face Liv, gnawing away at her lower lip, her arms tucked tightly around the waist of her thick down coat.

"What's wrong?"

She snorted a frustrated laugh. "Every time I want to talk to you lately, you think something's wrong."

She didn't belong here. The hardware store was his safe space, the space where he could get lost in his own thoughts and linger and tinker with tools until Earl kicked him out so he could lock up for the night. Having Liv here forced everything to tilt a little.

"All right," he said, keeping his voice steady. "What's up, Liv?"

"Maybe this isn't my place." She wrinkled her nose and avoided his eyes, her gaze landing somewhere near his chin. "Honestly, I don't know what my place is with you anymore. We're friends; we're exes; we're strangers."

"We're not strangers."

She shrugged, finally meeting his stare. "I have no right to ask you for any more than you're already giving. I know that. But I want to know what's going on with you and Sydney."

He stepped backward as if she'd punched him in the chest. "What?"

Her eyebrows lifted into her forehead. "I'm not blind. You walked into that store and the whole mood changed."

He breathed deep, weighing his options. No way could he admit to his relationship with Sydney. Liv wasn't in any place to have her boat rocked.

Suddenly her nostrils flared, and a blush bloomed in her cheeks. She chewed on her lip as tears formed and then there was blood, a tiny spot of crimson on her lower lip.

"Liv," he said, "you're bleeding. You chewed your lip so hard it's bleeding."

She touched her fingers to her lips and squeezed her eyes shut before looking up at him, her desperate face crushing his heart.

"I'm sorry. I don't want to make things even more tense between us. I'm not allowed to ask you for this, I know that. I just . . ." She blinked, glittering tears clinging to her spidery eyelashes. "Sam, if you fall in love with someone else right now, I won't make it. I can't. I can't keep fighting for my kid, for my life, for my sobriety, if I know that your heart is somewhere else."

It was unfair. They both knew it. But for as long as he could remember, he'd taken care of her. He couldn't stop now. He didn't know how.

"I'm sorry," she repeated. "It's messed up. You're allowed to have everything a normal guy should have. I just can't do this by myself."

"Liv." He chose his words carefully. "Nothing has changed with you and me. I made a commitment to you, and I'm not backing out of it. No matter what else happens. Trust me. All right?"

Her face collapsed and she burrowed into his chest, her sobs reverberating through his rib cage as if they were his own. All he had to do was get through the social worker's visits and the hearing, and then he'd launch her like a rehabilitated bird back into the world. She'd fly, God damn it. She had to.

chapter **nineteen**

These are probably better with whiskey." Liv's eyes took up half her face, and now they darted between Jorie and Sydney as if asking for permission.

"Liv," Jorie scolded. "You know you can't have alcohol."

"Oh God, of course. I'm sure you're on *strict orders* to babysit." Liv rolled her eyes and leaned back into the crook of the couch. "Gosh, sometimes Sam feels like a parent more than a friend."

Jorie sucked her lower lip between her teeth and eyed Sydney. Liv had run out of the store after Sam left, and they both noticed she'd come back a little looser and red-faced. Was she drunk? Sydney didn't know her well enough to tell.

"He just wants to help you make the right choices," Jorie said.

Liv hugged her arms across her chest as she looked up at Sydney. "I'm sure you've heard all about what a mess I am."

Only that you've derailed Sam's life and put your little boy's life in danger. "We all have baggage."

A tinny, twinkly tune played from Liv's purse, and she nearly spilled her eggnog lunging for it. Her formerly blotchy face lit up as she looked at the phone and answered the call.

"Baby," she cooed. "Hello, my heart. How are you?"

As Jorie's lips pressed into a sympathetic grin, a wash of shame forced Sydney to move away from the couch. Liv's kid. This was what it was all about. Reuniting Liv with her son. A sizzle reel of dirty memories flashed through her brain, and she took a sip of her whiskey-laced drink to steady her nerves.

"I know, babe." Liv's voice dropped to a whisper, and she pressed her fingers into her eyes, the pain clear across her delicate features. "You're being such a huge help to Mommy, though. Do you know what? Every day that you do what Nana and Papa tell you is another day that I can rest easy knowing everything in Ohio is going super well. And the better things go for all of us, the sooner I can get you back."

Jorie joined Sydney at the counter and leaned in close.

"Wow," Sydney said, weighing her words carefully. "She must be totally heartbroken."

Jorie's forehead wrinkled. The girl could tell a story with her eyebrows alone. "I don't know."

Liv stood up from the couch and held up a pointer finger, indicating she needed a minute, and disappeared out the front door. Once she was out of earshot, Jorie turned back.

"She's not heartbroken?" Sydney asked.

"She loves that kid," Jorie said. "And I'm a firm believer in a kid growing up with their mother. How could I not want Liv to have her son back?"

Sydney held her comments in as Jorie spouted the party line.

"But," Jorie continued. "I've seen this before. She gets sober, she holds on for a while, she thinks she has it all under control, and then she starts drinking again. Three weeks into 'I'm only having one beer' and she's calling me from the Pine Ridge PD drunk tank."

Jorie's nostrils flared, and she picked at invisible lint on her shirtsleeve.

"Is there anything different about her this time around?" Sydney asked.

Jorie shrugged. "She seems like she's really trying. She's going to all her meetings, even though she sometimes complains about them. She seems sober. I hope it's for real this time."

Sydney's stomach contracted. Jorie's speech sounded too much like Sam's. Cautiously optimistic.

"I want her to get better," Jorie said. "I do. It's just that she's been down this road before, you know? No matter how many people try to help her, she has to do it on her own."

Sydney swallowed down the honesty threatening at the gates of her mouth. What if Liv proved herself stronger than ever, got her son back, and Sam decided she'd made great enough strides to be with him again? What if the Liv who had cared for his mother showed her face again and won Sam over once and for all?

Jorie looked up at Sydney with a sad smile tugging at her lips. "Thank you for listening. It's nice having you around."

"Oh, I'm just using you to help get my mom's shop running again. Did you think we were, like, friends or something?"

Jorie's smile stretched, and she tossed a tiny balsam pillow at Sydney's head. "Just wait until your stupid book club comes around. I'm gonna hide fish in all the air ducts in here and then you'll be sorry."

"A romance book club that stinks like fish? Might hit a bit too close to home for some ladies."

"Oh God, that's foul," Jorie said, wrinkling her nose in disgust. "Terrible segue, but I'm spending the night at Matt's tonight. So, enjoy your alone time."

"I won't ask why fishy sex reminded you of your boy-friend."

Jorie laughed again and shook her head. "Thankfully, that's one issue we don't have."

After Liv and Jorie departed, Sydney settled behind the cash register to post on social media about the upcoming event at the shop. When she'd arrived that morning, three new voice mails greeted her. Instead of banks and credit card companies calling, Karen's debts had been turned over to professional debt collectors. The menace in their voices renewed the fear in Sydney's heart.

Her savings was gone. The car money was gone. If they didn't raise $9,000 by the end of January, Karen would lose the store and have to officially declare bankruptcy. The store's accounting ledger glared at Sydney from the cash wrap as if the book itself blamed her for its sad state of red.

She tapped on her teeth with a pen, trying to focus on a sparkly name for the Love Letters and Eggnog reading, but Sam's face kept breaking into her thoughts. Despite every-thing else weighing heavy on her mind, she couldn't forget him.

The night before had been a relationship unicorn; a ter-rifyingly bare-naked moment where she laid a deep insecu-rity at his feet and he, in turn, looked at her with even more warmth and dedication.

She'd always viewed sex as a tool. When it was purely for her own pleasure, it typically happened with a stranger or a casual date. When she needed something from a man, whether it was Connor's stress levels to subside or simply a body next to her in bed, she'd go through the motions and usually manage to achieve orgasm through various meth-ods of manipulation. Sex was perfunctory. A performance much like an actor hamming it up in the seventh of eight shows a week. Until Sam.

When they'd had sex in the lean-to, it was born of pure heat. She'd always been physically attracted to him, but in the months since they'd met, he'd crawled under her skin, wormed his way into the recesses of her brain, and burrowed into her chest. She wanted him with a desire deeper than her body.

It scared her. If sex wasn't just an act, and it wasn't a method of getting what she wanted, then what was it? Covered in layers of clothing and in front of a fire outdoors, being with Sam was animalistic. Splayed open on his couch while his eyes burned with emotions she'd never seen before, it was a different game entirely. A game that put her heart on the line.

Yyou're a stupid bitch, Debbie. If you can't see that your husband is BLEEPing someone else, then you're BLEEPing BLEEP."

Sydney shoveled another buttery cracker topped with peanut butter into her mouth, eyes and brain transfixed on the debauchery in front of her. As the trashy TV show went to commercial, she changed the channel to the Thursday Night Football game. Neither team was of much interest to her, but the football season was so short, she watched whenever she could.

A time-out on the field prompted a commercial break, and she hurried to refill her snack plate before the game started up again. Between the cold weather, the reduced drinking, and the alone time, snacking had become her favorite hobby. As she reached for the last sleeve of Ritz, she promised herself she'd start working out again soon.

The knock was so timid and soft she almost didn't hear it. She froze, her hand resting on the faucet, waiting to hear it again. *Rap rap rap.* This time louder. More certain.

The mountain town isolation still unnerved her a bit, and she peered past the curtain on the front door before she reached for the knob. As Sam's ruddy-cheeked face came into view, her shoulders slid down her back.

"Well, hello," she said, unable to contain her grin as she opened the door. He matched it tooth for tooth.

"Hello."

"Can I help you?"

He tilted his head as if to say, *Really?*

"Jehovah's Witness?"

"No," he said flatly.

"Girl Scouts? You seem a little old."

"Sydney."

"Magazine subscriptions? I already get *Teen People* and *Sports Illustrated*."

"Can you let me in, please? It's six degrees out here."

"Mm, I don't know. I'm still new around here, and I'm not entirely comfortable allowing you into my home when I'm here all by myself."

He lifted a single eyebrow, his intentions painted clear across his face.

"Oh," she said, her skin prickling with anticipation. "That's why you're here, huh?"

"Maybe I had a beer with Matt, and he told me he had to get home because Jorie was waiting for him at his house. Then he said some gross shit I won't repeat, but I'll say it led me to believe she'd be there all night."

She pressed her lips together, excitement turning her vision spotty. The blood had already rushed south, and pressure built between her legs. So this was how it was going to go. No illicit texts, no plans to meet up in seedy motels. Just pure, unadulterated desire whenever they were allowed. He wanted her in the same desperate way she wanted him, and he'd come here tonight on a whim to pursue that need. *Hey. Heard you'd be alone.*

"So," he said, lowering his voice and his chin. "Can I come in?"

Before she said, *Yes, please, God, come in and then come in and come in again,* she drank him all in. His eyes shimmered, glassy and bright in the cold, and his hands were shoved deep into his coat pockets. He swayed a little back and forth, and the subtle movement belied the bravado in his voice.

She didn't trust her voice to hide her desire, so she pulled the door open further and waved him in. His skin smelled of icy air and motor oil. The spicy scent of balsam wafted in after him, combining to create the world's most perfect fragrance.

Her eyes lingered on his beautifully bearded face as he peeled off his coat. When he turned, she breathlessly awaited his lips on hers, but instead, his eyes drifted over her shoulder to the TV in the living room. "Are you watching the game?"

"Yeah," she said. "Why?"

He hurried past her into the living room. "I hadn't really planned to come over here and watch TV, but since you've got this on . . ."

She huffed and followed him to the couch, settling in and leaving a respectable space between them. Being alone with him was like touching her finger to an electrical wire.

"Did I just cock-block myself?" she said.

He leaned into the couch, resting his elbow on the back and his head in his hand. He watched her. The intense scrutiny left her feeling exposed, despite the heavy sweats covering her body.

"I feel like a teenager," she said suddenly.

His lips turned up at the corners. Dear God, how did he get so attractive? His hair was mussed, his T-shirt rumpled, and his old jeans had a grease stain at the knee. But with all his attention focused on her and the power in his stare melting her rational mind, she wanted to lick him head to toe.

"Why?"

"I don't know." A laugh tickled her words. "You make me feel inexperienced somehow. Like I don't know what I'm doing."

He ran his hand over his mouth, oozing confidence.

Why were they still sitting there fully clothed? She wanted everything of his touching everything of hers.

"The Sydney I met back in October knew exactly what she was doing," he said.

She remembered acting like a drunken idiot in front of him at Taylor's, sure her cleavage and pouty lips would melt him like butter. Amazing how much could change in two months.

"That Sydney doesn't live here anymore," she said.

"I think you need to trust yourself a little bit more. Finding out who you are doesn't come from forcing one thing after another. Don't fight the current, Sydney Walsh."

Her name on his tongue was heaven. If she didn't move, she'd explode. Her skin would erupt into flames and she'd die on this couch. Sydney Walsh. Daughter, friend, sickeningly horny for Sam Kirkland.

"I know we'd talked about doing a clothed activity together," she said, "but I'm ready to abandon the non-naked hang. Unless my embarrassingly unsexy outfit killed your appetite?"

He flashed a smile. "I've never seen you in anything unsexy. Ever."

"Oh, please," she laughed. "My wardrobe up here is so bad. Layers upon layers, sweatshirts upon sweatshirts."

He tilted his head and raised one eyebrow. "White T-shirts. Tight jeans." He licked his lower lip and added, "Pink lace bras."

As if a switch flipped, all the hairs on her body stood on end. The look in his eye was undeniable. Pure hunger. His gaze dropped to her chest.

"See, the thing about the cold weather up here," he said, "is that you might be all layered up, but discovering whatever is underneath feels like finding treasure."

He inched closer to her, combing the hair away from her face. His fingers lingered on the curve of her jaw and then traced down her neck, leaving a trail of sparks in their wake.

"I have so much to learn from you," she said, a smile playing on her lips. "Tell me more, Mountain Man."

He closed the last inch of space between them and covered her mouth with his, sliding his fingers along the nape of her neck and pulling her close. She sunk into the kiss, reveling in the taste of him. Sweetness and salty skin. She traced her tongue lightly along his and curled her fingers around his thigh.

He pulled away enough to speak, but not so far that his lips were fully removed from hers. "You might be more of a visual learner."

She led him into her bedroom and closed the door, submerging them in a pool of darkness. He stood in the center of the room, the green glow of her alarm clock lighting him from behind.

Anticipation rippled through her, and before she stepped toward him, she willed herself to relax. *Get out of your own head. He's beautiful. And he likes you. Enjoy him.*

"Syd, last time—"

"No," she said. "Last time was just me being stupid. You don't care if I'm five pounds heavier now than I was in October. I'm not some insecure idiot who weighs herself every day and skips the bread on the turkey club, you know?"

Her eyes adjusted to the darkness, and his teeth gleamed as his lips pulled into a smile. "You're right, I don't care. But that's not what I was gonna say."

She swallowed. "Oh."

He stepped slowly toward her and placed his hands on her hip bones, working his thumbs underneath the elastic waist of her sweatpants and tracing the edge of her thong.

"I want to just enjoy you. And make you feel good. Okay?"

The breath rushed out of her lungs. *Oh, is that all?* "Okay."

"Whatever you like, let's do it. Whatever you don't like, we're not doing it."

"Good, 'cause what I'd like is to go back in the living room and watch the game."

His grin grew wider, and his thumbs sunk lower. "Non-naked hang time is officially over."

Tired of the layers of clothing between them, she yanked off her sweatshirt in one swift movement and revealed a thin white tank top underneath. He released a strangled exhale as his eyes lit on her chest.

She grabbed the edges of his T-shirt and pushed the fabric up and over his flat abs, past his smooth chest, and over his head. The curves of his torso were too much to ignore, and she leaned forward to trace his collarbone, the graphic flower tattoo, and his stomach with her tongue. With every inch of delicious skin, her senses heightened.

He ran a hand through her hair as she rested on her knees and loosened his belt buckle, popping the button on his jeans once she had access.

"Hey," he said, his voice raspy. "Only what you want to do."

"Mm, this I'm sure about."

She held his gaze for a lingering moment before tugging at his zipper and pulling his jeans past his knees. His muscular thighs flexed and lengthened, no doubt waiting for her touch, and she traced her fingernails up through the smattering of hair on his legs toward the promised land.

His strangled breaths came in regular intervals as she ran her fingers under the legs of his boxer briefs, momentarily brushing his taint. He shuddered and ran a trembling hand through her hair.

Some aspects of her previous sex life she was happy to forget. This wasn't one of them. She wanted to make him feel good, too, and bring him to the edge of explosive pleasure. As she dragged his boxer briefs past his hips and the firm, rounded curve of his ass, he released a muffled moan. Exactly what she'd hoped for.

His erection bobbed in front of her, begging to be

touched, and she wrapped one hand around the base, anticipation at the taste of him urging her onward. She looked up into his eyes one last time before slipping the soft tip over her lips and licking the head, gently at first.

She dragged her lips from the base to the tip, letting her tongue touch every half inch as he moaned. With a single expletive from his lips, she dipped the length of his erection into her mouth, wrapping him in velvety warmth.

"Holy shit," he muttered. "Go slow. Please, go slow."

She obliged, slowing her rhythm to a lazy, back and forth motion that still left him twitching against her. She trailed the fingertips of her other hand down the back of his thigh until he slowly pulled away.

"What's wrong?" she asked, gazing up at him. Had she accidentally dragged him with her teeth?

"Nothing," he said. "But if you don't stop, I'm gonna come, and that's not how I want this to end."

She stood to meet him, and he dropped his chin, resting his mouth on hers. He sucked on her bottom lip as his hands encircled her waist, fingers dropping to rest on top of her ass. With his erection pressing into her belly, he drew her hips into him and circled her tongue with his.

He ran his hands under her tank top and yanked it over her head, only breaking the kiss to let the fabric pass between them and to stare unabashedly at her chest.

"God, you're beautiful," he whispered. Her stomach caved at the compliment, not entirely believing it. There was enough conviction in his voice, however, enough fire in his eyes, to push her toward it.

He sank down to his knees, peppering kisses across her chest and the chasm between her breasts. When he arrived at her sweatpants, he unknotted the tie and slipped them down her legs.

He lifted his face to hers and licked his lower lip as every bit of electricity in the universe shot into her chest. Every time a man had gotten close to her sex she'd clammed up and either faked it or pushed him away. Now Sam hovered over it, tracing his fingers along the front of her thong while never losing her gaze, and she wanted his mouth on her more than anything.

"Can I take this off?" he asked. Her clit beat like a drum under the damp fabric of her white cotton thong. Should she let him try? *Get out of your head and go with it, you idiot. Look at his face.*

"Yes," she whispered.

He hooked his hands in the lacy straps and tugged, the middle of the thong catching where she was already soaked. All she wanted was him. For now, and for forever. If they could do this for the rest of her life, she'd die without another want in the world.

He tossed her thong aside and looked up at her again with those deep chocolate pools nestled under thick, dark eyebrows. Nerves fluttered in her belly as she waited for his mouth to find her clit, waited for the slick lash of his tongue against her heat.

Instead, his fingers floated up the outer edges of her thighs as he rose to meet her and kissed her gently. Her breasts filled his calloused palms as if fitting back into the mold they'd been crafted in. The nerves subsided. Maybe he'd sensed her fear and backed off.

"How do you feel?" he asked, lazily tracing his thumb over her nipple. The pink bud tightened further, and she nearly pulled back, her flesh as sensitive as it had ever been.

"Insanely good," she said, burying her face in his neck. "God, you smell incredible. I could bite you."

"Do it."

She pulled back to look at him and smiled at the joke.

"I'm not kidding," he said, although a grin tugged at one corner of his full mouth. "Do it."

"Crazy boy."

With deep-set eyes, he lowered his face to her breast and closed his teeth around her nipple, tugging and sucking until a choked moan floated past her lips. He tightened his bite as the pain and pleasure became indistinguishable, and suddenly an orgasm built deep within her.

"Holy shit," she gasped, placing a hand on his solid pec. He pulled away with a pleased grin on his lips and brushed her hair over her shoulder.

"I guess she likes that."

Who was this man? His only concern was pleasing her. She'd never met anyone like him. The yearning grew deeper.

She clasped her fingers behind his neck, savoring the sensation of his thick, soft hair between her knuckles. If this was somehow wrong, she didn't care. His eyes landed squarely on hers and pulled another soft moan from her lips.

"Do you have a condom?" he asked.

Her face collapsed. "Ugh. No, I don't. I definitely didn't pack any when I left New York, and it's not the type of thing I can pop into Pine Ridge Drugs for."

He brushed his lips across hers and gripped her hips, the length of his cock teasing her again. Whether they had a condom or not, she couldn't stop now. The magnetic pull between them was out of her control.

"Is it weird to rifle through Jorie's stuff in case she has one?" she asked, trailing a hand down his taut chest and resting at his hip bone. The curve of his hip careened into the dip of his pelvis, and every muscle stood out in brilliant, beautiful contrast. She'd never even seen him work out. But this kind of body was earned.

"Is it weird," he countered, "to already know where she keeps them?"

Her head jerked backward. If he was about to tell her he'd slept with Jorie, she didn't know if she could take it.

"It'll kill this insanely sexy mood we've got going here if I tell you the whole story," he said, "but I walked in on Matt and Jorie once doing it in the living room." He blinked the repulsion back and shook his head. "Needless to say,

they had a little box open on the floor next to them over-
flowing with condoms, and I've seen that box under her
bathroom sink."

"Oh yeah, the little wooden box? With the gold clasp?"

"That's the one."

She pressed her lips against him for good measure before scurrying out of the guest room and across the hall to
Jorie's bathroom. The cabin only had one small bathroom,
and Jorie was gracious enough to share it with her new
houseguest. The last thing Sydney wanted was to betray
Jorie in any way, but at the moment, she had one thing on
her mind.

She dug beneath the bathroom counter and came up
with the little wooden box. She popped the clasp and, sure
enough, tucked inside were enough condoms to last through
a very cold, long winter. She plucked one from the masses
and almost closed the box before she thought better and
grabbed two more.

When she returned to the darkened bedroom, Sam was
reclined on her bed, staring up at the ceiling with his hands
behind his head. His long, smooth erection rested on his flat
stomach, beckoning her like a call to serve.

"Grabbed a couple," she said, feeling once again like an
awkward teenager. "Just in case."

His eyes lit up. "Very, very smart thinking."

She placed the gold foil condom packets on the nightstand and took in a shaky breath. There was nothing to be
anxious about, no hurdles to jump. His gaze was honest and
true. And yet the nerves still churned.

"Come here," he said, pushing himself toward the wall
to give her maximum space next to him. "It's been a minute
since I shared a twin bed, but it's kind of cozy, right?"

She kneeled on the bed, and he raised a hand to her
stomach, letting his cool fingers slide across the skin and
trail over the space between her hip bones. He laid his palm
flat and ran his thumb across her belly button.

"You have the softest skin," he said. His dreamy eyes met hers, and all the tension relaxed out of her once more. Whatever he did, whatever spell of compliments and kindness he put on her, it worked.

She leaned forward, holding his scruffy cheek as she kissed his lips. His hand, still resting on her stomach, began its slow journey south until his index finger brushed the folds of her sex. A yelp escaped her lips, and his brow furrowed.

"That hurt?" he asked.

"No." She exhaled. *RE. LAX*. Maybe the next time she saw him she'd take a tranquilizer in advance. "It didn't hurt at all. I'm just so sensitive."

"I know." His face melted into a grin again. "I fucking love it."

He moved over farther, toward the wall, inviting her to rest on the bed. He made all the right moves, backed off whenever she needed. It was more foreign to her than if he'd danced around like a monkey and expected her to orgasm from that.

"Come here," he said. Reclined on the bed, he trailed his fingers lightly across her breasts, down her stomach, and farther down to where her thighs were clenched. They opened for him as if by command.

"Is that okay?" he asked, his breath hot on her ear. She exhaled a positive response, not sure what she said or if it mattered.

The pads of his fingers slicked over her wetness and dipped just past her lips. The touch was brief but electric, and when he slid back again, she opened farther for him. On the third pass, she ached for more contact.

"Look at me," he urged, mumbling directly into her ear again.

Her eyelids cracked, and there he was, that beautiful face hovering over hers. All the emotion and desire and want she'd always been so scared of radiated from that face.

As he brushed her lips with his, his fingers slipped inside
her.

"Oh God," she breathed.

"Good? Or not good?"

"So unbelievably good." Two long fingers slid easily
past her entrance, and she bucked her hips against his wrist,
careful to avoid her clit. If he brushed it, even gently, she
might shatter all over him, and she wasn't ready yet.

He removed his fingers, and as soon as they were gone,
she missed them with a hollow ache. His thumb pressed
gently against her sex, rocking back and forth in a concentrated effort that forced her eyes closed again.

"Good?"

"God yes," she groaned. "But I'm afraid I'm gonna come."

"Afraid?" His lips dropped to her ear, and he took her
earlobe into his mouth, sucking in perfect rhythm with the
two fingers that had slipped back inside her. "Go ahead and
come, baby. I'll do it again. And next time it'll be totally
different."

With each word from his lips, the pressure built. The
heat from his breath and the rough motion of his wrist and
the occasional brush of his thumb over her impossibly sensitive flesh made her head spin.

"No," she said, her breath ragged. "I don't want to come
like this. I want to come with you inside me."

He dragged his fingers out of her and repositioned himself so instead of lying next to her, he hovered over her. His
weight balanced on the tips of his toes and the palms of his
hands in an erotic plank that dragged the tip of his cock
across her hips.

She placed a hand on either side of his powerful hips and
pulled him down to lay on top of her, his weight pressing
her into the mattress and consuming her. She drowned in
him, and she'd never been happier to lose herself.

"I have never wanted someone so much," she said,
breathing the words into his ear as he cocooned against her.

He lifted his head and ran a thumb across her eyebrow, down her cheekbone, and over her lips. She tasted herself on his hand and opened her mouth to welcome his thumb.

She closed her lips over his thumb and sucked, gently rolling her tongue over the appendage. His eyes rolled back just before the lids closed behind them, and when she moaned against his hand, his hips dug into hers.

"Please," she begged. "I need you inside me."

He slapped at the nightstand, desperately grasping for a condom, and when he found one, she plucked it from his hand.

"Lift up," she said. The confused brows relaxed on his face as he realized what she meant and pressed back into the plank, each lean, curved muscle in his biceps popping out in stark relief. She tore open the foil packet and rolled the condom on, taking extra time to squeeze gently as she smoothed out the slick latex.

He used the tip of his cock to press down on her clit, subtly gyrating his hips until her eyes closed and she gasped. "Okay, okay," she breathed. "God, please do it already. I'm dying here."

With one firm press at her entrance, Sam slid inside Sydney, filling her up completely. "Jesus Christ," he whispered. His hips moved against her, slowly at first and gaining momentum as he went.

He rested his weight on his forearms, framing her face between them. The intense friction of his perfectly proportioned cock sliding in and out of her combined with the rolling rhythm of his pelvis brought her senses to epic heights.

She lifted her knees to straddle his waist, and he dove deeper still. Sweat collected on her lip, and before she could do something about it, his tongue lashed out and lapped it up. Her eyes flew open to find his flushed, creased face staring directly into hers. There was nothing precious about this moment. Whatever sweetness came before, and whatever would come after, didn't belong in the primal emotions coursing through them now.

Her gaze traveled down his chest to the abs rippling as he held his body above hers. But she wanted to feel him, really feel him.

"Lay on me," she said through labored breaths. "All your weight."

"I'll hurt you," he said, never breaking stride.

"You will not. Please."

With great care he lowered his body until they fused into one, her breasts crushed against his tattooed chest, and his face tucked into her neck. His bristly beard sent a thousand shocks over her damp skin.

This time it was her turn to grind against him. With all the pressure centered squarely on her most sensitive bit, the orgasm mounted. Pressure built like a tsunami and rose above her, threatening to crash at any second.

"God, baby, I'm gonna come soon," he said. The whisper of breath on her ear and one last thrust against him, and she crashed. She came hard and fast, a strangled scream pressed into his shoulder as she went.

"Oh my God," she gushed.

He trailed his cheek against hers and looked into her face, his brow still creased. He bit down on his lip and rocked his hips against her, slow but purposeful.

"Your turn."

His lips turned up at the corners and he ran a hand over her hair, tugging a few errant strands out of her eyes. He placed his mouth on hers, and she closed her teeth around his lower lip in a nod to their earlier exploits.

"You're so tight," he said.

His lips still brushed against hers as the lines in his face grew deeper. She clenched her sex, gripping him from within, and a single cry escaped his perfectly curved lips.

"Fuck." His teeth clenched as he seized up inside her, and after the last thrust, he exhaled into her hair and completely collapsed. His weight pressing her into the mattress provided the ultimate comfort.

For a minute, he didn't move. She trailed her lips across the freckles at his shoulder, ran her hands through the thick hair at the nape of his neck. He twitched and another trickle of pleasure wove its way up into her chest. She felt lit up from the inside out, as if she'd swallowed Christmas lights and someone had just plugged them in.

"That's it," he said, his voice muffled by the pillow. He turned his head slowly and nuzzled into her neck. "You killed me. I'm done."

"No way," she said, grinning. The curve of his back looked like a sand dune in a dark desert. "I'm going to need you to do that to me again later, please."

His cock twitched inside her again, and she burrowed further into his chest. "I guess he's up for it."

He lifted himself up and rolled onto his side, resting his head in his hand to look down at her. He traced her collarbone with shaky fingers and licked his lip as his gaze followed suit.

I'm so screwed. The deep sadness hit her almost as hard as the orgasm. Her feelings for him were on a slippery slope toward love. He was too perfect, too good for her, too good in general. He was everything Connor didn't have the heart to be.

"Okay, real talk," she said.

"Uh-oh."

"Where did you get this body? Are you a mechanic by day and Abercrombie model by night?" She ran a hand over his washboard abs as he laughed.

"I work out," he said. "But not like a maniac. I guess I just have good genetics."

Her heart rate finally slowed to a normal pace, and sleepiness set in. She knew it was too much to ask that he spend the night, but thinking about him climbing out of this bed made her heart hurt.

"Real talk," he said.

"Uh-oh."

A smile tugged at his lips as his fingers traced her collarbone and shoulders. "What was your favorite part?"

"You want a review? Like Yelp?"

His face broke into a laugh. "Yes, please. And at the end, please answer a series of multiple choice questions. Is this venue good for children? Is smoking allowed?"

"In all honesty," she said, rolling onto her side to be even closer to him, her lips pressing against his chin before she continued, "I wanted you to go down on me. Like, really wanted it."

His gaze deepened. "It's all up to you. Short of gerbils and extreme BDSM, I'll try whatever you want me to try. I love exploring you, having you tell me what you like. It's so hot."

"No gerbils?" she growled. "Get out of my house."

"I told you," he said. "I want to make you feel good. If you think me going down on you is going to feel good, then let's try it. If we try it and you hate it, we stop. It's as easy as that."

"But," she said, tiptoeing toward the truth, "what if I don't like it and it hurts your feelings?"

"Sydney," he groaned, burying his face in the pillow with flourish. When he looked back up at her, he shook his head. "You will not hurt my feelings. I promise."

It wasn't the only insecurity rattling around in her mind. The scene from earlier in the shop resurfaced, Liv speaking to Jay in dulcet tones. *She's trying.* She was trying. And yet here Sydney was, lying naked next to the man who'd help her get her son back.

"Are you sure you don't want to be with Liv?"

The words darted out of her mouth like a bird escaping a cage. The shock on his face matched her shock at having said them.

"No," he said. "I thought we talked about this."

"We did," she said. Shame burned hot on her cheeks. The question had been on her mind since that morning, but when Sam walked into the house unexpectedly, all rational thought fell out of her head and lust took over. But now, in the sober postcoital moments, the old fear wove its way back to her psyche.

"You don't believe me?" he said. He leaned back toward the wall, putting another inch of space between them. She refused the distance and curled her shoulders toward him.

"It's not that I think you're lying," she said. "But what if she does everything she says she will? What if she stays sober, proves she can be an amazing mother, and you realize you can find it in you to give her another shot? What if she's able to be sober-nurse-Liv all the time?"

He swallowed, his face relaxing. He traced the line of her frown with a rough-tipped finger. "Neither of us wants that. I sincerely hope, for Jay's sake, that Liv does everything she says she's going to. In fact, I'm counting on it. That optimism is why I agreed to help her in the first place. But I'm trying to focus more on my future than the past these days."

Her fingers trembled and curled into a timid fist. "Oh yeah?"

"Yeah," he whispered. "I like the idea of exploring my feelings for you."

Despite the fact that his condom-clad half erection brushed against her hip and his fingers traced lazily across her naked breasts, to hear him say he had feelings for her sent dazzling sparks through her limbs.

"You have feelings for me?" she teased.

He raised one eyebrow and one corner of his mouth. "If that wasn't perfectly clear, then I'm doing something wrong." He ran a lazy hand over his mussed hair. "Are you really okay with the way this is going? Because I tried to keep my distance, but once I found out you felt the way I felt, all my self-control kind of evaporated. I just don't want to put you in a bad spot."

"I wish it didn't have to be a secret. But I understand how it might upset things with Liv if we were open about it."

"We could . . ." He swallowed. "Wait. Wait until her custody stuff is over."

Sydney shook her head. "I feel better with you than I have in a long time. If you're in, I'm in."

On an exhale, he kissed her again. She couldn't quiet her thoughts. *Liv doesn't deserve your kindness.* When he pulled away, she consciously smoothed her brow.

"The game's probably still on," he said.

"Wow, sex and a football game. You're a lucky man."

He tilted his head toward hers and revealed his perfect white teeth. "Sorry, is this not your ideal night, also? Or was that somebody else at Utz's screaming about Derek Tahoe's terrible arm?"

"He'll never be a franchise quarterback. The Giants need to accept it."

He shook his head slowly, and the warmth pouring from his eyes made her squirm. It was all too good to be true. The other shoe would surely drop. Eventually.

chapter **twenty**

Sam took a step back and cocked his head. He crossed his arms over his chest. *Ugh*. It looked stupid. He wasn't good at this kind of stuff. Hand him a tree, and he could make you an armoire. Hand him a mess of parts, and he'd build you an engine. Hand him candles and decorative fabric, and he'd make you a rat's nest.

"I'm sorry," he said as Karen sidled up next to him, grimacing at his creation.

"Don't sweat it, scout," she said. "I'll fix it. Maybe decorating isn't your forte. Why don't you go across the way and see if Mrs. McDonagh needs help carrying over the pastries?"

"I was over there, and she told me to scram."

Karen giggled. "Sounds like your work here is done. Why don't you grab a beer with the other fellas over at Utz's and we'll take over?"

He looked around the shop and gnawed at his lip. He hated feeling helpless. But on this, the night of Sydney's

first book-club meeting, he wanted to provide any scrap of
assistance he could. Anything to make the night go more
smoothly for her.

The past week had been a dreamy blur of tangled limbs
and whispered conversations and screaming orgasms. She
was in his blood like heroin, and when they weren't together, he replayed scenes in his mind of the last time he'd
seen her.

Beyond the crushing sexual chemistry, he loved spending time with her. He couldn't decide which he enjoyed
more, laughing with her on the couch or stroking her in
bed. What he did know was that the thought of her leaving
town at the hands of a failed shop pressed on his chest like
a heart attack. He'd seen the past-due notices in the office,
heard the steely-voiced messages on the shop answering
machine. They were closer than ever to folding.

"Get out of here, will you?" Sydney said. "You're ruining everything."

She breezed past him, leaving him trembling in a wake
of her perfume. After torching several trays of cookies earlier with Jorie, she also smelled like burnt sugar. Even the
scent of failed baked goods on her skin tore him up inside.

"Okay, I'm officially bowing out," he said. "Seems embarrassingly sexist, though, to exile the men to a bar."

"It's all part of the draw," Karen reminded him. "It's a
boys' book club without the books while the wives spend
their evening here. Although if you fellas wanted to incor-
porate some reading into your beer drinking, we'd be happy
to supply the material."

"If I ever meet a man in this town who's read something
other than the *Pine Ridge Gazette*, I'll suggest it."

He took one last look at Sydney flitting around the shop,
making sure everything was perfect. Tonight she wore a
red plaid shirt unbuttoned to dangerous depths with multiple gold necklaces and tight black jeans. City Sydney and
Mountain Sydney combined. She rearranged candles on the

side table near the couch, and he felt privileged to know what she looked like underneath those clothes.

"All right, I'm out," he said.

She stood up and flashed him a smile. Her eyes darted over to the cash register, where Karen squinted over a to-do list, and in the moment when no one was watching, Sydney pressed a kiss to her fingers and waved it at him. *If she were a superhero, that would be her power. Decimating men's hearts with a press of her lips.*

With his head cloudy and his cock stirring, he slipped into his coat and headed across the street to Utz's. Another of Sydney's brilliant ideas—which popped into her head as they cuddled after a quickie in his garage office on Tuesday night—was to offer book-club drink specials at Utz's for anyone who brought his wife, girlfriend, or family member to the Loving Book Club.

He joined the table of beer drinkers in the back of the bar, flipping a chair around to straddle before leaning on his forearms.

"This is bullshit, right?" he said. "Relegated to the bar like it's 1950?"

"You'd rather be drinking wine and giggling over Fabio?" Matt said, guzzling from a pint.

"Wow, it really is 1950," Edith O'Hare's daughter said, taking a swig from her own pint. "Romance novels are nothing like that anymore. In fact, you should read one. You'd probably like it."

Sam grinned. He knew the guys at this table had no idea what romance was about. When he'd popped in on Sydney at home a couple of days ago, she'd been engrossed in a book about a professional baseball player and his high school sweetheart. She'd continued reading the chapter out loud. He made it through three pages of explicit words falling off her lips before he plucked the book from her hands and began hazily peeling off her clothes.

"Hell no," Matt said with a grimace. "I'd never read one. Plus, who's got time for books? It's almost playoff season."

Edith's daughter stifled a laugh and caught Sam's eye. They both raised their eyebrows at the same time. *Who's got time to read?* Who indeed.

Sam noticed a few empty pints at the table and went to the bar to order a round. "Hank. Give me a book-club special, please." After a moment's pause, he reconsidered. "Wait. Is the book-club special a strawberry mojito or something?"

"Boy, are you daft?" Hank said, laughing. "You remember who set all this up, right? Sydney ordered up a half keg of Saranac's Moonshadow Black IPA. Five bucks a pint while it lasts."

His body tingled as if he'd slid into a warm pool. Of course she'd ordered a limited edition IPA from a local brewery. It would get people in the door, and at that price, she'd drain the keg in no time. People would stay and drink after it had kicked, giving the bar great business in the slow season and giving spouses another reason to encourage their partners back to the next book-club meeting. Jesus, the girl was smart.

He carried three pints over to the table and set them in the center, snagging one for himself before two hands snatched out to claim the others.

"None for me?" Jared said as he shook snowflakes off his coat and settled down at the table between Greg and Matt. Greg begrudgingly handed over his full pint to Jared and waved at Hank for another.

"Just passed by the bookshop. Didn't see too many people." Jared took a long drink of the beer. "Shit, this is some potent stuff. Why didn't she do a Bud Light special?"

"'Cause she has taste," Sam said.

"Who all is over there?" Greg asked.

"Nobody you can bang," Jared joked, glancing around

the table to see who found him funny. No one laughed. He clapped Greg on the shoulder. "Sorry, man. Just kidding around."

"So it's a small turnout? The book club?" Sam asked, careful to hide his intense curiosity. Sydney needed this. He needed this.

Jared shrugged. "From what I could see walking by."

Sam swallowed a long pull of beer. The beer Sydney had selected. *God, please let this work.*

The telephone rang shrilly on the wall, and Hank snagged the receiver as Greg handed over another twenty. They'd officially kicked the half keg.

"Yeah?" Hank asked. His beady eyes darted over to Sam. "Yeah, he's here."

Worry lines creased Hank's brow, and Sam's neck prickled. A wave of dread crept over his legs like a slow-rising tide. Something was wrong. *Please be a tow. Please be a tow.*

"Sure thing, I'll send him over." Hank replaced the receiver and scanned the group before hitching up his pants and wiping his mouth. "Sam, you've been summoned."

"What's going on?" Matt asked.

Hank hitched his pants again, wiped his mouth. His eyes darted around the table, meeting the gazes of the town residents. "Eh, I think you better head over there and see for yourself. Seems Liv needs a hand."

The drinking. He knew it. He should've seen it coming. What was one year sober? From everything he'd read on alcoholism, relapses were all but guaranteed. He should've kept a closer eye on her, should've checked in more.

"Liv's drinking again?" Matt said, his voice laced with anger.

Sam shook his head. "I don't know."

He pushed back from the table and stalked out of the bar, neglecting the jacket hanging on the back of his chair. With the heat radiating outward from him, he wouldn't need it.

Eerie quiet met him at the Loving Page, save for the tinny Christmas music playing from a little speaker in the back. Matching lined faces that looked a lot like Hank's greeted him as he approached the modest group. He recognized each of the six faces, and another wave of disappointment washed over him as he realized Sydney hadn't gotten the turnout she needed.

"She's in the back with Sydney," Jorie said. She pressed her lips together and stared with wide eyes. "I don't even know where she got the booze, Sam. She seemed fine when she showed up."

"She brought it with her," Karen said, crossing her arms over her chest. "After she tossed her cookies in her coat, I noticed a flask in the front pocket."

"She threw up in her coat?" His throat turned to sandpaper.

"I think she was trying not to puke on the couch." Jorie tucked the paperback she'd been holding between the couch cushions and stood to meet Sam outside the closed office door. Something like sadness framed her eyes as she ran a hand across her brow.

"I'm so tired of this," Jorie said. "After everything we've done for her. Everything *you've* done for her. We believed in her. I really thought she could do it this time."

Sam forced a breath in and out of his lungs. He couldn't have this conversation now. He had to see for himself the mess Liv had created.

He pushed open the office door to find Liv hunched over a blue plastic pail, her white fingers clutching the sides for dear life. The putrid smell in the tiny space made him gag.

Sydney crouched next to Liv, her hand making gentle

circles on Liv's frail back. A pulpy, wine-colored splotch stained the front of Sydney's red plaid shirt.

"She'll be all right," Sydney said, her voice just above a whisper. "She's conscious, so that's something, I guess."

"Why is she back here?" he said. "The smell . . ."

"I know." She shook her head, her face blank and pale. "I didn't want her to embarrass herself in front of the other women. I haven't had the money to fix the toilet in the bathroom, so . . ."

Sam swallowed, his patience worn as thin as spring ice. "I can't take this anymore." His voice cracked.

"I know." Her eyes drew him in, held him. She physically comforted Liv, but her support surrounded him like a blanket. They couldn't say much, but he knew how she felt.

"Sammy." Liv's wobbly voice gurgled. "I'm so sorry."

He raked his hands through his hair and down his face. She was his responsibility now. And in order to get her out of the shop, he'd have to carry her past some of the biggest gossipmongers in town.

"Is she still throwing up?" he said.

"She's stopped for a minute."

Sam bent down and hooked Liv's bony arm around his neck, lifting her waif-thin body up to something resembling standing. She looked up at him through bleary eyes, a smear of purple vomit on her left cheek.

"I'm sorry," she said. "The social worker showed up today, Sam. I wasn't ready for her. I missed a meeting last week, and I don't know what's gonna happen now."

Her sour breath wafted toward him like a toxic wave. For the first time in years, he was overcome with the urge to set her down and leave her there. She'd made her decisions. Let her pay the consequences.

Instead, he lifted her through the office door, and as a hush fell over the book club, he pressed his lips together and dragged her past the reading nook. Fury filled his gut, spilled past his chest, and burned his throat. She ruined everything: her kid's life, Sam's efforts, and now the place Sydney had worked so hard to build. It was inexcusable.

As he carried her, toes dragging along the floor, he heard someone behind him whisper, "She doesn't deserve him." Whether they meant him or Jay, he had to agree.

The icy snow pelted his windshield and coated the roads. The treacherous conditions made the evening news, and he knew he shouldn't be out driving, but he couldn't stay cooped up for one more minute. If he'd stayed at his house, he'd have ended up tossing all her shit into the lake. Or worse.

He didn't know if his anger was warranted, but it bubbled up in him all the same. Yes, Liv had tried. She'd tried with everything in her. But it didn't hurt any less to know she'd failed and that he had a part in it.

He careened into downtown, and his truck slipped a bit as he pulled into a parking space at the curb in front of the Loving Page. The streets were empty. The women had all gone home, and even Utz's was locked up for the night. The desolation soothed him.

Inside the Loving Page, little red lamps and a few candles still burned, and as he neared the door, Sydney came into view. She wasn't alone.

He knocked on the shop door after trying the locked handle, and Jorie looked up, her brow twisted. She walked to the front and let him in.

"How is she?" she asked.

"Drunk." He shrugged. "I dropped her at her sister's."

"Wow, really? I thought they weren't speaking."

"Let her family take care of her for a while," he said. "I told her sister I'm done. Apparently she's still got a shot, but it's gonna be tough. I just can't do it anymore." The words caught in Sam's throat, and he pinched the bridge of his nose to fight back tears. They stung of failure.

"Sammy," Jorie said gently. She placed a soft hand on the arm of his jacket and squeezed. "You did everything you could. We all did. And now we're all done."

He coughed through the threatening tears and checked to see if Sydney watched. Her back was to them, but she didn't move.

"I don't want to talk about this right now," he said. "I'm beat. I just wanted to make sure everything was all right here."

Jorie tilted her head, examining his face. She'd known him for a long time, and she'd been on high alert since she caught him at her house under the ruse of borrowing a book. She had allegiance to both her friends, but he hoped she'd want him to be happy.

She shrugged. "Everything's fine here. But I think Liv lost some serious town support tonight. It's hard to overlook a girl's drinking problem when she brings a flask to a book club and then vomits right in front of your face."

"That's not even top on my list of concerns right now." He moved past Jorie and headed straight for Sydney. Secrets be damned. What did he have to lose now anyway? He needed to make sure she was all right.

"Hey," he said, placing a strong hand between her shoulder blades and peering down at her drawn face. "Y'all right?"

"Fine." She pressed her lips together in a forced smile. Her eyes shone up at him, brimming with tears. "I mean, that's that. All my hard work and six people came, and Liv vomited on one of them and spilled a full glass of wine on me. No one bought anything, and now I have to pay to have the couch cleaned."

She shrugged and a single tear slid down her cheek. Watching her cry broke him in half. He cupped her face and brushed the tear away with his thumb. Just as he remembered Jorie still stood in the same room, he heard the front door close. From outside, she sent him a short wave and a sympathetic smile, and then disappeared.

He turned his full attention to Sydney and wrapped his other arm around her hunched back, cocooning her into his chest. "You can be bummed tonight. You're allowed that. But that's not it. This isn't how this ends."

Her face lifted, and a warm breath passed over his lips. Tears clung to her lashes and brought out the most beautiful rosy hue in her cheeks. He planted a kiss on the corner of her lips.

"I can't work at this anymore," she said. "I'm tired."

He released a bitter laugh, and a strand of her mahogany hair lifted in response. "Trust me. That, I get."

A thousand words passed between them, but neither spoke. He wanted to brush off every responsibility he'd ever taken on, every burden he'd ever been saddled with, and disappear with her. Get in a car and go.

"I want to go home now," she said.

"Can I take you?"

She nodded. He wished he could explain how he felt about Liv in this moment, how much he wanted to be free of her. But even the mention of her name would sully the intimacy of their embrace.

They blew out the candles and turned out the lights, leaving the last bit of cleanup for the morning, and headed out into the cold. When they reached Sydney's car, she reached for a scrap of paper tucked under her windshield wiper. The icy rain hadn't yet ruined the ink.

"What's that?" Sam asked. He looked over her shoulder as they read the note together.

Spending the night at Matt's. The whole night. And the whole morning. See you around noon tomorrow. xx Jorie

"Huh," Sydney said, the corner of her mouth lifting as she looked at him. "Do you think she's onto us?"

"And it sounds like she approves?"

He didn't have the motivation or desire to wonder any

longer about who approved or who didn't. In the shitstorm of the evening, Sydney was a safe haven. He took her by the hand, led her toward his pickup, and helped her climb in.

Ten wordless minutes later, he shut off the engine in the driveway of Jorie's house. He peered out the windshield at the darkened structure and breathed deep. The place was finally theirs. No interruptions. No having to hurry home before Liv wondered where he was. They had a free night all to themselves.

"So," she said, "how do you want to play this? Do you want to see how many times we can get it in before dawn, or do you want to see how long we can go in one stretch?"

Surprise bubbled up in him like ginger ale. A smile played on her lips. "You're in a better mood."

"I want to forget about tonight," she said. "And I feel like Jorie's note was a gift for me to do just that." It was exactly what he wanted, too. To forget.

They climbed out of the cab and hurried inside as the icy wind whipped their faces. She tugged off her jacket and hung it on the hook near the door, and it was then that he noticed the red wine stain again.

"So she spilled wine on you, huh?" He ran a timid finger across the purple blotch.

"Yup. During her third retelling of the time you guys did it in a gas station bathroom." She puffed her cheeks out and bulged her eyes.

"That wasn't me." He shuddered at the memory of Liv telling him that exact same story. In her attempt at drumming up a sexy moment they'd shared, she'd inadvertently admitted she'd cheated on him.

"Thank God," she sighed. With a few quick flicks of her fingers, the shirt was unbuttoned and on the ground. A bra he'd never seen before, sheer black lace connected by thin black straps, waited underneath.

"This is weird," he said, tracing the cup of her bra with his thumb.

After the night he'd had, he didn't know what he wanted. The anger still coursed under his skin, reminding him of all the nights his mother received calls that she should pick up his father because he was puking somewhere in public, the nights when Liv never came home, the nights when a sick sense of foreboding settled into his bones and wouldn't quit.

At the same time, the woman who soothed all that anger and frustration stood before him in a slip of lingerie, her velvet-smooth skin begging to be touched. He understood now why sculptors created statues of the female form over and over and over again.

"What's weird?" she asked. She traced her teeth over her bottom lip and drew her eyebrows together as her fingers found his belt and tucked behind it. Her fingernails on his skin were heaven.

"I'm still so angry at Liv. I'm disappointed. But I want you so much at the same time."

"I have a lot of feelings, too," she said, stepping closer into him. She wrapped her cool hands around his neck and lifted her face to his. "But everything disappears a little when I'm with you. So right now, I'd like to just focus on that."

He peeled one of her hands from around his neck and lifted the knuckles to his lips, breathing in the scent of her delicious skin. Before he could make another move, she reached to the left of him and flipped off all the lights. The darkness swallowed them up, and for a moment, neither moved.

"It's too dark," he said, pressing his mouth against the soft spot behind her ear. "I want to see you."

"Just give it a second," she said.

Slowly, his eyes adjusted to the darkness, and the bold-faced moon brightened the space. She was brilliant, as if lit from within, her creamy white skin glowing against the black bra and dark jeans.

"Making love by moonlight," he said, unable to hide his grin.

"Making love, huh?" She pressed her lips together and tugged at a strand of hair as her chest rose and fell, pressing the flesh of her breasts against the bra cups.

"Yeah," he said. He was terrified to overstep his boundaries. But the way he felt about her was unrivaled. He cared about her, wanted to protect her, wanted to lift her up and make sure she had everything she wished for in life. "It's more than sex at this point."

She licked her lips, and the rapid speed of her breathing increased. "I think so, too."

Her long, slender fingers unzipped his coat and pushed it off his shoulders before unbuttoning his flannel shirt. Tonight he wore nothing underneath, and she ran her hands across his biceps and chest as the shirt fell to the ground.

"Let's take our time," she said, her voice a whisper against his shoulder.

He hoped tonight she finally gave in to what she'd been hinting at all week. He didn't know why she held back, but if it had anything to do with protecting his feelings, he'd tell her it didn't matter anymore. He was an open book with her. His heart laid bare.

She peeled off her own jeans, the curve of her hips bending and flexing as she moved. Her black thong matched her black bra down to the tiny bow stitched at the middle of each, and he wanted to taste her in both places.

He bent his knees and wrapped his arms around her waist, lifting her clear off the floor. A laugh rolled out of her throat as she tossed her head back, and her hair trailed behind her. He'd give his soul for that laugh.

He pressed his mouth against the space between her breasts and then worked his tongue past the right cup until he felt the nub of her nipple in his mouth.

She'd said to go slow, but as her legs squeezed around his waist, the warmth and wetness from between her legs dampened his lower abs and made his cock harder than ever. Maybe they could get the first orgasm out of the way so that the next one lasted.

She hugged her arms around his neck, and he buried his face in the chasm of her chest, breathing in the soft scent. He reached a hand up her back and popped the bra clasp, helping her out of the garment before her breasts spilled out toward him.

He filled his mouth with the satiny flesh before him, sucking at her nipple and dragging his teeth across her skin until she choked out a moan. He moved to the left and did the same on the other side, this time eliciting an "Oh God."

"I wonder if I can make you come like this," he said, growling against her chest.

"Do you feel how wet I am?" she said. With that, she pressed her hips into him, and his cock responded accordingly. The jeans were torture.

"Hold on," he said. He removed his arms from her body and she clung to him, grinning down as she gently rolled her hips from side to side. Knowing he made her that hot only turned him on more.

He unhooked the button on his jeans and kicked them off as she remained glued to his chest. When he tugged off his boxer briefs and stood completely upright, the tip of his erection brushed the bottom of her ass.

"Jesus," she said, cradling his face between her arms and stretching her tongue into his waiting mouth. He closed his lips around her tongue and sucked briefly, her thighs tightening around him in response.

With great control, and all the while holding her gaze, he lowered her body an inch until the tip of his cock rested perfectly between her cheeks. Her eyelids lowered and she tilted her hips back, sliding her seam over his head.

He was a fraction of a moment away from sliding her thong to the side and slipping inside her. Suddenly, she removed one arm from around his neck, reached down, and moved the thong herself.

They locked eyes, and she used the same free hand to grip his erection and carefully dip the head just past her lips. He couldn't see straight. His arms and legs were numb, as if every nerve ending in his body had rushed to his cock.

"Jesus Christ," he choked.

"I can't get enough of you," she said, trailing her full lips over his mouth. "I know we shouldn't do this without a condom, but you feel so good."

She said what he was thinking, and before they could act on it, he pulled away and set her down. Her chest deflated, but he wasn't saying no.

"Not yet," he said, covering her mouth in an eager kiss. "I want that, too. Just, not yet."

He took her hand and led her to the bedroom, closing the door behind him and flicking on the small bedside lamp.

"Is that okay?" he asked.

Every time they'd been together after the lean-to had been pitch-black. He needed to see her as much as he needed to feel her.

"Yes," she said, lowering herself to the edge of the bed. He kneeled in front of her like a peasant in front of his queen. Whatever she wanted him to do, he'd do it.

"Can I touch you?" He ran his hand over the smooth skin at her belly button and trailed it down over the space where her thighs met.

"I hope you never stop," she said. Thank God for the light. Her cheeks were spattered with blush, as if the blood couldn't decide where it wanted to pool. Her long dark hair cascaded across her slender shoulders and brushed the tops of her breasts, and he pushed the strands back for maximum view.

"You're sure the light's okay?" he asked. If she wasn't comfortable, she'd shut him down, and he wanted her perfectly at peace.

"It's fine," she said. She scraped her fingers through his hair and leaned back onto her elbows with an eager grin.

As his index finger trailed across the tops of her thighs, the space between them opened slightly. She was letting him in. He gazed up at her for more reassurance, and her bright eyes shone *yes*.

She was completely bare, and her delicate folds glistened with all the anticipation he'd felt on his stomach earlier. As he traced across her lips with shaky fingers, he took in the sight before him. She was beautiful. Perfect.

He pressed the pad of his middle finger against her clit, and her hips rose to meet him, her head falling back with a sigh. His bottom lip quivered, desperate for her taste on his tongue.

With two fingers already slick with arousal, he massaged her up and down and then used his thumb to tease the soft space below her entrance. He slowly dipped his two fingers past her lips, and her legs parted even farther.

"You like this?" he asked, his words catching in his throat.

"Yes," she choked out. She lifted her head, her hair wild and her mouth swollen. With a half-closed stare, she said, "I want you to taste me."

He paused, frozen between her legs. "Baby, we don't have to."

"You have never made me feel like I had to do anything," she said. She gasped and rolled her head like a woman on the verge. "Right now, all I want is your mouth on me. I need it."

With great care, he slid his fingers out and looked up one last time. "You're totally sure?"

"More than sure," she said, leaning forward to touch the hair at his temple. "*Please*, Sam. Please."

A nervous thrill ran through him, his lips tingling with fear. Pressure weighed squarely on his shoulders. If she didn't enjoy it, he'd feel terrible. And that would make her feel worse in return. All he could do now was listen to her body and give her more of whatever she liked.

He traced his tongue in the space at the crook of her thigh while pressing his broad shoulders against her legs for maximum access. His thumb rested at the base of her entrance, where her blood pulsed like crazy.

Once she pressed her own thighs back until she was nearly in a split, he knew he was doing something right. He placed his mouth over her sex and rolled the tip of his tongue back and forth, back and forth. She squirmed underneath him, gasping, while barely perceptible yelps escaped her lips.

"Holy shit," she breathed. He closed his lips around her clit and sucked while sliding a single finger across her seam. She pulsed against him, and her thighs spread wider still.

He removed his finger and placed his mouth over her sex again, returning to the gentle tongue strokes, while he reached both hands up to lightly pinch her nipples. With a few more expletives, she clutched the bedspread underneath her and began to lift her hips.

"Oh God," she groaned. "Oh God . . ." He dragged his hands down the front of her, hooked his forearms under her thighs, and squeezed as his tongue dragged across her from one end to the other.

One more time, he covered her sex with his mouth, inhaling the sweet scent of her as it flooded his nostrils, and pumped out a rhythm on her clit.

With a deep, guttural groan she shouted, "I'm coming." Her hips pressed up against his mouth, and as he continued to stroke her with his tongue, her pussy throbbed against him with the rapid-fire release of an orgasm.

He placed a delicate kiss on her inner thigh and sat up slowly, savoring the dramatic rise and fall of her stomach and the way her skin glowed in the soft yellow lamplight.

"Oh. My. God." Her head hung back as if a puppeteer had dropped a string, and Sam crawled across the mattress to lie next to her on his back. He turned his head, waiting for the review.

"You're not faking it, are you?" he teased.

Her head rolled to the side, and a wide, drunken smile covered her face. "No. Hell no." She ran a hand through her hair and held the tangled strands in a mass on top of her neck. "I think you melted my brain."

"That's what I was going for."

As he watched her breathing, the rise and fall of her chest slowing over time to a normal rate, thoughts of Liv slipped into his mind. He'd never felt anything close to this with Liv. And yet he'd made so many sacrifices for her. Sydney hadn't asked him for a thing.

"What's that look for?" she asked, trailing a fingernail across his brow.

"Nothing," he said. His thoughts were too much for the moment. He wanted to hunker down in this room, this space, this settled corner of the world, and enjoy her over and over again. At least until tomorrow.

chapter **twenty-one**

The clanging noise of jingle bells startled Sydney from her daydream. *About time she took this stuff down.* Karen struggled to cram the last of the Christmas decorations into clear plastic storage bin as the snow swirled outside.

"This is my least favorite day of the year," Karen said for the fifteenth time that afternoon.

"Most people take their Christmas decorations down on New Year's," Sydney said. An older man poked around the bookshelves, a befuddled stare on his face. "Sir, can I help you with anything? I'd be happy to make a recommendation."

"Oh, no. I, um—" His weathered face dropped in surprise. "Well, I was thinking maybe something for my wife. I don't know. Maybe it's too . . . salacious?"

A grin spread over Sydney's lips. She loved proving people wrong when it came to romance novels.

"Not all romance is salacious." She hopped off her stool

behind the register and joined him at the shelves. "Some is faith-based, some is rated 'PG,' if you will. Do you know what your wife typically reads?"

He rattled off a few titles, and Sydney plucked some suggestions from the Amish-romance section. The front door of the shop opened, and Jorie rushed in, nervous energy vibrating out of her limbs. She blinked rapidly and waved at Sydney.

"I'll leave you to browse a bit on your own," Sydney said, leaving the man with a stack of suggestions. She hurried over to Jorie, a gnawing sense of dread in her gut.

Tonight was the second meeting of the book club. If it drew a sparse crowd for the second time, she'd start to consider her next steps. With all the online promotion she'd done, business had increased slightly but not nearly enough to cover the debt.

What they needed now was a slam-dunk promotional gem that would draw people out of the surrounding tourist areas for something they couldn't get anywhere else in the North Country region. Sydney so badly wanted that "something" to be a warm, welcoming shop featuring a wider selection of romance novels than ten bookstores combined. But at this point, it seemed like a distant dream.

"What's going on?" Sydney asked.

Jorie nearly bounced out of her winter coat, her eyes sparkling. "You're gonna flip. Remember my cousin? The one with the weird taxidermist husband?"

"Sure." Sydney remembered the evening she and Jorie spent nearly an hour on Facebook giggling over photos of squirrels wearing raincoats.

"Well," Jorie continued. She clutched Sydney's forearms. "Her former coworker is a romance author."

"No shit."

"Yes shit! Her name is Sophie Miller. But guess what her pen name is?"

Sydney's stomach retracted, afraid that her guess was a

leap too far. Her gaze flickered over to the cover blowup positioned near the shop door of tonight's book-club read: *The Duke's Deal* by Rowena Willow.

"It couldn't be," Sydney said, her voice barely above a whisper. But Jorie's head was already nodding so furiously Sydney was worried it might bounce clear off her neck.

"Rowena Willow!" Jorie shrieked. "And listen to *this*. When my cousin realized the connection, she called Rowena to tell her about what you're doing here at the shop, and Rowena freaked out. She thought it was such an amazing idea. She's coming. Tonight. To the book club."

A shimmering breeze fluttered over Sydney's skin, raising layers upon layers of goose bumps in its wake.

Rowena Willow was one of the romance genre's most sought-after authors. Her social media following was a tidal wave of influence, and a tweet from her was worth its weight in gold. Sydney froze in place.

"Tonight," she whispered. "Rowena Willow. Here. Tonight."

"Yes, babe." Jorie's eyes glistened with tears. "She can't wait."

The next three hours dissolved in front of Sydney's eyes as she raced around the shop, dusting and straightening and tearing down the last of the tinsel hanging across Sam's bookshelves.

The pressure of tonight's meeting weighed on her chest like a brick. What if Rowena Willow walked in and Sydney and Jorie were the only meeting attendees? What if their talking points were unintelligent drivel? What if Rowena Willow anticipated Aspen and realized upon arrival that Pine Ridge had none of the charm or beauty?

At six forty-five, Sydney watched with horror as the snow fell in curtains outside the front window of the Loving Page. While residents of the town were used to the weather, she also knew some of the older folks liked to stay home when the roads were as bad as they were now. She feared she wouldn't see Edith O'Hare or her sister tonight.

She shook out the nerves in her hands and fidgeted with the platter of decadent cookies Jorie had delivered for the evening. Swirls of pink frosting topped each petite blond sugar cookie. Prosecco chilled in champagne buckets on top of the coffee table along with stacks of Rowena Willow's newest title. Sydney was as ready as she'd ever be.

"Phew, is it shitty out there," Jorie said as she entered the shop. She hung her snow-spattered coat onto the coatrack and shivered. "I passed by Sam's truck towing somebody out of an embankment about a mile back."

Sydney ran a hand across the back of her neck, pinching to ease the tension that had settled there overnight and refused to quit. "What if Rowena Willow can't get in?"

"Oh, she's here!" Jorie said brightly. "I spoke with my cousin half an hour ago. She's all settled into her B and B, and she's planning to walk over in a few."

Relief flooded Sydney's chest. The guest of honor had arrived. Now all she needed were a few attendees. She'd been tweeting and posting on Facebook and Instagram all day, hoping that at least two or three interested readers would be suddenly compelled to attend.

"You look hot," Jorie said, touching the sleeve of Sydney's black silk dress.

"Thanks," Sydney said. "It's not too much?"

She'd dug deep into the recesses of her suitcase for tonight's event and selected a ruffled black silk dress that cinched at the waist along with opaque black tights and lace-up high-heeled booties.

"Not at all," Jorie said, despite her own sweater and jeans combo. "You're the emcee of tonight's festivities. You have to look the part."

Sydney cracked her knuckles and tugged at the collar of her dress. She thought the holiday party and the first meeting of the book club would loosen her up a bit for tonight's main event, but the nerves churned all the same. To top it off, today was Liv's court date.

Sydney had heard through the Pine Ridge rumor mill that Liv spent the week at her sister's trying to prepare for the court date while also dealing with her relapse. Sydney knew that as soon as the court made its decision, it wouldn't be long before the news made its way to the bookstore.

"Oh, look!" Jorie pointed at the front window as a small huddle of women shuffled along the sidewalk and burst into the Loving Page. Edith O'Hare, her sister, and her daughter looked as if they'd been out in the storm for hours, although Sydney suspected they'd simply walked a few feet from Edith's car.

"Isn't this cozy?" Edith said, her pink-lipped pout pulled tight into a grin. "Oh, Sydney, I'm so glad you didn't cancel tonight. I've so been looking forward to it."

Tears threatened, and Sydney looked upward at the overhead lights to keep them at bay. Maybe, even if she couldn't pull her mother out of debt, she'd still done something positive in this town.

As Jorie helped the older ladies get settled into the reading nook, the shop door opened again, and two more Pine Ridge residents walked in.

"She forced me to read tonight's book," the taller of the two women said with a roll of her eyes and a thumb at her friend. "And I, uh . . . I kind of liked it. So here I am."

"She loved it!" the other cooed. "She read it in two freaking days. Look at her face. When I told her Rowena Willow was coming tonight, she almost cried."

The first woman's cheeks filled with an embarrassed blush, but she simply shrugged and pushed past Sydney with a dog-eared copy of *The Duke's Deal* tucked firmly under her arm. *Maybe it's working. Maybe this crazy idea is actually working.*

As two more readers entered the shop and then two

more, Sydney took a moment to stand back and soak in the scene in front of her. Someone plucked a lip gloss from the front counter and handed it to Karen behind the register to purchase. Edith O'Hare's daughter snatched a T-shirt that said *A Well-Read Woman Is a Dangerous Creature* from the clothing rack, eyes aglow, and checked the price tag before hurrying over to pay Karen.

"Excuse me? Are you Sydney Walsh?" A lilting female voice carried over Sydney's shoulder, and she turned expectantly. The face from the back cover of *The Duke's Deal* grinned at her from behind brightly painted red lips.

"Rowena Willow," Sydney said. She extended her hand, and Rowena shook it, bringing with her a fresh, floral scent that Sydney breathed in without thinking. "I can't tell you what an honor it is to have you here. Thank you so much for making the trip from New York."

"The pleasure is mine," Rowena said. Sydney knew the woman was in her fifties, but her impeccable makeup, flawlessly colored bright red hair, and tailored blazer made her look forty, at most. "When Anna told me what you ladies were up to, I had to see it for myself. I think it's fantastic that you're bringing romance readers together."

Sydney tucked her bottom lip between her teeth and breathed deep. Her nerves hummed like generators. "Please come in. Can I get you anything? We have prosecco and cookies for the meeting, but I also have water, coffee, tea . . ."

"Prosecco and cookies!" Rowena said, clapping her hands together. "Out of my way." She winked at Sydney and passed by on another cloud of perfume.

A rap on the window caused her to jump. Sam stood just outside, snowflakes swirling around him and his cheeks bright with color. A grin occupied half his face.

"Hey," he said, slipping in the front door and keeping his voice low. "Just wanted to pop in before the meeting got started and let you know that Utz's is packed. Hank said the keg is almost kicked already, and if you ladies want to come over after you're done, he'll whip up something special for you."

"It's working," she said, all the emotion from the past three months stuck in the base of her throat. Tears threatened again. "I don't know what changed, but it's working."

"You did it," he said. The pull between them was magnetic, but Sydney hung back.

"What happened today?" She couldn't avoid the question any longer. "With Liv? Did you hear anything?"

A dark cloud passed over his face, and his chin dropped to his chest. When he looked up again, he pressed his lips together. "Yeah, her sister called me about an hour ago. They denied her shared custody. I guess they're going to appeal, but it doesn't look good."

The air whooshed out of Sydney's lungs on one gust. After everything that had happened, she still couldn't feel good about this. "Wow. That sort of breaks my heart."

"Yeah. Between the social worker's visit last week, and Kevin testifying that he thought she was drinking again, she didn't have a shot. So Jay's gonna be with Kevin and his parents in Akron for now. Probably for the best." His jaw worked back and forth, and he forced a tight smile. "But, um, I'll tell you about it later."

"Sydney!" Karen's voice called over the low din of voices.

Sam's grin widened. "Go. Have fun. I'll talk to you after."

He touched her elbow, and searing heat traveled through the thin fabric to her skin. Maybe they'd finally be able to touch in public. The possibilities made her dizzy.

He raised his eyebrows, and with one more tug of his lips, walked out.

Come on, come on. Sydney and me. Is here good? This is cute, right? In front of the historical romance section?" Rowena Willow placed a hand on her hip and posed as if she'd been doing it all her life. Sydney dropped her chin in a vague attempt at looking as confident as Rowena.

"Beautiful!" Karen snapped the photo and handed Rowena back her phone.

"Smart move with the stamp inside the books," Rowena said.

Sydney had stamped each purchased romance novel with the store's social media handles, encouraging readers to post when they were finished reading. Rowena tapped at her phone, using the stamp as a guide.

"So," Rowena said, a bright smile on her face. "I hear there's an after-party."

Edith O'Hare hooked Rowena's elbow, promising to lead her across to Utz's herself, and Sydney surveyed the room. All sixteen of the book club's attendees milled around the shop, purchasing additional books and buzzing about the next meeting's title, *Broken*.

"Maybe the author of this one will show up, too!" someone behind Sydney trilled.

She grinned. At this point, anything seemed possible.

"We'll clean up later, right?" Sydney asked her mother as Karen finished ringing up the last of the evening's sales. The last shred of cynicism had officially vanished from Karen's demeanor. Tonight, even she'd been won over.

"Heck yes," Karen said. "Tonight, we celebrate. If we keep having nights like this, we'll be all right, Suds. I can hardly believe it."

Sydney, buoyed by the positive outcome of the evening, followed the stream of people from the Loving Page across the street to Utz's, and when she entered, the crush of people pushed her back. The place was busier than she'd ever seen it. Hank's wife joined him behind the bar to help with that night's onslaught of patrons, and on the specials board, Sydney's keg was crossed out. Warmth rolled over her.

"Hey." A strong, calloused hand grasped hers from behind.

Sam drew her in, no doubt using the crowd as an excuse to be close. His body heat radiated outward, warming her extremities and begging her to be closer.

Since their first tryst in the lean-to, they'd kept their relationship quiet. No matter how the town or Sam felt about Liv, he'd wanted to remain respectful until everything came out in the custody hearing. But even now, she didn't know how far to go.

"Congratulations," he said, lowering his dark eyebrows. She licked her lips, wishing they were his.

"Thanks." The word disappeared in the mess of voices. She breathed in as he breathed out, catching the scent of him on her tongue. "We're still probably not allowed to kiss, huh?"

The left side of his mouth curved into a grin, and he trailed his thumb across the palm of her hand. "Maybe not just yet."

"Okay, well I'm going to go get a beer. And maybe while I'm gone you could ugly yourself up a little. Otherwise, being around you in public is going to be really difficult for me."

As she turned toward the bar, his hand brushed against her ass. She sent a shocked look over her shoulder, but he just winked. "Whoops. Sorry. I think my watch got caught on your dress."

She leaned over the bar and caught Hank's eye, nodding when he asked if she wanted an IPA. She hadn't had a drop of alcohol all night, and now, in light of her success, she felt a celebratory drink was in order.

"Where is she?"

The single question floated over the crowd without discernment like a leaf on the wind. But since the disappointing end to the first book-club meeting, Sydney had been on high alert for that voice.

"Oh, nobody knows, huh? Where the fuck is she?"

Upon the voice repeating, Sydney stood up straight and turned slowly over her shoulder toward the entrance. The crowd quieted, but Sydney couldn't see over the groups of tall men to the distraction.

"There she is!"

Heads swiveled toward Sydney, most blinking in confusion. A path cleared. Just inside the front door, wearing a stained white T-shirt and ratty jeans with no coat, her hair hanging in limp strands around her blotchy face, was Liv.

"Liv?"

"Yes, hello." Liv's eyes floated in their sockets, and the dank scent of booze wafted off her as if she'd been soaking in it.

"Are you okay?" Sydney asked. Everyone in the bar turned their attention to the spectacle at the front. Even the music seemed to lower.

"You're a bitch," Liv spat. "Did you know I don't get to have my kid?"

Red-hot shame sliced through Sydney. Liv couldn't know what had been going on between her and Sam—could she? And yet the weight of responsibility sat heavy on her shoulders.

"I heard," Sydney said. She was desperate not to have this conversation in front of the entire town, but Liv's awareness of others seemed nonexistent. "I'm so sorry."

"You're not sorry. You're not sorry one tiny little bit, are you? Because all along you've been out to get Sam, and I was the only thing standing in your way."

"Liv, honey," Jorie said, appearing from the crowd and approaching Liv. She placed a hand on Liv's wiry arm. "It's not Sydney's fault."

Liv swatted her friend's hand away and pinched her chapped lips together until they went white. "What, she's won you all over? Everybody's Team Sydney now? Screw you, Jorie. You haven't been a real friend to me in years."

Jorie sent Sydney a helpless frown, as Liv was beyond reason. Whatever was on her mind, she had to get it out. Sydney gritted her teeth and prepared for the worst.

"Maybe we should go somewhere quiet and talk," Sydney said.

"Oh yeah, you'd like that, wouldn't you? Because you don't want anybody to know what you did." Liv's face settled into a challenge, and Sydney swallowed. What was she talking about?

"I haven't done anything," Sydney said, while scenes from Sam's garage, her bedroom, and the office of the Loving Page flashed through her mind. She shook the tremors from her voice. "Liv, please. Let's go outside and talk."

"No!" Liv screamed. She pushed a hand through her stringy hair. "No. We're not going outside. I'm done trying to be nice to you. Everything was fine until you showed up. But you know what, Sydney Walsh? You fucked up. He'll never want to be with you now. Not after you slept with his brother."

A collective gasp stole the oxygen from the room, and for a moment, everything stood still. Sydney's neck prickled, and her eyes went dry.

"What?" Sam's voice hit her in the chest with the force of a Mack truck.

"I did not."

"You did!" Liv shrieked, her eyes wild.

Sydney turned to Sam, terrified of what she'd see. His face was still. Waiting.

"That is not true," Sydney said. Her voice trembled and cracked.

"What the hell?" Sam's voice squeaked, breaking Sydney's heart in half.

"I did not have sex with Jared," Sydney said, every molecule in her body pulsing like a bass drum. Panic swelled.

"I have a picture." Every head in the room swiveled back to Liv as she held her phone high above her head. Sydney's mind reeled. Was it possible Jared took advantage of her, snapped a photo, and then lied about it? Her memory after they left Utz's was nothing but static.

Liv dropped the phone into Jorie's timidly outstretched hand. Jorie frowned at Sydney before craning her face toward the phone screen, squinting. When her gaze lifted, Sydney knew. Something on that phone incriminated her, and she'd never get out of this unscathed.

Jorie handed the phone to Sydney, and a sick sense of dread brewed. She looked down, and staring back at her was a grainy photo, possibly taken through windows with dirty screens. The woman and the man were most certainly she and Jared, both still in winter coats, reclined on the guest room bed.

An almost imperceptible huff of relief escaped her lips. Jared had set her down on the bed. Nothing more. She knew it.

Tingling began in her legs and crept north until the entire expanse of her skin prickled. Hot breath on her neck brought her back to life.

"You gotta be kidding me." Sam's voice floated over her shoulder.

"See, it's nothing," Sydney said.

"Nothing? You're at his house. On a bed. At night." Sam's face contorted into a mask of disgust.

"No," she insisted. "I mean, yes. But we didn't sleep together. This is nothing. Nothing sexual."

The words rose up but stopped in her throat. She couldn't explain. Remove the sexual element and still, it sounded absurd. *No, he just took me back to his place, and I was incredibly drunk, but nothing happened.*

"You have to admit this doesn't look good," Jorie said. Her jaw set, her arms crossed tightly over her chest. A thousand questions etched on her face. "Why were you at his house?"

"He was taking care of me," Sydney said. The hot flush

crept up her neck and into her cheeks. What did happen that night?

"Taking care of you?" Jorie said. "Why? What happened?"

"I don't remember." Sydney's voice bordered on manic.

"You don't remember?" The vein in Sam's neck pulsed, his words scraping across her skin like prickers.

"No, I remember . . . well, I remember part of it." She remembered tequila and crying and Jared's strong arms and the John Stockton poster. She remembered the way Jared looked at her when she stumbled out of his guest bedroom, the frown of pity on his lips. "I know we didn't sleep together. I know nothing happened."

"You know but you don't remember?" Sam said. His voice raised an octave, his lips parted. "Sydney, give me something here."

Fury and chaos crashed over her, the murmurs of disbelief rising out of the crowd. Where was Jared? He could tell them. She searched the room, gazing at every face hoping to see his, but Jared was nowhere to be found.

In one last desperate attempt at easing Sam's distrusting mind, Sydney blurted out, "Even if something did happen, which it didn't, it was before you and I had even kissed."

The words slipped out before she saw them coming, and as soon as they landed, she gasped. Sam's eyes flew open, the emotion intensifying with a violent rush of blood to his neck.

"Kissed?" Liv's shaky voice asked.

The room spun, becoming a swirling mass of confused faces. Her breath stuck in her throat, unmoving and cutting off all air supply to her lungs.

"Whoa," Greg said, "you guys are banging?"

"Ah," Sam said, raking a hand through his hair. "This is bullshit."

"No, Sam, it's nothing," she said, taking a step toward him. She needed him to understand. It was a moment of weakness, a product of too much tequila and fear of losing all control over her life. "Jared was just taking care of me because I was drunk."

As if the key had turned in the lock, his face fell. Those magic words, *I was drunk*. She regretted them the second she'd said them.

His eyes blazed, wilder and filled with more pain than she'd ever seen. "You were drunk, you don't remember, but you're sure nothing happened? Where have I heard that before?"

The words drove a stake through Sydney's heart. She'd been stupid and careless and now she knew what he really thought of her. Just another person in his life who'd chosen alcohol over him.

"I can't take this." He shoved past anyone standing between him and the exit, disappearing through the front door and leaving Sydney trembling. She pressed her full beer into the hand of someone next to her and raced out after him.

The snow had slowed to a delicate shower of lazy flakes, but she relished the cold. It shocked her back to life.

"Sam." She called out after him as he jogged across the street, her voice nearly swallowed by the heavy snow drifts. She struggled to keep up in her high-heeled boots, determination urging her forward. "Sam!"

A few feet down the road, in front of a cluster of white-trimmed pine trees, he spun around, and the undisguised sadness on his face knocked her backward. Deep creases were etched on his face, and his lips pressed into a thin line.

"I don't want to talk to you." His words dripped with disappointment. "I'll say something I'll regret. Just leave me alone."

"No." She wrapped her arms tightly around herself in a futile attempt at warmth. "This is insane. You know me, Sam. You know I wouldn't sleep with Jared, and I especially wouldn't sleep with Jared and then lie about it."

"Do I know that?" He stepped toward her, dropping his

chin and huffing out a short breath. "All right, fine. Maybe you didn't sleep with him. But how many more times am I expected to put up with this? How many more times can I be put in the position to believe one person's word over another because of fucking alcohol? I can't. I can't do it anymore. I'm exhausted."

Her chest ached. If she could, she'd go back in time and save him from everyone who'd hurt him, everyone who had made him feel small and unimportant. But she wasn't one of those people. And she deserved better, too.

"Please don't let this ruin everything that's happened between us. It's too special."

"Don't *let* this ruin everything?" His red-rimmed eyes widened. "So this is on me? If I *let* this ruin everything, then it's my fault?"

"No," she said. Her voice betrayed her. She sounded like a whimpering mouse. "No, it's not on you. It's on me. It was stupid. When I first got to Pine Ridge, I had no idea how to handle anything, and I drank too much that night, but . . ."

"When was this exactly?" he asked. "What night was it that you needed somebody to swoop in and save you?"

Damn it. The night you were supposed to fix the shelf on the bookcase you made me. The night you offered to set me up with your friends on the radio to promote my event. The night you spilled your guts to me about your alcoholic father.

"Early November," she said.

He nodded slowly, and she could see the wheels turning. He was searching for a date. "The night you met him, right? The night you did tequila shots at Utz's?"

The tears pooled in her eyes. She was a fool. Every time she seemed to pull it together, one mistake sent it all crashing down around her. She'd always be the lawyer one panic attack away from losing it all. The woman who turned to alcohol when she needed a break from reality.

"Yes." She tried to swallow, but her throat was as dry as

summer dirt. "But you had Liv. At that point everyone, including you, told me I should stay away, that nothing could happen. I was barely allowed to hang out with you unsupervised. I didn't do anything wrong, Sam. I made a stupid mistake. People are allowed to make mistakes. I didn't sleep with Jared, and even if I had, it wasn't against the rules."

The lines on his face smoothed, and now he looked at her, slack-jawed and still. His calloused hands that had once touched her skin so gently now clenched and released into tight fists.

"Right. You're right. I'm being overly sensitive. You didn't do anything wrong. I thought we had feelings for each other at that point, but it turns out I was just another idiot crushing on the new girl."

"No, Sam, stop."

"Nah, I'm not doing this again." His lips pursed, and for a brief moment, she thought he was going to walk toward her. Touch her. Give her any shred of hope she hadn't messed this all up. Instead, he shook his head. "I think I need to be alone for a while. Try to figure out why I keep doing this."

"Keep doing what?" The icy wind sucked her breath away, and she struggled for air.

"Giving too much to people who don't deserve it."

With one last blistering glare, he turned and walked away. She watched with deepening sadness as his figure got smaller and smaller, eventually rounding the curve of the street and vanishing from view.

And suddenly Sydney had the unquenchable urge to disappear.

chapter **twenty-two**

Jorie reached over the chipped Formica countertop and tipped the carafe until the steaming dark-roast coffee poured out into Sam's waiting mug. The solemn look she'd worn all morning deepened as she replaced the carafe on the hot plate and leaned against the counter with her arms crossed.

"Donut?" she asked.

Sam exhaled, the dripping plastic bag of ice crinkling as he adjusted it against his throbbing eye socket. Fine, he deserved it. The lecture, the screaming curse words, the sucker punch. But damn if it didn't hurt all the same.

"Nah."

He sipped the hot coffee and grimaced as the bitter liquid burned his tongue. Great. A busted eye and a burnt tongue. Might as well chop an ear off while he was at it.

"Don't you dare go feeling sorry for yourself." Jorie trailed a hand over her still-flat belly. She needed to be careful with that particular gesture if she wanted to wait the full twelve weeks to tell everybody the good news.

"Practicing your mom voice already?"

She raised a single eyebrow.

"Jesus, Jorie. I just got punched in the face. Can you cut me a break?"

She released an audible breath before snagging a plate from the counter, plopping a plain donut on it, and shoving it toward Sam. She never stayed angry for too long. The lack of frosting seemed to be the best she could do today.

"So Jared was pretty pissed, huh?"

Sam shook his head, immediately regretting the motion as the pain pulsed in his cheek and spread briefly to his temple and forehead. "Beyond pissed. Besides that one time he kissed my girlfriend when I was thirteen, he's never given me a reason not to trust him. He's an idiot, but he'd never go after a woman I was interested in. Even in these, the most absurd of circumstances."

Jorie sighed, her face finally softening. "Oh, Sammy. I don't blame you for reacting the way you did."

He lowered the bag of ice and stared at her with raised brows. In the ten days since the showdown at Utz's, he'd barely heard from her. Any friend of Jorie's knew that meant she was unhappy.

"Oh, you don't?"

"No, I don't. You were well within your right to question something you felt uneasy about. Were you well within your right to insult her by holding her past against her? Or demanding she share every bit of herself with you while refusing to do the same yourself? No. No, you were not."

There it was. He lifted the ice to his eye again, mostly because it hurt but also so he'd have to look at her disapproving face with only one eye.

"I tried to see her the morning after," he said. "She'd already left."

Jorie nodded. She knew. She'd been there when he showed up at her door, hat in hand, and asked to speak with Sydney so he could apologize. Jorie's face had twisted up as she explained that Sydney had already packed up her stuff and taken a train back into New York, claiming she needed a break from Pine Ridge.

The knife had twisted in his heart. The night of Liv's big reveal at Utz's, he'd been so heartbroken, split wide open after watching her hit rock bottom, that he couldn't expend a single ounce of energy more in kindness toward Sydney, a woman who held his heart in her hands. Years of pain built up over his father, his mother, and Liv spilled out over Sydney. The one person who didn't deserve it.

But Sydney hadn't even given him the courtesy of letting him explain himself. Instead, she'd simply up and left. As if what they'd had never mattered at all.

"Have you tried calling her?" Jorie asked.

"Yes." He didn't want to have to say out loud that most of his calls went straight to voice mail, and every text he'd sent went unanswered. Maybe it was still too soon. Maybe she was still too angry.

"So, what now?" Jorie asked.

The doorbell over the bakery door jingled as the Cruz family entered, their seven-year-old twins bouncing around the shop, proving they didn't need any more sugar. Sam slinked backward to avoid an awkward inquisition about his busted eye and took the opportunity to think things over.

What now?

The easy thing would be to forget Sydney Walsh had ever existed. Return to his life without anyone or anything tying him down. Maybe he could meet somebody new.

His eye pulsed with fresh pain as he realized he'd applied too much pressure on the ice bag. A bitter laugh escaped his lips. Sure. Meet somebody new. Easy as that.

Visions of Sydney played in his mind—her skin, her

hair, her lip-press-into-smile—and his anger melted like the ice on his face. He didn't want to forget her, didn't want to move on with someone new. He wanted her. No substitutes.

As the Cruz family exited, the twins even more amped up than when they'd entered, Jorie waved and ran her hand across the front of her apron.

"So," Sam said. "A Valentine's Day wedding, huh?"

Jorie grinned. "Yeah. I know it's cliché, but the timing works and the church was free. I just hope this little nugget stays hidden until then. I've always dreamed of wearing my mom's dress, and an extra inch of belly makes it impossible."

Sam tossed the dripping ice bag into the trash and shoved the plain donut into his mouth, crumbs scattering down into his beard. He remembered Sydney's fingers on his chin the night they'd first kissed. Tremors began in his belly and traveled upward.

"Does she know yet?" His voice growled, giving him away.

Jorie raised an eyebrow. "Not yet. I was going to call her tonight."

His heart thumped away in his chest. Anger mixed with sadness and tore up his insides. "You think she'll come? To the wedding?"

Jorie shrugged. "I hope so. She was pretty hurt when she left. But maybe a month is enough time to cool down and give you another shot. If that's what you want."

He clamped his teeth down over his bottom lip, ignoring the pain of bone on flesh. "Maybe a month will be enough time for both of us."

The buzzer forced Sydney's heart into her throat. She wasn't expecting anyone, and all of Bee's friends knew she was staying at her boyfriend's for the next couple of months. Maybe a delivery guy with the wrong apartment number?

She tossed the blanket off her lap and crept toward the door as if two dead bolts didn't stand between her and a possible intruder. Only a few weeks back in New York City and already her defenses were sky-high.

Let somebody try to break in. She dared them.

"Who's there?" she asked into the intercom.

"Suds, it's me."

Her nostrils flared, a soft spot opening up in her chest. Without another moment's hesitation, she pressed the button to open the building's front door and allowed her mother inside.

Sydney glanced around her borrowed apartment and hurried to tidy the empty cracker sleeves, water glasses spotted with residue, and haphazardly discarded clothes. Her mother knew all about her emotional state, but the living situation was another story.

"Hun?"

The front door creaked open, and Sydney stood bolt upright with a sticky cereal bowl in hand. She swallowed down the wave of sadness and forced her tears back. Karen grinned, her lips pressing into her lined face, and shoved her hands into her coat pockets.

"Hi, Sweets."

"Hi, Mom."

Sydney closed the space between them and wrapped trembling arms around her mother, sinking into the comforting scent of cold winter air and Pert Plus shampoo. Though she stood at least four inches taller than Karen, her mother cradled Sydney in her arms and patted her back.

Sydney pulled away and blinked back the threatening tears. "Come on in."

"Not a bad place." Karen moved through the apartment, nodding at Bee's minimal studio. "Guess you were smart to keep at least one good friend in New York."

The corners of Sydney's lips turned up. "Yeah, she's the best."

"It's close to work, you said?"

"Just a couple blocks."

The day after the Utz's debacle, Sydney accepted a sales position at the Prada flagship store in SoHo. Towering heels and a pencil skirt constituted her uniform, and although constricting, the outfit and the job kept her mind off Pine Ridge.

Karen plopped down onto the stiff couch cushion and grimaced.

"I know," Sydney said. "It's a terrible couch."

Karen raised her eyebrows. "So. You're all right?"

Sydney swallowed and begged the nerves fluttering in her stomach to quiet. All right? She lived, breathed, ate, slept. Sort of. Was that all right?

"Sure. I'm all right."

Karen peeled off her functional army-green winter coat and glanced around again. "You're lucky you had a friend to loan you a place."

Sydney raised her eyebrows and sucked on her lips. Bee had been Sydney's most reliable friend since college and hadn't hesitated when Sydney called in a panic on the train ride down from the mountains. She promised Sydney she spent most of her time at her boyfriend's place anyway.

Saved from homelessness twice in one year by women in serious relationships. The irony.

Sydney perched next to her mother on the couch and watched as Karen's veiny hand reached over to squeeze her knee. Karen tilted her head and grinned, her lips curling but her eyes remaining steady and questioning.

"Guess I'm not doing a very good job of getting the truth out of you. Thought maybe showing up unannounced would scare ya into a confession." She raised her bushy eyebrows. "How long is this vacation from reality going to last?"

Sydney huffed out an indignant breath. "Vacation? New York is the vacation in this scenario?"

"Drop the tough-girl act." Karen winked, her voice smooth as honey. "You forgot how to do it, and it's not very convincing anymore."

Sydney stood up and went into the kitchenette in search of water. She poured a glass, took a sip, and turned back toward her mother, slightly better prepared to face the lion.

"I don't belong in Pine Ridge."

Karen barked out a single bitter laugh. "Try again."

Sydney gritted her teeth and reached for the truth. The same truth she'd been trying to bury since she crossed the Adirondack Park line. "Fine. Pine Ridge is Sam. I can't continue to be there if he's there. Simple as that."

The grin of satisfaction stretched across Karen's face. "That's more like it."

"I'll figure it out. I'll stay in New York and I'll get a better job. Or maybe I'll stay in retail. I don't know." Saying the words out loud summoned the yawning chasm of sadness in her stomach.

"Or you could try something really crazy and talk to Sam."

Sydney clutched her water glass tighter, staring into the tepid liquid. Talk to Sam. She wanted nothing more. Her pride wouldn't let her.

"I know what you're thinking," Karen continued. "He was a jerk. You're right."

"Mom, we've been through this. . . ."

"I know, I know." Karen held up her hands in defeat. "But you were so angry when you first left, and now the dust has settled. Three weeks later, and you should see the guy. He still mopes around town with a black cloud over his head. He's always in the shop, fishing for information on you."

A flicker of hope sparked in Sydney's chest. In her darkest fantasies, Sam had already moved on.

"How could I be with someone who has that low of an opinion of me?" She joined her mother on the couch, her jaw and stomach clenched. "Like I'm some drunk. Like he didn't know me better than that."

Karen patted Sydney's hand, her face clear and hopeful. "He messed up. People do that sometimes. If anybody's got an excuse to be rash and peg somebody as a drunk who might hurt him, it's Sam Kirkland."

Visions of slurring, stringy-haired Liv floated into Sydney's memory. What destruction she'd caused. "I shouldn't have to pay for someone else's mistakes."

Karen nodded. "No. You shouldn't. I'm not saying forgive him all his sins and pretend like he didn't hurt you. I'm saying don't cut and run. He's not perfect. But he deserves more than that."

Sydney exhaled, the unsteady breath floating past her lips. She hadn't slept well lately, thrumming headaches plaguing her from morning to night. She remembered what he'd said.

I get these tension headaches. . . . I went to the doctor once, and he said it's just stress. That's the only cause. Stress. And when I'm with you, they go away.

She licked her lips, the ache that had replaced him pulsing at her temples.

One more shot.

Maybe.

She met her mother's wide-eyed stare. "How's the shop?"

chapter twenty-three

Jorie gasped as the white curtain fell back into place behind her. Her Barbie-doll blue eyes, framed in frosty sapphire eyeshadow, widened as they fell on Sam. Who had done her makeup? She looked like a clown. But a woman's wedding day was probably not the right time to criticize her eyeshadow.

"What are we gasping about?" Sam asked.

"She's here."

Sam dragged both hands over his face as the skin on his arms and chest prickled. He didn't think he was physically capable of experiencing even more anxiety, but anxiety laughed in the face of whatever tortured him now. This was being-hunted-in-the-woods pure terror.

"I'm not gonna do it." He peered past the gauzy white curtain into the church nave and found Sydney immediately. Her chestnut hair was pressed into waves, and every ten seconds she turned toward Karen with a pained expression on her face.

She didn't want to be here. It was obvious.

"You're freaking doing it." Jorie sipped a bottle of ginger ale and wiped a finger around her lips. "I'm the bride, it's my day, and I say you're doing it."

"That's just it," Sam said. "It's your day. Nobody wants to see the love-drunk asshole making a speech to the girl he lost during someone else's wedding."

"Sure, in most places with most people this is frowned upon. In Pine Ridge? With you and Sydney? And with the bride and groom's permission? People will be disappointed if you *don't* do it."

The knotted tie at his throat cut off his air supply, and he tugged at it, the stiff fabric remaining taut. His new, custom-fit white shirt clung to his back with sweat. Why had he gone to the trouble of new clothes? It wasn't his wedding.

Maybe it would matter to Sydney. If it mattered to her, it mattered to him. A month apart had been just enough time for him to realize her place in his life and how if he didn't try to get her back, he'd never forgive himself.

"Okay, sugar! It's time." Mrs. McDonagh appeared, flanked by her husband and the pastor, and clapped her hands. "Sam, get the hell out of here. My daughter's about to get married."

The champagne glittered in plastic flutes, tiny bubbles floating up in time to the disco beats pulsing from the DJ booth. Half of Pine Ridge crammed into the reception hall attached to the church, grooving to the music and taking full advantage of the free booze.

Sam gulped at his water, the cool liquid doing nothing to soothe his parched throat. Sydney sat across the room at a round table next to her mother, the same pinched and pained expression on her face as earlier in the church.

This was crazy. He couldn't do it.

Could he?

A month ago, he'd done everything wrong; he'd doubted himself, doubted her feelings for him. He'd pushed her away because if the past had taught him anything, it was that people had the power to hurt you if you let them.

He'd never counted on meeting someone like Sydney. But Jorie's wedding gave him the opportunity to right the ship. All he had to do was face Sydney and the town and admit he'd been wrong.

"Hey, man." Matt clapped him on the shoulder, shaking him from his daydream. "You want a little liquid courage?"

Matt held two shots in his meaty paw, but Sam balked at the booze. "No, thanks. I think this is something I've gotta do sober."

As Jorie and Matt took their places at the sweetheart table, the DJ announced the speeches, and Jorie's dad took the mic first. Sam's throat constricted. Could he do this? He couldn't do this. He'd never been sweatier in his life. He'd hurt Sydney. How could she ever give him another shot?

"Sam?" Mr. McDonagh held the microphone, shaking it above his head like a prize. That thing was no prize. It was the gateway to Sam's public embarrassment.

"Right." He stood and approached the sweetheart table, taking the mic from Mr. McDonagh with a shaky hand. He cleared his throat, unfolded his sheet of notebook paper, cleared his throat again. Was it suddenly hotter in here? His face flushed.

"Uh, I've known Matt and Jorie for as long as I can re-member." His gaze lifted, preparing to lock eyes with Sydney.

Instead, an empty chair. Wait. Was that where she'd been sitting? Edith O'Hare, Karen, empty chair. That was it. She was gone.

"Sam," Jorie hissed, pointing toward the rear of the re-ception hall where the door swung closed behind a blue patterned dress. "Go!"

His blood froze in his veins, turning him into a solid block of fear. Not fear of embarrassment but fear of losing. If she ran out on him now, he'd lost his shot.

No fucking way.

He tore through the reception hall, bumping elderly Pine Ridge residents who cheered him on with cries of "Go, Sam!" and "Get her!"

Get her get her get her. The words rang out like a call to action, the only directive in the world worth listening to.

"Sydney!" His voice rang out in the empty lobby, bouncing off faded blue walls and bulletin boards touting God's love and potluck dinners. Among the layered papers on the cork board was a bright pink postcard for the Loving Book Club.

A bitter laugh escaped Sam's lips. Even the church wanted her back.

"Hey." Her voice slipped into his ear, down his jaw, and past his neck, raising goose bumps in its wake. She stood near the door, coat in hand, with wide eyes and her bottom lip tucked between her teeth.

"You're leaving?"

She shook her head, silky tendrils of hair sweeping against her jaw. "No. Just needed a little air."

He swallowed down his desire. Maybe she didn't want him anymore. Maybe she was terrified, too. But through everything swirling around them—the hurt, the fear, the past—something else tethered them to each other. A crackling thing, like the first licks of a fire. He'd felt it the first time he'd laid eyes on her, and they'd tended that fire until it raged within him, untenable and wild.

She had every right to turn him down now. But he'd be in love with her for the rest of his days anyway. What did he have to lose?

"You ran out on my speech," he said.

Her lips parted, and her brow furrowed. "Sorry if I

couldn't sit there and listen to you talk about love and commitment and everlasting devotion. Maybe you're over it all, but I'm not."

Over it all. Would he ever be over it all? Not if he could help it.

"If you'd stayed, I think you would've enjoyed it." On uneasy legs, he moved toward her, closing the space between them.

She stiffened, her arms tightening around her heavy coat. A blush rose in her smooth cheeks, and a memory flashed in his mind of the first time they'd made love by the campfire, her face pink from both the cold and the heat.

"Sam." Her quiet voice held a warning. Just like the first time he'd kissed her.

"Sydney." Only a few inches separated them, and he clutched the now-damp paper in his still-trembling hand. He glanced down but knew he didn't truly need the script. "I've known Matt and Jorie for as long as I can remember. And since the rest of you have known them most of your lives, I don't have to tell you how perfect they are together. They're so great, they both insisted I use this opportunity not to talk about their love and commitment to each other but instead about how I fumbled and lost somebody I could've shared a similar future with."

The tiniest whimper escaped Sydney's lips, and he blinked up to catch her reaction. Same flushed cheeks. A new tear in the corner of her eye. Her brow still creased in the middle, urging him to continue.

"I was a colossal idiot. I let myself believe all the things I wanted to believe, because when most of the people you've loved have let you down, you tend to believe everybody who comes after them will, too. Sydney didn't deserve the blame for my father or for anyone else who'd hurt me."

A strong hand gripped his wrist, and he stopped short. That was it. She really was too hurt to forgive him. When he met her eyes, the pained expression on her face cut him deep.

"I'll stop."

"No." Her voice was a whisper. "No, don't stop. I just needed to touch you."

The pressure of her fingers on his wrist anchored him down, reminded him that the past was the past but he had control of the future.

"You needed to touch me?"

"I've missed you so much."

A deep breath escaped his lips. A release. "You have?"

"Yes." She lowered her chin, the crease between her eyebrows deepening.

"Even though I was a complete asshole?"

"You definitely pinned some stuff on me that wasn't mine to take." Her hand slipped from his wrist to his waist, and her fingers crept under the flap of his jacket to the thin shirt below. The heat from her hand penetrated the fabric and branded his skin.

"That's putting it lightly." He took one step closer. "I am so sorry I hurt you."

"I'm sorry I ran."

"You were allowed to react however you wanted to react. But I'm not the only one here who misses you. I got a ration of shit for pushing you out of town."

A smile creeped onto her lips as she dropped her coat on the floor and their bodies finally met, hips pressed against thighs, breasts against ribs. The pressure of her exquisite frame against him was like slipping into a warm bath. Every inch of him eased.

"I've been thinking maybe I'd come back." The smile threatened to stretch, but she tamped it down. "Rowena Willow signed on as a silent partner, you know. Not sure if anybody told you."

So Karen *had* kept mum, just as she'd promised. Sam

had become a regular fixture at the Loving Page, desperate for any connection to Sydney he could get. He was there the morning Rowena Willow had stopped by to sign the paperwork.

His hands stayed pinned to his sides. Was he allowed to touch her yet? He couldn't make a single wrong move. Not now. "So, you might come back, huh? Help expand the shop?"

"Yeah. Maybe. Among other things."

"I tried calling you."

Her lips pressed together, and her nostrils flared as her gaze focused on his chin. "I know. I wasn't ready yet. Being in Pine Ridge made me feel more like myself than I ever have before. I needed to know if this place was the reality or the escape."

Did he dare jump to a conclusion? She was here, wasn't she? Nimble fingers dancing along his abdomen as if his body belonged to her?

"And?" he asked.

"It's both." She huffed out a laugh and met his eyes. "I didn't know that was possible."

His pulse, after racing for the better part of the day, finally slowed. She did that to him: infused his blood like heroin when she wanted to and soothed his soul in the very next breath. Despite Liv and her all-consuming addiction, no woman but Sydney had ever had as much power over him. He'd let her take him anywhere she wanted to go.

"So," she said. "Was that the end of your speech?"

She was close enough to kiss, her plump pink lips begging for it. But not yet. Not until he'd said it all.

"No." He didn't need the paper. "Sometimes in life we think we know exactly what we're headed for, we can see the map of our future laid out before us. I was content with that life. Until I met Sydney. And when you meet someone who shows you all the ways life can be so much better, it's hard to go backward."

Her grip on his waist tightened, her fingers hooking under his belt as she looked up at him curiously.

"Sydney, I'm in love with you. You are passionate and stubborn and smart. I'm glad you hit me with your car, and I'm glad Connor had no idea what a prize he had, and I'm glad your mom's store was on the verge of bankruptcy."

Her face collapsed as she laughed, two tears breaking free as she went. "Oh, you're glad for all that, huh?"

"Did you miss the part where I said I'm in love with you?"

"No, I didn't miss it." She reached a hand behind his neck, burying her fingers in his hair. "I've been waiting for that for a long time."

"I'm sorry, I'm so unbelievably sorry."

"I know you are. I think I just needed to hear you say it."

Before he could linger on the ways she soothed him, filled him up, eased his troubled mind, she laid her soft lips on his. She sucked gently on his bottom lip, sending up a flurry of sparks in his chest.

"I'm in love with you, too." Her breath warmed his chin. "And when I move back to Pine Ridge, I'd like to see what could happen between us."

"Move back. To Pine Ridge."

A smile tugged at her lips, and his focus darted between the sight of that gorgeous mouth and the sensation of her fingers lazily trailing over his neck. He swallowed down the last whisper of fear. She'd forgiven him. At the very least, she'd agreed to put it behind them.

"Yeah," she said. "I think this is where I belong."

He grinned. "I think you're right."

ACKNOWLEDGMENTS

Where to begin? This book was a colossal group effort, and I'm not sure it would've happened without each person below.

Thank you to my tireless agent, Eva Scalzo, who believed in this story enough to polish it, help build a series from it, and then pitch it to the world with all the enthusiasm I never dreamed someone could have for something I'd created. Thank you for supporting my work and my career, for fighting for me, and for being a friend.

Thank you to Sarah Blumenstock for championing this story, and for your guidance. I'm so proud to have my very first published work as part of your roster, and I'm beyond excited about what's next for us.

Thank you to the team at Berkley for welcoming me into your family. It's a dream come true to be one of your authors.

Thank you to Brittany Kelley, Michelle McCraw, and my #RChat ladies for literally turning me into a better writer. You have offered unbridled enthusiasm when I needed it, tough love when I really needed it, and the kind of friendship I never thought I'd be lucky enough to find in adulthood.

Thank you to David Glenwright, Jenna Gerry, Kerri Farrell, Meagan Drillinger, Meredith Mooney, Michelle Onufrak, Saskia de Jonge, and Timothy Meola for being the best cheerleaders a girl could ask for. For the early manuscript reads, the photoshopped covers, the shared joy, and the encouragement. Your positivity means everything to me.

Thank you to my parents, Chuck and Joanne Miller, who always "knew" I'd make it, even if we didn't always know exactly what I'd be making it at. Thank you for giving me the gift of the Adirondacks and for always having my back.

And to Josh. Thank you for your unwavering, relentless belief in me, and for making even the craziest pipe dreams seem possible. I know I wouldn't be here now without you. I love you so much.

Ready to find
your next great read?

Let us help.

Visit prh.com/nextread

Penguin
Random
House